PRAISE FOR *PRIMETIME PRINCESS*

"A page-flipping, witty beach read, it also contributes to the ongoing discussion about whether or not women can really have it all and what the somewhat mystical 'all' actually entails."

—PopMatters

"Be prepared to laugh out loud, shake your head in disbelief but, mostly, cheer as heroine Alexa Ross navigates her way through. I should have been writing my own book, but I couldn't stop reading *Primetime Princess*!"

—Mary Jane Clark, *New York Times* bestselling author

"This examination of what one wants, and what lengths one is willing to go to get it, touched my funny bone and my heart!"

—Samuel L. Jackson, actor

"*Primetime Princess* is a completely engaging, thoroughly entertaining read—with a vitally important message deftly woven in its pages."

—Jill Conner Browne, *New York Times* bestselling author of the Sweet Potato Queen books

"This is one of my favorite books this year!"

—Megan Crane, author of *I Love the 80s* and *Once More with Feeling*

ALSO BY LINDY DEKOVEN

Primetime Princess

THE SECRET
LIFE *of*
WISHFUL
THINKING

LINDY DeKOVEN

LAKE UNION
PUBLISHING

Published by Lake Union Publishing, Seattle

www.apub.com

Amazon, the Amazon logo, and Lake Union Publishing are trademarks of Amazon.com, Inc., or its affiliates.

ISBN-13: 9781477821398
ISBN-10: 1477821392

Cover design by Kathleen Lynch/Black Kat Design

Library of Congress Control Number: 2014949071

Printed in the United States of America

To my husband, David Israel,
who asked me to say he is perfect in every way . . .

There is a special place in hell
for women who don't help other women.
—Madeleine Albright

PROLOGUE

It was the most humiliating day of her life.

Yet, it had started off so well.

A limo picked Kenzie Armstrong up at the Regency Hotel at precisely eleven o'clock in the morning to deliver her to Avery Fisher Hall at New York's Lincoln Center. She slipped into the backseat and quickly began rehearsing her keynote address, entitled "The Hollywood Studio: Reinventing the Strategies, Platforms, and Revenue Streams," for the annual Ad Age Digital Media Summit. She'd gone over it repeatedly, memorizing exactly what to say, where to pause, and when to emphasize a point.

"Miss Armstrong, there's water in the side pocket and snacks in the middle console." Fernando, her driver, took great care of her. Ordinarily she'd tear into the small bags of Dylan's candy he'd carefully placed near the water. But not today.

"I'm not the least bit hungry, Fernando."

"Not even the peanut butter pretzel bites? Oh, you must be anxious."

Fernando winked in his rearview mirror, and she smiled back.

"Anxious is putting it mildly. I'm terrified. This is the biggest audience yet, and there's a lot at stake."

"You'll be fine, Miss Armstrong. You are what your name says. Strong. Very strong." Fernando drew to a stop, then turned around and smiled.

Kenzie forced a smile back, hoping it looked self-assured and confident.

But she was scared shitless.

They pulled up to the back entrance of the auditorium. Waiting outside was a young production assistant with the name *Charlotte* on the clear plastic tag that hung from her neck.

"Much good luck, Miss Armstrong. You'll do great," Fernando said as he opened the door to let her out.

"Thank you, Fernando. I'll meet you back here after my speech." Fernando nodded as Charlotte grabbed Kenzie's garment bag and ushered her inside.

A petite brunette with freckles, Charlotte told her they had little time and then whisked her off to a dressing room. As they approached, Charlotte pointed to a black nameplate next to the archway. There was her name: *Kenzie Armstrong*. Engraved in white lettering. Kenzie immediately thought to take a photo to send to her mom. She'd be so proud that—

But reality set in. These moments were the worst—those flickers in time when Kenzie forgot, just for a microsecond, that her mother was gone.

Six months ago, her mom had succumbed after a long battle with leukemia, and Kenzie was still struggling with the loss. Almost everything upset her. The aroma of lilacs in bloom brought back the memory of her mom's favorite hand lotion. Bakeries reminded her of her mother's burned cookies at bake sales. And sometimes just the sight of a middle-aged woman with a particular hair color, or a certain build, or a familiar expression could bring her to her knees.

Kenzie knew it was the order of things, but still she wondered why she got to live and her mom had to die. The pain remained fresh. Kenzie seemed stuck at the first stage of grief.

At twenty-eight, Kenzie was the youngest executive at a major Hollywood studio. Her ascent had been swift after she'd created a social media campaign for a low-budget Fox film the studio had already written off. When it surged to number one opening weekend and stayed there for weeks, beating one superhero after another at the box office, the entire industry was stunned. Suddenly she was the flavor of the month—and one without a contract. The big brass at Victory Studios swooped in and offered her a position and salary no one her age could resist.

Today was her coming-out party. Her public debut to the film, TV, and digital communities. She'd made speeches before, but none at this level. The audience included Wall Street power brokers, high-ranking advertisers, digital media experts, techno-junkies, and the media elite. This was an important event.

She'd prepared for weeks. She wasn't going to make a single mistake. She'd even replaced the rubber soles on her heels to avoid tripping across the stage. The unseen audience watching on TV and live streaming the event might be in the millions.

While Charlotte waited outside her dressing room, Kenzie changed into her black knit skirt and matching jacket. Her blond hair was wrapped neatly in a bun at the back of her head, and a few wispy bangs graced her forehead. She probably looked more like a nun than a marketing maven.

A knock sounded. "Miss Armstrong, you have ten minutes," Charlotte said outside the door. Kenzie pictured her staring at the clock in the hallway. She took one last glance in the mirror, straightened her suit, checked her makeup, applied a little more lip gloss, and took a deep breath. This was it. She was ready.

Charlotte led Kenzie down the hall and into the wings along-side the stage. Kenzie peered out from the curtain at the crowd. The theater was enormous. Every seat was occupied. Her knees weakened.

The cacophony of voices filled her head. Her lips trembled slightly, and her right eye began to twitch. Charlotte said Kenzie would be on in five minutes and offered her water, which she declined. Instead, she felt the need to run to the restroom.

As Kenzie raced to the ladies' room, she heard Charlotte marching close behind. Charlotte would suffer the consequences if Kenzie didn't get to the stage on time. From inside the restroom, Kenzie heard Charlotte whispering updates into the mic attached to her headphones. Washing her hands, she heard Charlotte shout, "Three minutes!"

But when Kenzie opened the bathroom door, Charlotte was frantic. Kenzie had already been introduced. The audience was applauding her arrival. She grabbed Kenzie's hand and yanked her out of the restroom and across the hall, back into the wings. What had seemed like a short walk before felt like a journey of a thousand miles now. Frenzied and out of breath, Kenzie ran after her, trying not to lose her balance in her heels or trip across the cables that lined the corridor. Charlotte grasped her arm and jerked her back and forth like a rag doll as they flew toward the stage.

Kenzie said, "I thought I had three minutes."

Charlotte yelled, "No, I made a mistake. One minute. Not three!"

They reached the arena, and Kenzie leaped onto the platform. The auditorium rumbled as she took the stage of the magnificent theater. A round of applause greeted her entrance, and Kenzie's ankles wobbled.

She managed to catch her breath, slow her pace, smile broadly, and then calmly walk toward the podium at the center.

The lights shone brightly on her face. The room was a sea at night. Dark and vast. She squinted to see if she could make out a single face, but she couldn't. All she could see was the illumination of the teleprompter with her opening words waiting to be read.

Kenzie began the speech, which felt as familiar as her name. After a few moments she began to relax. She talked about her plans to propel Victory Studios to the top of the industry in the digital and social spaces. She revealed the Twitter handle for their new film, *Sydney's Monkey,* and then moved out from the podium and turned her back to the audience so she could point to the digital orangutan on the jumbo television screen erected onstage. She announced that the studio had already earned more than two hundred million engagements across social media platforms.

As she walked back to the podium and plunged deeper into her talk, she grew more confident and at ease. She remembered to speak slowly and to use her hands for emphasis.

But from the moment she took the stage, she'd thought she heard suppressed laughter from the audience. She wasn't sure what it was about. Maybe she was imagining it. Her speech wasn't funny. In fact, it was incredibly dry, full of numbers and big words. So she ignored it and kept going.

But the laughter grew louder.

And then, out of nowhere, a stage manager appeared at her side. He whispered something in her ear that she couldn't make out. Then he stepped behind her and gently tugged at her skirt.

Kenzie's heart fell through the pit of her stomach and to the floor.

In her rushed departure from the restroom, her skirt must have become entangled in the waistband of her thong—her shocking-pink thong, she remembered—exposing her entire rear end. It had been on display from the moment she took the stage and was featured in all its glory when she turned her back to the crowd just moments ago.

Kenzie stared at the audience, her face on fire.

People began to howl. They applauded, cheered, and heckled.

She felt the cool breeze of the air conditioner on her neck. A single bead of perspiration trickled down her left temple. A strand of hair had come loose from her bun and hung awkwardly behind her ear.

She was hot and sweaty. Her chest caved and her mouth was dry and desperate for water. Her cheeks felt warm. She started to lose her balance but quickly grabbed the podium with both hands.

She fought to get past the humiliation. She knew she had to move on. Pretend nothing had happened. Make a joke. Laugh. At herself. With others. Rise above it. That was what she should do.

But she couldn't.

Kenzie, c'mon, you can't just freeze. You have to do something. Anything. Open your mouth. Keep going. After all, the show must go on. It always goes on. Doesn't it?

But instead she stood motionless, gaping at the audience. A tear slid down her left cheek. Jumbled thoughts raced through her head. How could this happen? Where was Charlotte?

The audience had grown quiet and still, but Kenzie couldn't move. Her arms were locked on either side of the podium. Her neck worked hard to support her head, which seemed as heavy as a bowling ball. Her whole body was stiff and tense. She brushed away the tear, which had settled on her upper lip.

While the audience waited patiently for her to continue, she drew in the stink of stale dust and worn-out sneakers that permeated the auditorium and wondered why she hadn't noticed it till now.

Kenzie learned later that the video of her bare butt on the stage of Avery Fisher Hall had already gone viral at that point. In fact, it had spread from Stockholm to Sacramento and on to Shanghai before the stage manager had even approached her. YouTube had gathered over five million hits in just a few hours. The morning talk shows, the cable networks, tabloids, talk radio, and the late-night comedians were already preparing gags and showing the clip, with her rear end blurred for broadcast, over and over. By the end of the day, millions of people in all twenty-four time zones had seen her defining moment. During her speech she'd observed tiny bright flashes from cell phones, but, of course, had failed to realize their significance.

When she was hired at Victory Studios, the critics claimed she was too young and inexperienced to assume such a lofty post. Despite her reputation as a tough warrior and fierce competitor, many believed she was too green for such responsibility.

As she stood stone-faced, gazing into the audience and unable to go on, Kenzie began to wonder if, in fact, they were right.

KENZIE

Four Years Later

"Hey, tootsie, what's the plan?" Leo DiSanto stormed into Kenzie's office, trailing the scent of freshly mowed grass from the paddock. "We gotta do something special for opening day. Something big. Gotta get new fans. Wanna put Grayson Downs on the map. Whaddya got?"

Kenzie glanced out the sliding door that opened onto the paddock where the horses would be saddled and paraded when Grayson Downs Racetrack in Palmdale, California, opened in just six months.

For the past four years she'd been happy to begin each morning working on the track's backstretch as a hot-walker, leading racehorses around a ring until they cooled out following a race or workout. Then she'd give them baths before returning them to their stalls. It was quiet and peaceful. The horses' calm, accepting nature soothed her, and no one relied on her for anything except taking care of the animals.

But two weeks ago Leo had offered her a position as director of marketing for the track. Anyone would have been thrilled to say yes, but not Kenzie. Had she not been down to her last dollar, she never would've accepted.

She hoped she could handle the stress. She didn't want to become overwhelmed with anxiety and endure another panic attack. The one she experienced onstage four years ago had destroyed her career and nearly destroyed *her*.

"I'm working on it, Leo." She hoped her voice didn't sound as uncertain as she felt.

"Ya gotta think of something," Leo pushed. "It's time to get moving, tootsie."

Before Thong-gate it had been Kenzie's time.

Back then she was a different person. Wildly ambitious. Referred to as the "Energizer Bunny," she'd wanted to run the world. Featured in magazine stories, gossiped about, she was on her way. She was going to have it all.

And then it was over.

Life had changed.

From the time she was a child, Grayson Downs had always held a special place in her heart. Max, her maternal grandfather, had taken her mother and her here often over the years. Grandpa Max was a racetrack regular, always looking for the next big score. For Kenzie, Grayson outings were magical in a different way. While Grandpa Max stood in line to place his bets, anxiously watching the horses and the tote boards, Kenzie and her mom watched the races, talked about life, and shared stories, unconcerned about winners and losers.

Grayson was a refuge, a place she found exciting but also tranquil and relaxing. Even now she could shut her eyes and smell the grass, the hay, the musky, earthy scent of the horses. It was as if her mother were there again, sharing an ice-cream cone, pointing out details about every single horse, pulling Kenzie to her feet to cheer with her at the top of their lungs for ones with the longest odds.

"It's easy to applaud the winners," her mom used to say. "But who encourages the ones who are down on their luck?"

But as soon as Kenzie opened her eyes, reality sank in. Those days were long gone. Along with her mom.

She blinked to clear her blurred vision and saw that Leo had perched on the edge of her desk, a layer of skin squeezing up over his too-tight pants and hanging over the waistband as he leaned too close, pressing her for an answer.

"Can it wait till Monday?" Kenzie hedged. "I'm about to meet my friend Gemma for dinner. But I'll have it all for you then."

"Okay, tootsie, but we need to get chicks to the racetrack," Leo said. "Why don't you get that new person I just hired for you to help bring in the gals—ya know, that Indian girl?"

"Leo, she has a name. It's Sarita. I don't think she likes it when you call her 'that Indian girl.'"

"Let's call her Rita. That's good, dontcha think? Need to Americanize it."

Kenzie tapped a pencil on her desk, her heart pounding as she debated whether to share the out-of-the-box idea she'd had. "I'm thinking about . . . Well, I've been thinking about a women's expo," she offered hesitantly.

Leo's fleshy face scrunched up on itself. "Really? What the heck are we gonna do with a women's expo?"

Kenzie cleared her throat, feeling her face heat. "Well . . . I was thinking maybe free manicures, massages, career experts, various other services that women might enjoy."

"And what does it have to do with the track?" Leo asked.

She shrugged, feeling foolish. "Nothing. I mean, not really. But the idea is to get women here, right? Isn't that what you want?"

Leo's thick lips were pursed, and his eyebrows drew together like mating caterpillars. "I don't know. Sounds like a lot of work, and it's just you, me, my assistant Glenn, and your gal Rita till we bring on more staff in June when the racetrack officially opens." He stood up, giving her what Kenzie felt sure was meant to be an encouraging smile, if it hadn't been threaded with condescension. "I tell you what, tootsie. Why don't you mention it to Brynne Tomlinson and get her input? She owns the most horses in training here. She may have some ideas, okay?"

Kenzie nodded numbly, wishing she'd never mentioned the idea.

* * * * *

"I'm wondering if I should quit my job," Gemma Haskins said as Kenzie approached the table inside the restaurant. "That's why I wanna see Annalisa tonight."

"Oh no. That's why we're meeting here at Johnnie's? So you can go next door and see your psychic?" Kenzie asked, sliding into the booth. It had been a long day, and Kenzie was glad that she could just sit and relax with her best friend, whom she'd known since college. Gemma was always looking for someone to give her the answers. It was literally how they met—when Gemma asked Kenzie how to make a cappuccino at the café they both worked at one summer.

"Yes. I need some good news."

"Well, she'll give you lots of that, as long as you line her pocket with bills," Kenzie said. "Come on, Gemma, it's a sham. Don't you get that she's just taking your money?"

"Look, times are tough. I'm thirty-three, can't get promoted, and my love life sucks."

Kenzie shook her head but held her tongue. Gemma never seemed to get the breaks so many others did. If the psychic offered some kind of hope, some kind of opportunity for her, then fine.

Gemma ripped through her meal and wrote notes to herself to make sure she had all her questions for Annalisa, then checked her watch.

"Oh, time to go. Wish me luck!" Gemma tore out of the booth.

"I'm gonna grab dessert next door," Kenzie called after her. "Text me when you're out of there. I'll wait for you."

"Sure thing. Fingers crossed!" Gemma shouted as she raced outside.

Kenzie paid the bill, walked next door, and ordered a small cup of chocolate frozen yogurt with chocolate sprinkles. She watched as a young man and woman nibbled on each other's cones. The woman was pretty, with delicate features. Her boyfriend was handsome, with an affable grin. Kenzie watched as they gazed into each other's eyes, and wondered if she'd ever feel that way about anyone.

She'd had only one serious boyfriend, Scott Semple. They hadn't spoken since they broke up her junior year in college, but he'd friended her on Facebook recently. Now he was a car salesman in Yuma, Arizona. Married. Two kids. He and Kenzie had gone out for maybe a year, and then he'd dumped her when he'd met Alison James. A bimbo, in Kenzie's humble opinion, but Alison was better suited for Scott. Kenzie's ambition had turned him off. It turned a lot of guys off. She wanted to work, to have a career. It was the twenty-first century, after all. But she was left with zero male prospects. In fact, she had been so busy building her career and then taking care of her mom, Kenzie hadn't dated in so long she wasn't sure she'd even know what to do.

She ate the remaining chocolate sprinkles in her cup, tossed it into the metal can by the door, and returned to her beat-up black pickup truck, which was a far cry from the fancy BMW she'd driven in her previous life. She knew Gemma would be finished soon, so she sat in her truck and played *Flappy Bird* on her iPhone. Just as she was about to start a new game, Gemma burst out of Annalisa's Psychic Lounge wearing a huge grin.

"I got a fantastic reading! So excited," she shouted. She jumped into Kenzie's truck, which had been waiting by the door. "Can you drive me to my car? It's on the other side of the parking lot."

Kenzie started the ignition and put the truck in gear, unable to resist smiling at Gemma's enthusiasm. "Okay, so what did she say?"

"Oh my gawd, it was unbelievable."

Kenzie rolled her eyes. Gemma had a flair for the dramatic. Kenzie was pragmatic, businesslike, and levelheaded, whereas Gemma was more starry-eyed and idealistic.

"I know you think this is crazy, 'cause I saw your eyes roll, but according to Annalisa, I'm gonna get a promotion soon." Gemma sorted through the contents of her purse, looking for something. "Let me find my notes so I can read her exact words to you. Something about seeing me in a big office, no longer someone's assistant. Lots of people want to meet me. Dang it, where are they?"

Kenzie backed out of her parking space. As she did, the door to Annalisa's Psychic Lounge opened again, and a heavyset woman shuffled out the storefront. She had frizzy gray hair and was wearing a white caftan and silver gladiator sandals—and she was moving quickly toward them. The woman flapped papers, trying to get Gemma's attention. Kenzie stopped and waited as the woman she presumed was Annalisa staggered over to the driver's window. She was having a heck of a time walking and was out of breath.

"Yo, Jenifah," she said in a gravelly voice. "Your notes. You forgot 'em." She reached across Kenzie's chest and handed the papers to Gemma. Kenzie couldn't believe Annalisa didn't even know Gemma's name.

Annalisa grabbed the frame of the driver's side window to stabilize herself. She was so winded she could barely get the words out. "The good stuff . . . the good, is in here."

Gemma smiled broadly and blew her a kiss.

Suddenly, Annalisa's hand fastened itself to Kenzie's arm.

Kenzie tried to pull away unobtrusively, but Annalisa's grip was like steel. "Okay," she said uneasily. "That's great. We're gonna head home now."

Annalisa lowered her head and peered through the window into the truck, still clutching Kenzie's arm too hard.

"Your ring," Annalisa said. "Where . . . where did . . . you get that . . . that beautiful ring?"

"Oh, this?" Kenzie looked at her right hand, which was on the steering wheel. "Um, well, thank you. I found it on the beach. There was no lost and found. I put it on Facebook, Twitter, and Instagram, but no one claimed it."

"It's lovely," Annalisa said. She finally let go of Kenzie's arm, but then reached inside the window to take hold of Kenzie's finger, examining it closely. Kenzie shifted uncomfortably, trying to catch Gemma's eye. But Gemma was staring in equal fascination at Kenzie's ring.

"Looks like an amethyst, pearl, and a beautiful peridot . . . Whew . . . Quite a find." Annalisa inspected it carefully, as if she were a jeweler.

"Really? Uh, I don't think so." Kenzie laughed. "I think it's fake. I saw one like it at the 99-cent store. But thank you."

Annalisa released her finger and then placed her hand on Kenzie's shoulder. She leaned in close. Her face was about an inch away from Kenzie's. She stared directly into her eyes, which Kenzie found unsettling.

"I'd . . . take good care of that ring . . ." Annalisa was breathing heavily. "It belongs . . . to him . . . to your future husband."

"What?" Kenzie asked.

Annalisa released her hand from Kenzie's shoulder and took a step back from the truck. She was ghostly pale and continued to gasp for breath. Kenzie asked if she was all right. But Annalisa didn't respond. Instead, she closed her eyes and tilted her head back toward the sky.

"He'll come . . . into your life . . . He will . . . sometime . . . sometime in the next six months," Annalisa said. And then she stumbled backward and collapsed to the ground.

"Annalisa!" Gemma cried.

* * * * *

"She *died?*" Kenzie almost dropped the sack of groceries she'd been carrying the last two blocks from the market to her apartment.

"Last night on the way to the hospital," Gemma sobbed. "I was her last client. Maybe it had something to do with me."

"I doubt it. She couldn't breathe." Kenzie held the phone closer to her ear. "I'm really sorry. I thought that when the paramedics arrived, she'd be okay."

"Me too," she said. "I feel terrible."

"Oh, Gem," Kenzie said. "I know how much you liked seeing her."

"I did. I'm going to miss her," she said. "She got nearly everything right. I came to depend on her. Even you benefited from her abilities."

"Really? How?"

"She said your ring belonged to your future husband and then croaked. I mean, God—what're you going to do?"

Kenzie reached the ancient white-stucco apartment building on her narrow, tree-lined Pasadena street and hiked up the artificial grass staircase to her studio apartment on the second level. This place didn't come close to the elegant condo she'd owned in West Los Angeles, complete with a concierge and doorman. But it was a different time. She placed the grocery bag on the kitchen counter and tossed her purse onto the metal end table that came with the four-hundred-square-foot dive. Then she crashed onto the gray couch that would serve as her bed later that evening and stared at the cottage-cheese ceiling, clutching the cell phone to her ear.

"About what?" Kenzie asked.

"About finding your future husband! Don't you want to?"

"Seriously?" Kenzie pulled herself up from the couch. She went to the fridge and grabbed something to drink. "It was a ridiculous thing to say."

"Really? Why?"

"Well, for starters," Kenzie said, gulping down the flat Diet Coke that had been sitting, opened, in the refrigerator door, "unless my future husband is five years old, I can't imagine him wearing a ring that came out of a gumball machine."

"Annalisa didn't think it was a cheap ring," Gemma said.

"Annalisa didn't know what she was talking about."

"Did you take it to a jeweler?"

"No, that never occurred to me." Kenzie returned to the fridge.

Gemma was quiet as Kenzie opened the fridge door again and saw one lonely tomato.

"Aren't you even curious?"

"Not really. You know I don't believe in that stuff." Her tone was curt, matter-of-fact.

There was a long pause.

"It's a suffragette ring," Gemma announced.

"Huh?"

"I found an image of a ring that looks like yours online. I'm texting it to you now." Gemma could barely contain herself. "Look at it. It's the same one, isn't it? It looks like an amethyst, pearl, and peridot in eighteen-karat gold. Just as Annalisa said."

Kenzie looked at the photo. Gemma was right. It sure looked like the same ring.

"Wow."

"Get off your butt," Gemma said. "It's Saturday. Let's go see Harriet at XIV Karats and get this thing appraised. My boss gets his wife's bling there. Or rather, I pick it out and he gifts it. Let's see what she says. Meet ya there in an hour, okay?"

Kenzie had so many errands to do, but she had to admit that Gemma had piqued her curiosity.

She wondered what the heck she'd found.

* * * * *

Gemma and Kenzie met at the jewelry store and learned that the ring was real. The design had first appeared in the 1890s, but it wasn't produced for the campaigners to wear until 1918, when the first women were enfranchised. The green stones stood for hope; white, for purity; and violet, for dignity.

Kenzie was speechless as she listened to Harriet Fuller, a sophisticated African American woman in her forties, explain more about the ring and its history. Harriet said interest in suffragette jewelry had increased and prices had risen.

Kenzie slipped the ring back on her finger and thought about whose it might be. It was a suffragette ring. But why would it belong to a man? Harriet wrote down the name of a woman who was a feminist historian and encouraged Kenzie to contact her to learn more about the ring.

"Boy, you have all the fun," Gemma said as they exited the shop. "I get a reading about a possible promotion, and you get one about your future husband."

"Hey, you've worked really hard and deserve a promotion. At some point you'll get one. It's not that hard to predict. That's why psychics are scam artists. They listen to what you want and just repeat it back in a different way."

"Don't be such a skeptic."

They walked to Kenzie's truck, parked down the street. When they approached her parking space, Gemma took Kenzie's hand and softened her tone. "I want you to try to live a little, Kenz. You've been walking horses around a shedrow at Grayson for four years, and now you're director of marketing there. It's an exciting time. You should wear that ring more often. Maybe it'll bring you good luck."

"Well, I'll need some luck in this new job. It appears the pressure's on me." Kenzie took out her car keys.

"Why on you?" Gemma asked.

"Richard Grayson III, the track's owner, wants to tear it down and build a commercial development. Leo begged him to reconsider and promised he'd increase attendance, draw a younger crowd, and figure out a way to attract more women."

"Ah, that's where you come in."

"It seems like a tall order for a track that's only open the first three weeks in June, and part of the Antelope Valley Fair and Alfalfa Festival next door."

"The what?" Gemma laughed.

"It's a small track. Accommodates seventy-five hundred fans. But they've only gotten about nine hundred a day the past five years. Has to be improved or the place gets knocked down. There's no turf club. No restaurant. Just a few hot dog vendors. Let's just say it's nothing like Churchill Downs."

"Well, you have quite a challenge. But you know that track well."

"I do. Aside from working there these past few years, for me it holds wonderful memories." Kenzie kept her eyes on Gemma and then lowered them. "I spent many good times with my mom and grandpa there."

"Well, then Leo hired the right person." Gemma rested her hand on Kenzie's shoulder. "If anyone can turn this around, you can."

"Thanks for the support. But, you know . . . I'm a little scared . . . Like, what if I can't do this?" Kenzie asked softly.

Gemma squeezed Kenzie's arm. "You can do it. You're good at this."

"I hope so, but I haven't gotten all my confidence back."

"You'll get there," Gemma said. "Meanwhile, how about giving me a lift to my car? It's uphill and I'm feeling pretty lazy today."

They got into the truck and pulled out of the parking space. While Gemma opened her compact and put on lipstick, Kenzie glanced at her friend's dark-brown shoulder-length hair and billowy white blouse tucked neatly inside her midrise jeans. She always appeared fresh and immaculate.

Kenzie did not.

Her sweater was frayed and carried the scent of the track. Dirt collected at the hem of her jeans, probably from the walk on the backside yesterday. And she hadn't applied makeup since this morning. As Kenzie watched Gemma smack her lips, she wondered if all this primping was about seeing *him* later. Gemma was obsessed with him. She didn't want to ask, as it had become a sore subject. In fact, she didn't know if Gemma had seen him at all. But she didn't want to broach the topic.

Gemma took the keys out of her purse as Kenzie pulled her truck up alongside Gemma's car.

"Glad you insisted that I come out here today," Kenzie said. She leaned across the console and hugged Gemma good-bye.

"I know you don't believe in psychics," Gemma said as she reached for her purse and jumped out of the truck. "But just keep an open mind, okay? I mean, you never know. She could be right."

GEMMA

Gemma wasn't ready to tell Kenzie more about Jeffrey Kahn. Especially since Kenzie had begged her to stop stalking him. But Gemma couldn't help herself. She was determined.

She sank further into her seat as she drove slowly by Jeffrey's home. It was the fourth time this week. She just wanted to get a glimpse. She figured he must've driven by her house, too, at one time or another.

A few weeks ago, on one of her drive-bys, she'd discovered what she thought was Jeffrey's home. But now it was empty and for sale. She'd scoured the Internet to find out where he had moved. But there was no information. Days passed. Where the heck was he? Gemma searched the Web, but there were too many Jeffrey Kahns to really narrow it down. After a while, she reluctantly gave up.

But then the mystery was solved. Just the other day she had a fortuitous encounter with a local paper at her dentist's office, which produced the clue she'd been hoping for. The paper was full of photos of fancy community fund-raisers. As she flipped through the pages, a small photo at the bottom corner of one caught her eye. The caption read: "Mr. and Mrs. Jeffrey Kahn attend People

Assisting the Homeless fundraiser." Gemma was fixed on the photo, which featured an attractive couple in formal attire. She ripped out the page and stuffed it into her purse.

This Jeffrey Kahn was a lawyer at Davidson, Marks & Rogers, served on the board of directors of PATH, and lived with his wife, Emily, and their children, Scarlett and Dylan, in a lavish home in Brentwood. This was the same law firm listed at the top of the agreement Gemma had discovered just a few weeks earlier. This was the right Jeffrey Kahn. It had to be him.

Now she wanted to meet him. But it had to be done the right way.

After Kenzie had dropped Gemma off at her car yesterday, Gemma had gone home and again searched the Internet till she found Jeffrey's correct address. Earlier today she had parked on his street. She was mindful of the security cameras, so she didn't stay long.

The gate opened and a black Range Rover with tinted windows drove away. She followed it to a private school a few blocks away, where she parked and watched as Jeffrey's two kids got out and ran onto the school grounds. Then she followed the SUV as it wound its way through the business district and into a CVS parking lot. She parked a few rows away. And then there he was.

Her father.

She guessed he was in his midfifties. She saw him walk briskly into the pharmacy. He had dark hair, gangly arms, and a muscular build. Was he left-handed like her? Was his second toe longer than the rest like hers? What other characteristics did they have in common?

She had so many questions. She wanted to know him. But first she needed a closer look.

She hopped out of the car, entered the store, and grabbed a red handbasket. She intended to fill it up with random items so as not to appear suspicious and follow him through the store. But Jeffrey grabbed a single item and quickly took it to the checkout stand.

Gemma stood right behind him as he placed a small bottle of aspirin on the conveyor belt. She examined the wiry black hair on his knuckles and his short but well manicured nails. She even detected clear nail polish.

Jeffrey tapped his index finger on the counter, then pulled out a shiny silver money clip stuffed with cash and gave the clerk a twenty-dollar bill. He put the change in his pocket, smiled, and took off. But in that one moment, Gemma's eyes met his. Just long enough for her to see that they were green.

Just like hers.

Gemma was shaking. Her heart raced and her knees were weak. But the memory of his green eyes lingered.

* * * * *

A few hours later Gemma sat at her vanity and examined her eyes in the mirror. She wondered if he knew who she was. She'd searched everything but the Homeland Security database for more information about him. Had he ever done the same?

Gemma picked up her cell and dialed.

"I saw him today," she said the second Kenzie answered.

"You did?" Kenzie asked. "What happened?"

"I followed him into a store. I didn't say a thing. But guess what? He has green eyes!"

"Wow. So what're you going to do?"

"I'm going to talk to my mom tomorrow."

"Are you sure you want to open this up?" Kenzie asked.

"I want to know him. He's my father. And I want to know why I never knew about him."

Gemma knew Kenzie understood, because both of their fathers were sperm donors. It was one of the craziest things they'd found out they had in common when they first became friends. Except Gemma had learned recently, and by accident, that her mother had some kind of relationship with her father.

"I'm glad you finally saw him so you don't have to search anymore."

"Yea." Gemma rubbed the back of her neck, which felt tight and tense, and decided to change the subject. "How's the new job going?"

"Well, let's see . . . Earlier today Leo told me that Brynne Tomlinson, the biggest horse owner at Grayson, hates my guts because he hired me instead of her cousin. Nice, huh?"

"She obviously doesn't know your background and how successful you were," Gemma said.

"I can hardly wait to work with her," Kenzie sighed. "Anyway, Gem, I'd much rather talk to you. However, I've got to get back to work. But I want to know what happened with your dad. And . . . I wonder why your mom never told you about him?"

"Yes, I have those questions and many more."

* * * * *

The next day Gemma drove up her mother's driveway and parked her car. She took a deep breath and marched along the walkway to the front door. Inserting her key, she let herself in.

"Hi, honey. Good to see you. It's your lunch hour, isn't it?" Her mother's eyes were fixed on the ball of yellow yarn that had just fallen off her lap onto the living room floor. She reached for it with one hand while the other clung to the knitting needles, trying to hold the last stitch. Gemma walked over to the sofa, kissed her mom lightly on the cheek, and then took a seat across from her.

"Is everything okay?" Her mom's needles resumed their clacking. "You never come by during the week. Is something wrong?"

Gemma's left eye was twitching and her mouth was dry. It surprised her that what she thought would be so easy was suddenly difficult.

Her mother stopped knitting and leaned forward. "What is it, Gemma?"

Gemma stared at the ground.

"My dad," she said softly. "He wasn't a sperm donor."

They both sat still. "Why would you say that?" Her mom's voice was tight.

"Because I know."

"What is it that you know?"

Gemma took a deep breath and looked up at her mother. "Several weeks ago I came over to borrow your green purse. Remember, you told me it was on the top shelf in the front closet? When I reached for it, another bag tumbled down and a bunch of papers fell out. I noticed a document labeled *Agreement Between Jeffrey Kahn and Karen Haskins*. I was curious, so I read it."

Her mother let several seconds lapse and then carefully placed the ball of yarn and needles in the knitting bag. Gemma could see her eyes were brimming with tears. She reached for a tissue and handed it to her mother.

"Mom," she said softly, "it's time. I want to know the real story. I want to know about my dad."

"Oh, Gemma . . . it's only because I wanted to protect you . . . I didn't want to hurt you and—"

"Mom, I want to know." Gemma interrupted and sat forward in her seat. Her voice was strong and determined. "I *need* to know. I'm angry that you never told me."

Her mom sat up straighter. "Well, there was a reason."

"Good, then tell me."

Her mother wiped the tears from her eyes and took a deep breath as Gemma relaxed back in her upholstered chair.

"I lived in a rundown apartment, worked as a medical transcriber, and cared for your grandfather after his Parkinson's set in. Money was a struggle," her mom said, and paused. "A friend asked if I'd help serve drinks at a bachelor party one evening." Her right hand gripped the edge of the sofa. "It was quite rowdy. A large group of young men, all drunk and horny."

Gemma bit her lip as she sat and listened with rapt attention. She could tell this was difficult for her mom, because her legs were trembling.

"I was groped and fondled until one obnoxious drunk guy pushed me up against a wall and ripped at my clothes. He roughed me up pretty good and then disappeared." Her mom stopped, averted her eyes, and gazed out the large picture window that overlooked the small front yard. Her voice was shaking. "I remember holding my arms across my chest, trying to protect whatever modesty I had left while my underwear hung at my knees. It was awful."

"Oh, Mom . . ." Gemma said.

Her mom got up, went to the kitchen, and poured herself a glass of wine. She never drank in the middle of the day. Then she turned slowly toward Gemma, who remained seated.

"Jeffrey was a guest at the party. He saw what was happening and rushed over." She took a long sip of wine. "He wrapped his jacket around me and helped me into the alley outside. He handed me a beer and a cigarette. I can't remember the conversation. I was a mess. Then he offered to drive me home."

She stopped, blinking into the air, seemingly lost and unaware of the tears streaking her face.

Gemma stood up and walked over to her mom, then put her hand gently on her back. "Come on, Mom. Let's go sit down." She followed her mom wordlessly back to the sofa, and when they were seated side by side, Gemma handed her another tissue.

"I'm embarrassed to say I had too much to drink and was exhausted by the time we reached my house," she said, dabbing her eyes. She waited a beat and then continued. "I remember little except making love in the backseat of Jeffrey's Camaro. It wasn't one of my better moments. He walked me to the door and said he'd call but never did."

"So what happened?" Gemma asked. But she had a feeling she knew.

"Nine months later, I tracked him down and asked that he take a paternity test because I wanted him to know the baby was his." She looked away from Gemma. "He was furious. I didn't even want to tell him, but my dad insisted. I knew Jeffrey wanted nothing to do with me. In fact, his own bachelor party was the weekend after you were conceived."

"Oh my God," Gemma said.

"Jeffrey was convinced the pregnancy was a con job to get him to support me and my dad," she said. "He wanted no part of me or the baby. He hired an attorney and offered me a deal."

Gemma shook her head, her cheeks feeling cold and her hands burning hot. "That was the legal agreement I found, right?"

"Yes," her mother said. "The agreement stipulated that Jeffrey would provide child support till you were twenty-one. It would be sent by check every month from his attorney to a post office box. There was to be no contact. We were never to be part of his life." She reached up and tucked a strand of hair behind Gemma's ear, a sad smile playing over her lips. "It's why I never told you about him."

Tears had welled in Gemma's eyes.

"Oh, honey." Her mother pulled her close and wrapped her arms around Gemma. "I'm sorry, baby. I really am. I accepted the agreement without ever thinking of the consequences. I regretted it, but, honey, I never regretted having you. Not for one minute. You're the light of my life."

Gemma nodded against her mother's shoulder, but she wasn't ready to pull away and leave the comfort of her arms, or look her in the eye.

For a moment Gemma wondered if she should have left well enough alone.

But it was too late. There was no going back.

SARITA

Sarita Mahajan's new job at Grayson Downs was her ticket to freedom.

Sarita had never been to a racetrack before her interview a week ago. She'd had no idea what to expect. A friend who worked at another racetrack told her that Grayson had an opening for a social media coordinator. The pay was decent, so Sarita went for it.

She'd been hired to work for Kenzie Armstrong, whom she'd Googled the second she left her interview with Leo, Kenzie's boss. Sarita was impressed with Kenzie's background.

"The first thing we need is an online presence," Kenzie had said to Sarita on her first day at work earlier this week. "I'm going to depend on you to get Grayson on the map. We need to improve the website, start a blog, get on Facebook and Twitter, and build the brand." Sarita sat across from Kenzie at her desk, taking notes. "We also have to focus on opening day. We'll need to prepare a promotional video so everyone knows when the track opens and then start soliciting vendors for the expo. You with me?"

"Yes, I totally get it," Sarita nodded solemnly.

"Don't be afraid to ask questions. In fact, I'm going to ask Keith Brackpool, who runs Santa Anita Park, to put you in touch with their digital manager so you can learn what they've done to attract new fans," Kenzie said. "I know this is your first job out of college, but I'm confident you can handle it."

Sarita was thrilled and excited about her new challenge.

But her father had other plans.

Mohan Mahajan expected that she'd work in the family business importing undergarments from India. It wasn't meant to be a career because her dad's goal for all his daughters was to marry them off by the time they were twenty-five. So far he'd succeeded with her two older sisters. But that wasn't going to work for Sarita.

Why rush to get married? At twenty-two, Sarita had other plans. Freshly armed with her college degree, she'd been eager to get a job and start carving out her own future.

Except things hadn't exactly been moving as quickly as Sarita would have liked.

She had been living at home for four months, under her father's thumb. An utter nightmare. After being away at college, home was like . . . Well, it was like prison. She had one goal: To get her own place. Quickly.

Her father was all about family and traditions. But Sarita viewed the latter as rules. And she hated rules. She broke them constantly. The more rules, the more she rebelled. In high school she drove to San Francisco without a driver's license. The next year she was caught stealing earrings from a drugstore and later arrested for smoking weed in the girls' bathroom. Her father condemned her behavior, but Sarita was her own person. Papa had no idea how far and deep it went. And she wanted to keep it that way.

"You can do as you please, my darling," her mother said as she dried the dishes from supper one night. "But you must be home Thursday evenings, as that is when Papa will entertain suitors."

Mama wouldn't consider a dishwasher, as an appliance could never clean the family china the way she could by hand.

Sarita rolled her eyes at the insanity. Everyone had a dishwasher, for God's sake. Her mother lived in another world. When she moved back home, she'd been surprised to see how little had changed. Her room was exactly as she'd left it. It was as if time had stood still.

"I don't know that I can be home every Thursday night, Mama," Sarita said as she lifted the silverware from the table and set it in the sink. "I have a job now. I may have to work late."

Her mother stopped drying the dishes and stared at Sarita. Sarita looked the other way and removed the rest of the plates from the table.

Sarita was familiar with the matchmaking tradition. She'd watched her older sisters sit at the dinner table, their eyes lowered, listening to their father as he held court. And then if the suitor was worthy, following dinner Papa would escort him to the study to meet privately with his daughter. After dinner Sarita's sisters would laugh and sometimes cry. Sarita never understood why they didn't object to this practice.

"I'm glad you enjoyed your first week at work," Mama said levelly. "Did you make friends there?"

"Mama, it's not like the first week of school," Sarita said. "And my intention wasn't to make friends. I want to make enough money so I can move into a place of my own."

Sarita couldn't wait to see the world. She was a modern young woman. Someone who wanted to do more with her life. A husband and family might come, but they weren't high on her list. At least not now.

"Well, did you enjoy it there?" Mama asked. Sarita felt sorry for her. Her mother was clueless. And so agreeable. So much so, it made Sarita angry. She wanted her mother to argue, to have her own opinion. Not her father's.

"It was fine," Sarita said as she rinsed off the silverware. "The big boss, Leo, is kind of strange. I overheard him asking someone why I didn't have one of those red dots on my forehead. He saw it in *Slumdog Millionaire*."

"Ah, he's not particularly evolved," Mama said as she stacked the dishes and then put them in the cupboard.

"Hardly," Sarita quipped. "He has no idea what social media is but heard he should hire someone to do it, as it could benefit the track. He didn't seem impressed that I had a college degree. But he thought my ability to realign the icons on his iPhone was pure genius, so he hired me on the spot."

"He'd better be careful. One day you could have his job," Mama said.

"No," said Sarita, laughing. "That's not what I want to do. But I like my immediate boss, Kenzie. She seems nice and easy to work for. I'm a little nervous about this woman Brynne Tomlinson, though. Apparently she's difficult. We have to be nice to her. She's rich and an important horse owner."

"Are you going out tonight?" Mama asked as she exited the kitchen. Sarita knew her mother didn't want her to leave. She wanted to talk, to "catch up." Mama always wanted to catch up. She'd wanted to know every detail of Sarita's life when she was studying in New York—"in the big city," she'd say. Her mother couldn't imagine what it would be like going to school in Manhattan.

Deveeka Mahajan enjoyed living in Desert View, their small Hindu community where everyone knew one another. Almost all were either first- or second-generation immigrants from India. Few moved away. Their adopted home suited her mother well.

But Desert View was a town of few secrets. Everyone knew Sarita had been arrested for smoking dope in high school. It was a community tragedy, in that it brought shame upon the family. Her parents lived in fear of shame. Her father had sent her to a psychologist, hoping the therapist would put an end to his youngest daughter's unbecoming behavior. But the counseling had no effect on Sarita. Instead, she just made sure to cover her tracks better and shared less and less of her life with her parents. She knew they'd never approve of her lifestyle.

"Yes, Mama, I'll be going out," Sarita said as she wiped down the counter and removed her apron. "Please don't wait up for me. I might not be home till very late."

"My goodness, but don't you have to get up early for work? Where are you going?" Mama asked as she started up the stairs.

Sarita cringed. How would she get through the questions? The prying? The spying? She shuddered at the thought.

She'd grown, but her parents hadn't. As far as they were concerned, their youngest daughter had returned to the nest. In their eyes, as always, she was the same. But she wasn't.

Not by a long shot.

"Mama, please don't worry about me. Just meeting a friend tonight. I'll see you in the morning," Sarita said.

Once Mama had ascended the stairs, Sarita picked up her cell phone and checked her texts, then smiled. She tiptoed up the traditional dark-wood staircase to make sure her mother was out of sight. When she heard the muffled noise of her parents talking in their bedroom, she continued down the hall to her own room. Just before she entered, she reached up to the ceiling and quietly pulled on a cord that released a trapdoor. Sarita reached inside and unfolded a wooden stairway, then climbed up into the attic. After a moment she returned down the steps, carrying a red wig and a black corset under her arm. She slid the stairway back up then tiptoed down the stairs and out the door . . . and disappeared into the night.

BRYNNE

Brynne Tomlinson, a tall, elegant-looking woman in her early forties, sat high in her chair across from Leo, who was perched behind his desk.

"A women's expo at the track? It makes no sense," she said. "Why would I want to get a manicure at a racetrack? The whole thing is ridiculous. It was obviously conjured up by someone who doesn't know or understand this world."

"You hardly know her," Leo said. "Why don't you talk to her? I'm sure she'd love to hear some of your ideas." He stood, indicating the meeting was over.

"She doesn't want to hear my ideas." Brynne rose from her seat. "You need a man in this job, Leo. You know that. Men understand racetracks."

"Kenzie is highly qualified. You're just angry that I hired her instead of your cousin. But his résumé didn't come close to Kenzie's. Give her a chance."

Leo held the door open and Brynne swept through.

Brynne was furious. She stood outside his door and picked at microscopic lint that had collected on her designer jeans. She brushed it off, then continued across the long second-floor hall-way in her short black boots. When she reached the reception area downstairs, she straightened her black jacket and sunglasses. She opened her small yellow clutch bag, pulled out a mirror, checked her makeup, and then headed out the door and stomped across the parking lot.

Leo made her angry. But fine, she would speak with Kenzie. Horse racing was a man's world. Only certain women, like Brynne, could participate. There wasn't a place for most women on that turf. All she knew about Kenzie was that up until last month, she had been a hot-walker, for God's sake. The lowest of the low. And now she was a marketing executive with Grayson? Leo must be screwing her. There was no other explanation.

Brynne marched to her white Jaguar convertible. She got inside, put the top down, and drove out of the parking lot. She shouted a telephone number into her hands-free phone and sped up the freeway ramp on her way to Bel-Air Estates, where she, Martin, and their perfect fourteen-year-old twins, Brianne and Marianne, resided.

"Get me Miss Armstrong. It's Brynne Tomlinson!" she shouted into the speaker.

"It's me, Brynne. How can I help you?"

"Miss Armstrong," Brynne said, "I don't think you really under-stand racetracks. And creating events to attract women is just . . . Well, it makes no sense. I think it's best you find something else to do."

There was a long moment of silence.

"Well, first, you can call me Kenzie. And second, I'm open to any ideas you may have. In fact, my colleague Sarita Mahajan is on the phone, too, so please feel free to share your thoughts with us."

"I would discard the entire concept." Her tone was terse.

"Um, is there some reason you don't want Grayson to attract more women to the races?" Kenzie asked.

"It's a male sport. Women don't care for it," she said matter-of-factly. "Miss Armstrong, are you married?"

"No."

"So, then I'll assume you don't have children. Well, I'm sorry. And how old are you?"

Kenzie sighed. "I'm thirty-two."

"Oh, well, you'd better get started. You're not getting any younger. Maybe that's where you might want to focus your attention. On finding yourself a good man. And then maybe have some children."

Brynne reached her exit and slowed to a stop at the bottom of the ramp. She noticed a car full of teenagers next to her. The girls were twerking and jerking and showing it all off. She peered into the car and noticed they were half-naked in their short shorts and tiny tops, their nipples erect and fannies showing. Good Lord. What was the world coming to? These girls had lost their minds.

"I've made choices in my life," Kenzie said politely. "Some may not be ones you would've made, but they were the right ones for me. I think I have some time."

No one had ever challenged Brynne, particularly a low-level employee. Someone who, just months ago, was walking a horse in a circle making the same wage as the woman who cleaned her bathrooms. Who the heck did this Kenzie think she was? It didn't make sense. And whoever she was, she thought thirty-two was young? Oh dear. Thirty-two was *old*. Her eggs were probably rotten already. Had she not heard of infertility? One needed to get knocked up early in life, because later it was all downhill. The body deteriorated. It sagged. Everything fell. Sex wasn't what it once was. It just wasn't.

"We'd really like to include your thoughts in our plans, Mrs. Tomlinson," Sarita interjected. "I hope you'll feel free to offer some suggestions."

Brynne clenched her jaws. Now this little . . . *underling* was weighing in, too? "Unfortunately, I think you're both focused on the wrong thing," she said frostily. "A women's expo does not belong at a track. Period." She hung up.

She drove up the street toward her gated home, pressed the security button, and watched as the six-foot black iron gates slowly opened. She continued up the long circular driveway and parked right in front of the massive white marble pillars adorning the entryway to her Southern-inspired mansion. Elena, a Hispanic woman dressed in a gray housekeeper's uniform with a name tag and white gloves, met Brynne as she stepped out of her car. Brynne handed her purse to Elena and swept through the thirteen-foot hand-carved nineteenth-century pine doors, which she had salvaged from a building in São Paulo, Brazil.

"Martin? Martin? I'm home, darling. Where are you?" Brynne's voice echoed through the entryway, which featured a graceful staircase and glittering chandelier. An oversize oil painting of Brynne, Martin, and the twins lay beautifully against the wall above the gold-and-silver stairway.

Tall with broad shoulders, Martin Tomlinson had been the finest Jackson, Mississippi, had to offer. He was destined for greatness, and he'd found it managing his father's oil wells in Texas. But California had brought him even bigger success as he'd purchased vast acres of undeveloped land outside Bakersfield, eventually erecting strip malls and condominiums. Martin Tomlinson did exactly what he had planned. He wanted it all, and he got it. And Brynne enjoyed everything that came with it. Her job was simple: She would be the perfect wife. She knew exactly how to perform those duties. It was all she ever wanted.

Martin and Brynne were a portrait of the good life, attending elegant parties and philanthropic events. Proud members of the top 1 percent. While Martin toiled away making more and more money, Brynne cultivated her hobby, which was breeding, racing, and selling Thoroughbreds. Martin wasn't the least bit interested in her hobbies, but Brynne loved her horses. She had twenty, all magnificent. And she was the sole owner. No syndicates or partnerships for her.

"Mother," Marianne said as she climbed down the long stairway, "Elena's going to take us into Beverly Hills today. We're going to Barneys. We want to see if they have the new Lanvin clutch bags." Marianne's blue eyes twinkled with excitement as she and her identical twin, Brianne, blew kisses.

"While you're there, check out the winter coats," Brynne said. "You'll need something warm. It's going to be cold in Connecticut when you return to school next week."

The girls, in their skinny designer jeans, silver flats, and embroidered tank tops, flew by Brynne into the chauffeur-driven black Mercedes, which was waiting for them. As they drove away, Brynne marveled at how grown-up they were.

When Brynne was fourteen years old, life had been different. She hadn't had the chance to live away at a fancy boarding school back East.

Northern California in the seventies had presented all sorts of opportunities. It was a time of change, but Brynne had wanted none of it. She grew up in a middle-class home but couldn't wait to escape. She wanted to be far away from the recently enlightened and liberated women in the community. She longed for a traditional family in which the father worked and the mother stayed home. Hers was anything but that 1950s ideal. Her parents were divorced. Her mother worked hard to make a living, and her younger sister suffered from epilepsy. Life was rough. Brynne wanted an easier one. She didn't want the difficult path her mother had taken. She also wanted nice things and was determined to get them.

Brynne couldn't wait to get to Ole Miss. She read *Gone with the Wind* repeatedly and dreamed about life in the South. The second she touched down on Mississippi soil, she knew it was for her. She fell in love with the dialect, the antebellum architecture, and the rich Southern cooking. She made friends quickly, attended church with them, and relished their conservative politics. She loved Southern hospitality. Once she married Martin, she became a fixture among those in high society, a true Southern belle.

"Did you have a good day at Grayson, darling?" Martin said as he sifted through their afternoon mail, his eyes focused on each item. Brynne draped her arm around his waist and kissed him softly on the cheek.

"Not really, dear," Brynne said. "But that will change. I have to get someone fired. Then all will be fine again."

"I'm sure that won't be a problem."

"Of course not." Brynne smiled.

KENZIE

"Hey, you must be Candy!" Chase Fielding was a hugger. He jumped out of his seat in the reception area, shook Kenzie's hand, and embraced her like they'd known each other for years. But they'd never met. Chase, a film director, wanted to shoot some footage at the track, and Kenzie had arranged to show him around. "Thanks for having me out here today."

"It's *Kenzie*," she said, "and it's nice to meet you, Mr. Fielding. Glad you could come."

Chase had deep-set brown eyes. Most of his chocolate-brown hair was hidden beneath a blue Los Angeles Dodgers cap. He sported a carefully groomed goatee. There was a paunch beneath his ratty beige windbreaker that suggested an affinity for rich food and cold beer.

"Well, I'm eager to get a tour. Shall we?" he asked.

They moved quickly from Kenzie's office to the stables. She was happy to tell Chase about Grayson. One month into the new job, she already had a potential film being shot there. She'd sent word to the local film commissions that Grayson could be a wonderful venue, which sparked interest from a few studios.

Kenzie was eager to talk to Chase, but as they walked he took one phone call after the next. They hardly spoke. When they approached the back side of the track, he hung up the phone.

"I'm so sorry. I didn't mean to be rude," Chase said. "Trying to get a lot done in a short period of time."

"Oh, no problem. I know you're busy," Kenzie said.

"So the barns are on the left?" Chase asked as they approached horse trainer Shrader Clement's barn, which housed a few Thoroughbreds.

Kenzie nodded. Chase took an abrupt turn, walked swiftly around the perimeter of the stable, and glanced inside. Kenzie noticed how quickly he surveyed the premises.

And then he was finished. He signaled that they should head back to her office. Kenzie was surprised. She'd thought he'd have a million questions. But Chase was on a mission, and he'd apparently gotten what he needed. He continued texting and talking on the phone as they walked back to Kenzie's office.

As Chase tended to his calls, Kenzie smiled when she saw Matt Gibson drive up the road. He waved and rolled up alongside her.

"Hey, how come we never see you on the backstretch anymore?" Matt shouted out the window of his silver full-size pickup. "You too good for us now that you're a big exec?"

Kenzie used to be intimidated by Matt, a big, handsome dude who looked like an ex-jock of some sort, with broad shoulders and a muscular build. He had a wicked sense of humor and often caught her off guard with a joke that played well with the guys but was lost on her. She'd smile and laugh, even though she hadn't a clue what he was talking about. Then he'd call her on it, which made her feel worse. While working on the backside, she'd learned that Matt was not only the leading jockey's agent but also a former local sportscaster. She couldn't get over how the guys showered him with attention and praise, like he was a famous athlete. At first she was kind of interested in him but had noticed he wore a wedding band.

"I just gave a director a tour of Clement's barn. He's thinking of filming some scenes for his next movie here," Kenzie said. She crossed in front of Matt's truck and around to the driver's window. Folding her arms across her chest, she stared up into the cab.

"Calling it *Fifty Shades of Hay*?" he asked.

"Very funny, but Fiftyshadesofhay isn't trained here. That horse is at Bob Baffert's barn in Santa Anita. Owned by Mike Pegram, Karl Watson, and Paul Weitman. I'm sure you know that." Kenzie watched as Matt chewed on a toothpick.

"Impressive," he said.

"Hey, I'm just a font of information. At your service."

"Really?" He chuckled, peering down from the cab. "At my service? Great, let me tell you what I need." He winked.

"Very funny. I didn't mean it that way."

"Then what way did you mean it?" He smiled coyly.

Kenzie uncrossed her arms as their eyes met. She was tongue-tied. He had that effect on people. He'd first caught her eye with his broad, sexy smile. Matt's snappy repartee kept her off balance. But whenever she encountered him, it felt like an army of butterflies invaded her stomach.

"I just meant . . . you know." Kenzie lowered her eyes and gazed at the bits of hay, dirt, and gravel under her feet, then spotted a copper penny embedded in the ground. She reached for it, flicked off the dirt, and showed it to Matt.

"Look. A lucky penny!" she said.

"I guess. But it's only lucky because you found it while talking to me. I have that effect on people."

"Okay, sure," said Kenzie, smirking. "Then it'd better bring me good luck. I'm counting on you." She raised it high in the air before placing it in her back pocket.

"You don't need good luck, Kenzie. You're doing great."

"How do you know how well I'm doing?"

"I just know." Matt rested his elbow on the frame of the open window and stared directly at Kenzie. "Hear stuff."

"You don't know anything about me." Their flirtatious banter began to make Kenzie feel uncomfortable and a little guilty. Matt was married.

"Well, then how does one get to know you?" Matt asked. His unyielding gaze intimidated her. "How does one get through that protective armor?"

Kenzie put her hands in her back pockets and glanced at the morning ritual around her. A colt and its groom strolled beside them, while another horse stood patiently awaiting his morning bath. An exercise rider mounted a mare and began making her way to the track. It was like Kenzie never left this place. The backstretch. Her home for the past four years. Out of the corner of her eye, she saw Chase, who was way ahead of her now.

"I've gotta get going." But she remained there, staring up at him.

"I'm sure you do," Matt said as he settled back into the driver's seat, the toothpick flicking between his lips. He waited a beat before he put the truck in gear. Then he gave Kenzie a big smile, waved, and sped up the road.

Kenzie walked slowly at first, and then realized Chase was probably already at her office. She glanced back at Matt's truck, which took a turn into another barn.

"Yup, we'll do the scene here," Chase said as soon as she walked into her office. "I'm going to text Marty, my location scout, and have him work the dates out with you."

"Well, great, Mr. Fielding, I'm glad it works for you," Kenzie said as she returned to her desk.

Chase sat in the seat opposite hers and then reclined in his chair. He took a deep breath, looked around the office for a bit, and seemed to relax a little. She felt his eyes on her as she keyed something into the computer.

"So what do you do here?" Chase asked.

"Oh, promotions and events for the track," Kenzie said simply. She turned away from the computer to look at Chase.

Chase spotted the small refrigerator behind her desk and, without saying a word, got up and pulled out two plastic water bottles. He handed one to Kenzie and returned to his chair.

"Ever wanted to be an actress?" he asked.

"No. Never crossed my mind."

"Hmm. Kind of refreshing," Chase said as he guzzled about half the bottle.

She turned back to her computer and finished typing.

"Nice photo." Chase nodded toward a frame on her desk.

Kenzie shifted her attention to the picture of her and her mother. Her mom was sitting on her front porch, smiling wistfully at the rosebushes she had recently planted.

"Thanks. My mom and me. Few weeks before she passed."

"Oh, I'm sorry," Chase said. He fell silent as he stared at Kenzie and took another long sip of water. "I hope it doesn't make you uncomfortable if I tell you that you're extremely attractive."

"Well, thank you. I appreciate that." She blushed slightly as she pulled her chair in toward the desk, sat up straight, and looked at Chase. "Really glad you think Grayson might work for what you need. Please let me know if there's anything more I can do."

"Thanks. Like I said, Marty will get back to you with the dates. I think this place will be just great."

"Good. I'm glad," Kenzie said as she got up and walked with Chase to the door. There was a pause as their eyes met. He reached for her hand and offered a firm handshake. His hand was smooth and cool, with no calluses—unlike the hands of the racetrackers like Matt, which were dry, rough, and leathery. Chase held on to her hand longer than necessary and then let go.

"So I was wondering," Chase said, "would you like to go out sometime?"

Kenzie felt her face flush. "Sure." She said it without even thinking. Being with Chase reminded her of the past. The world of filmmaking and fun. For a moment she remembered it fondly.

"I'll call you," he said, and exited.

Kenzie was left standing at the door.

She wondered if Chase might be someone she'd like to date. And who knew where it could lead? If they had a lot in common, then maybe—

She stopped the thought before it could finish itself. Ever since Gemma's psychic had collapsed outside her car and then died, she couldn't get the woman's last words out of her head. About her "future husband." It was ridiculous—childish. She hated herself for even entertaining the foolish thought.

Yet she couldn't forget Annalisa's dying prophecy.

* * * * *

Two weeks passed before Kenzie received the call. But it didn't come from Chase. It came from his assistant, asking if she'd meet him for dinner that evening. Kenzie didn't appreciate his employee calling to ask her out on a date. And at the eleventh hour.

"I'm not sure—" Kenzie said.

"I know this is last-minute," the assistant interrupted. "But Mr. Fielding's schedule changed, and he'd like to see you if possible."

Kenzie was curious. She wanted to go out with Chase. She'd felt a tiny spark of interest when they were together and was curious whether there might be something there. He could've called himself, but she remembered what her own crazy schedule was like four years ago. "Well . . . okay," Kenzie said.

* * * * *

When she arrived at the restaurant that evening, she was astonished to see Chase already seated at a table of six assembled in the corner. She'd thought it would be just the two of them. But when the hostess brought her to the table, she realized she was the last to arrive. There were two other couples.

Chase stood, reached for her hand, and kissed her cheek.

"Kenzie, let me introduce you," Chase said. He gestured toward each person, starting on Kenzie's left. "This is Fred and Patty. And sitting next to you are Martin and his wife, Brynne. Martin and Fred will be providing the financing for my next film."

Wait a second, Brynne? Kenzie's eyes darted from Patty's short blonde bob and Fred's manicured beard to Martin's yellow bow tie and then back to Brynne. What was she doing here? It couldn't be. It was. Kenzie looked at Brynne again to make sure she wasn't hallucinating. Yep. It was her. Brynne offered a smug, saccharine smile.

"Chase, darlin'," Brynne said, "this girl works at the racetrack."

"Yes, she does," Chase said as he helped Kenzie into her seat. "Oh, of course, you'd know each other. I'd forgotten that you had horses at Grayson."

"I suppose this is a new girlfriend?" Brynne asked.

Kenzie was sick. His date must've canceled at the last minute. She felt like a fool.

"Brynne, I can always count on you for entertainment," Chase said.

"Glad you could join us," Patty said.

"Well, why don't we order? I'm kinda hungry," Chase said, apparently trying to move things along.

"I read you might get Scarlett Johansson for your new film," Patty said. "Is that true? I love her."

"Depends on her schedule," Chase said, his eyes focused on the menu.

"I have a meeting at ABC tomorrow," Patty said. "Brynne, do you wanna go with me? I don't really want to do it alone."

"Oh, you'll be fine. I don't think you need me," Brynne laughed.

"She needs to find a writer," Fred chimed in. "We have the rights to a book that Patty believes will make a good TV series."

Kenzie couldn't figure out who these folks were, what positions they held in the entertainment industry. She'd never been around the finance types, as she'd worked mostly with film executives and producers.

"I hope you're doing okay," Chase whispered in Kenzie's ear as the others conversed.

"Yes, I'm fine," Kenzie said. "Just not sure who everyone is. Well, I mean, other than Brynne."

"These guys aren't in the entertainment business. But they want to produce movies. So they offered to put up money for one I may do next summer. Haven't decided yet. They're kind of courting me." He scooted his chair a little closer to hers. "And the wives . . . Well, I guess maybe they need something to do."

"But they pitch shows to the television networks?" she whispered back.

"Everyone's a producer." He gave her a pointed look. "These guys have a lot of money, so the studios take a few meetings with their wives. You know, to appease them." Chase smiled conspiratorially, as if Kenzie would understand what he was saying. The truth was that she did understand. She'd been in that business. But she wasn't about to reveal her past to Chase or to anyone else at the table.

"So what exactly do you do, Kenzie?" Patty asked as the waiter took the last of their orders. Kenzie felt the women's eyes on her as the men engaged with their cell phones, which they held discreetly under the table.

"Marketing for Grayson Downs. Events. Promotions. Things like that," Kenzie said. The less said, the better.

"By yourself?" Patty looked at her incredulously.

"Just me and a social media coordinator." Kenzie forced a smile, trying to deflect the attention.

"Oh," Patty said. "Well, anyway, Brynne, dear, I have to come back with an entire story worked out. We'll have to get together this week, 'cause I'd love for you to help me with this."

"Oh, I can't this week." Brynne's bottom lip jutted in a sulky pout. "We're sending the girls back to school on Thursday, so I want to spend every waking minute with them before they leave."

"You must miss them so much when they're gone. I understand. Our son, Sam, is away at college this year. They grow up so fast," Patty said.

"You can't imagine." Brynne sighed deeply. "But they wanted to go to boarding school. What can I say? I'll definitely be able to help with your idea. I'll need a distraction."

Kenzie was trying to keep her jaw from hitting the floor. Didn't these women realize that simply watching a movie didn't qualify one to be a producer? Did they think they could be ballerinas because they attended the ballet? Or writers because they knew the alphabet? She was stunned by their naïveté.

Chase reached for Kenzie's hand and squeezed it, but Kenzie left her fingers limp in his grasp. She didn't fit in and wished she hadn't accepted this date. Chase seemed exactly like the men she'd met at Fox and Victory who were consumed by work, their personal and professional identities melded as one. She wondered why he even asked her to dinner that evening. Maybe it was just a prelude to a hookup later. She'd met plenty of men like that.

"Hey, Fred, what do you think of that new deal with Netflix?" Chase asked. This created a lot of discussion. Kenzie was thrilled to just eat her dinner. It was the kind of dinner she hadn't enjoyed, well, since she'd had an expense account. Each bite reminded her of those good ol' meals she'd left behind.

This dinner brought it all back. The business lunches, the travel, the hours with her BlackBerry in one hand, an iPhone in the other, and sometimes her Android at her side as well. Calls in the middle of the night, emails, faxes, texts. No sleep. The frenetic pace, the anxiety. She took a few deep breaths, peered around the restaurant, and noticed women with plunging necklines, Botoxed foreheads, full enhanced lips, and diamond rings the size of . . . well, the size of horse turds. Then she noticed Matt Gibson sitting at a table, presumably with his wife and another couple.

"Chase," Patty said, "I hear you'll be leaving soon to direct your next picture. Where will you be going?"

"Melbourne for five weeks, then back here for three." Chase reached for his glass and took a sip of wine.

"Well, that's great," Brynne said. "And what will you do, Kenzie, while Chase is away? Will you be going with him? Giving up your job?"

"Uh, we just met, Brynne," Chase said. He looked at Kenzie and smiled. But she glanced at the exit, ready for this night to be over.

"I'd like to make a toast to Chase's date," Fred said out of the blue. He stood up and raised his glass toward Kenzie. His tone was firm and his eyes were bright with anticipation. "To Kenzie, the girl with the beautiful ass and the sexy pink thong."

Kenzie had just taken a sip of wine, but it went down the wrong way. She began coughing hard and struggled to catch her breath.

Fred's drunken behavior wasn't lost on anyone. As Kenzie continued to cough and clear her throat, Patty urged Fred to sit down. But he continued to run off at the mouth, crowing about the incident onstage.

Kenzie slumped deep into the back of her chair. Her face was on fire. Her heart beat rapidly in her chest. Fred reached across Patty and grabbed Kenzie's arm.

"Hey, I wasn't there," he beamed. "But I saw the video. Nice butt is all I can say."

"Oh, my dear God, that was you?" Brynne was radiant. She took out her phone, insisting that despite it being four years, she still had the video saved. "It must be on here somewhere. I'm sure it was transferred to this phone. I'll find it."

Chase whispered so only Kenzie could hear. "Was that you?"

She nodded and slumped further into her chair. It was like being onstage all over again.

"Wow, I didn't see it, but I remember hearing about it at the time. Must've been awful," he said.

"Wasn't great," Kenzie said.

"Hey," Fred continued in his drunken stupor, "are you wearing a thong tonight? Wanna show us?" Patty pushed him back into his seat and tried to keep him quiet.

Abruptly, Kenzie threw the napkin off her lap, stood up, pushed in her chair, and walked away from the table without uttering one word. Chase called after her, but it was too late.

She was gone.

GEMMA

"What a nightmare," Gemma said in a hushed tone as she stuffed a handful of popcorn in her mouth. "Brynne Tomlinson sounds horrible. I'm sure you couldn't wait to get out of there."

"I couldn't stand it," Kenzie said under her breath as the lights in the movie theater dimmed. "It was like I had no control over my body. It just leaped out of the seat and tore out of there."

"Don't worry," Gemma murmured as she patted Kenzie's knee. "You did the right thing. Let's watch the movie and get your mind off it."

The opening credits ran over a sequence featuring a young mother and daughter flying a kite on the beach. Gemma immediately thought about the times she used to do that with her mom. She smiled at the memory. But as the credits continued, her mind continued to wander.

Gemma watched the movie but wasn't the least bit engaged. All she could think about was the story her mom told her about meeting her father. It had been a week and she still couldn't get it out of her mind. The more she thought about it, the more she hated Jeffrey. And now she was sure that he hated her, too. She realized it was unlikely he'd ever sought her out or stalked her the way she had him.

As the movie played on, Gemma wondered if over the years Jeffrey had regretted his actions. Maybe he felt bad that he'd offered such a harsh and inflexible deal. Maybe his parents had driven it, not him. She'd heard stories like that before. Thirty-three years was a long time.

Maybe it was time to reconcile things.

Gemma had wanted to tell her mother that she saw Jeffrey at the pharmacy. And that she'd discovered where her green eyes came from. But after hearing her mother's story, she knew her mother wouldn't approve.

Gemma had her own thoughts as to what might happen next. Once Jeffrey met her—his *daughter*—once he got to know her, things might be different. Eventually he might even accept her into his family. He might never embrace her mother, but surely he would want to see his child. What parent wouldn't?

"Interesting relationship between them, isn't it?" Kenzie's question interrupted Gemma's thoughts. "The mother in this film always telling the daughter that she's not being realistic. Sound familiar?"

"Hmmm," Gemma said. Of course she related to that. Her mother considered her a dreamer and often accused her of living in a fantasy world. "Stay in reality," she'd say. Just thinking about that reminded Gemma of what her mother said after she revealed the story about Jeffrey Kahn: "I know what you're thinking, Gem. Please don't get your hopes up. I don't believe things have changed. I wouldn't approach him. I don't think it's wise."

But her mom's words would not deter her. In fact, Gemma felt emboldened. Inspired. The more she thought about it, the more determined she became. She wanted to know her father. She'd introduce herself to Jeffrey. She just had to find the right time and place. It had to be well timed, perfectly orchestrated.

Gemma started to conceive a new plan.

SARITA

"What're you doing up there, Sarita? Mama has your dinner." Papa's voice made her cringe.

"I already ate. At work!" Sarita shouted from her bedroom. Then she heard her mother's footsteps approaching and a light tapping on her door.

"You already ate?" Mama asked. "You don't want to eat with your family at dinnertime? I saved leftovers for you. You can just heat them up. What's gotten into you? Open this door. Please."

Sarita rolled her eyes, jumped off the bed, and opened the door. A crack.

"Mama, really, I'm not hungry. I love your dinners. But not tonight. I had to stay late at work, and we had dinner brought in," Sarita said softly, sensing her mother's disappointment. "I'm tired. I'll see you in the morning."

Without saying more, her mother turned and walked away, and Sarita slowly closed the door, then lay down on her bed and stared at the ceiling. She'd lived in this room since she was six years old. It reflected nothing about who she was now.

Once she heard that her mother had descended the stairs, Sarita jumped up off the bed, stuffed some clothes into a plastic bag, and tiptoed down the hallway. With her bag in one hand, she dislodged the door that led to the attic, unfolded the stairs, climbed up into the darkness, and closed the hatch.

She'd discovered that the attic extended beyond the area that held the old boxes with family heirlooms. There was a room tucked farther back, over the garage. The past few weeks, Sarita had made that space her refuge.

She erected a big wall of boxes with a small opening she could slide through. Over time, she arranged lace doilies, vintage glass ornaments, fringed and beaded lampshades, vampire figurines, black and red velvet pillows, masks, coffin purses, skulls, a collection of Anne Rice and Stephen King paperbacks, silver bracelets, and ticket stubs featuring the Black Veil Brides, Alter Bridge, Bullet for My Valentine, and Siouxsie Sioux. And then she hung a black lacy mosquito net from the low ceiling. It was her sanctuary.

Sarita set the plastic bag aside, then sat on a small beanbag chair she'd hauled up the previous weekend and lit two beeswax skull candles, which offered some much-needed light. She adjusted her earphones, closed her eyes, and sang along with Chibi, the lead singer of the Birthday Massacre. She made sure to sing softly. She didn't want to call attention to herself or raise suspicion. She sang the same song over and over, as if studying for a test, making sure she knew the exact words. She looked through the window and saw the moon hovering over the mountains. Her phone vibrated. It was a text from Kenzie.

Sorry to bother you so late. But can you come in earlier tomorrow? I want to go over the promotional video with you.

Of course, Sarita texted back. A little over a month into the job, she was really enjoying it. She especially liked working for Kenzie.

8. My office.

Sarita reluctantly typed *Okay* in reply. She looked at the time on her phone and hoped her parents were in bed. It would be a long night, so she knew she'd better get going.

She dumped the items from the plastic bag onto her chair and then ripped off her jeans and replaced them with black skinnies and eyelet combat boots with buckle chains. She put on a black shredded skirt adorned with big silver safety pins, a spiked collar around her neck, and a pair of purple velvet arm warmers. The fingerless rainbow gloves and black strappy jacket went on last. She stood up and peered into the small, curvy black baroque mirror superglued to the wall and began applying black liquid eyeliner, burgundy lipstick, three applications of black eye shadow, and a heavy black brow pencil. The red synthetic wig, thick with bangs, and ten thin, spiked silver bracelets on each arm went on last.

She crouched down as she moved toward the only window in the attic, then yanked on the rope attached to the folded emergency escape ladder that was lying under a tarp on the ground below. As she pulled on the rope, the ladder unfolded. She attached the anti-slip brace securely to the outside of the window frame. Then she slid out the window and made her way down the ladder into the shrubbery below. Fortunately the attic window was at the side of the house, so she left the ladder hanging in case she needed to get back in later. Because she wanted to avoid a late-night encounter with her parents, Sarita walked to the bus stop instead of taking her car, which was parked in the driveway.

When she arrived at the Deathrock Bar, a line of similarly clad young men and women stood in line. The daytime Sarita was no match for the Sarita who came here. This was her element. These were her people. Everyone knew her. She'd been part of this community for a while. The waters parted when she entered. She was a star.

"Hey, you're going on in a second," Levi Evans said as Sarita waltzed by the bar leading to the stage. "Got Bristol's band tonight."

Sarita high-fived Levi as she made her way through the densely populated and loud smoke-filled room toward the stage, and then took a seat at a small table with four guys.

"You almost missed your set." Damien Storey's ghostly white face, heavily made-up eyes, dark-purple lipstick, and bright-green Mohawk stood out even in this crowd. His half-inch-wide stainless-steel O-ring stretched across his earlobe, as large as the button on her winter coat.

"My parents. Had to make sure they were in bed." Sarita sighed, then kissed Damien softly on the lips.

"You're on soon. Ready?" he asked.

"I am."

Sarita smiled. She kissed Damien again and then attached a narrow stainless-steel nose hoop through her nostril. Damien wrapped his arm around her back and drew her close.

Sarita poured herself a beer, drank it, then drank another. She waited for her name to be called. She wasn't nervous. In fact, she scooted her chair closer to Damien's and relaxed, her head on his shoulder, as he took a sip of his drink. The band was so loud they could barely hear each other.

Even though they had only been together a few months, Sarita felt connected to Damien, a twenty-eight-year-old from Newport Beach who'd dropped out of college but who was already an account manager at Ernst & Young. Sarita admired his intelligence, tenacity, and unfailing support. She'd been smitten the second they met shortly after she returned home from college. She wanted to be with him all the time but knew it wouldn't be possible until she moved out of her parents' home. In the meantime, she sneaked out often so they could rendezvous at the club.

Damien had asked her to move in with him, but Sarita wasn't ready for that, nor for the drama it would create within her family. She lived on the edge, enjoying half her life with Damien and their friends, and the other with her family and coworkers. At any second it could all fall apart. But she felt at peace and happy in this environment and counted the hours in between.

"Okay, next up, Sarita!" The moment she heard her name, Sarita bolted out of Damien's arms and rushed to the stage. She grabbed the mic and within seconds was belting out the words to "Stargazer," a song recorded by Siouxsie and the Banshees. Sarita loved this upbeat, guitar-driven pop tune because the lyrics were about someone who looked up at the stars and wished for a better life.

Sarita clutched the microphone and held it close to her lips, singing the words with conviction and passion. She hoped her face reflected the pain and anguish of someone trying to break out of one world into another. At the end of her performance, she put down the microphone and was greeted by wild applause.

When Sarita returned to the table, her friends high-fived her. She tumbled into her seat next to Damien and drank another beer. Draping his arm across her back, he whispered congratulations.

However, as the night wore on, Sarita became less exuberant. Like Cinderella, she was facing her own midnight deadline, because she had an early meeting the next day with Kenzie. But on the way out she was asked to return a week from Thursday to compete with five others for the chance to be the lead singer in a new industrial band called the Witches of Skeletal Symphony, which had been recently formed by Moody Gray, a famous Goth guitarist. And because Moody got his start at the Deathrock Bar, he'd decided to hold a contest to find a lead singer for his new band there.

"Really? They want me to compete in the contest? Oh, wow!" Sarita was elated. She covered her mouth with her hand and gave a small yelp.

Damien drew her close and muttered softly, "You crushed it, baby. But of course, I knew you would."

Damien drove them to his apartment, where they shared a cold pizza. He was supposed to take Sarita home, but they could barely keep their hands off each other. Soon they were in Damien's bedroom making love. Sarita had fallen hard for Damien. She hated leaving him. They relied on texts and FaceTime because their time together was so limited. She thought about him constantly. She'd never had a boyfriend as attentive. If only her parents would approve. But they never would. He was hardly the kind of man they had in mind for her.

As 3:00 a.m. approached, they both lay in bed staring at the clock. Sarita had to be at work in five hours. It was time to leave. When Damien took her home, he encouraged her to think about entering the contest, but she laughed. She desperately wanted to compete, but she couldn't. She reminded him of "suitor night" on Thursday evenings, which she had to keep open. Not being present for one of her father's matchmaking sessions would create havoc. They thought about all kinds of excuses, but none were feasible.

Damien pulled alongside her house and watched as she climbed up and through the open attic window. She folded the ladder and brought it inside. He waited until she waved that she was in safely, and then she watched him drive away.

* * * * *

Four hours later Sarita was awakened by her alarm. She looked in the mirror and was horrified to see that she hadn't removed her makeup from the night before. She ran to the bathroom and shut the door.

"We didn't see you the entire night," her father said outside the door. "What is wrong, my dear one? Why are you so distant? We are so happy to have our youngest back home, and yet we never see you. Never speak to you. You tell us to leave you alone. And we do. But dear one, we've no idea what your life is like. We worry for your safety."

"Papa, I'm really tired," Sarita said from inside the bathroom. "I work. You know that's what I do. And when I come home, I do more work, and then I sleep. I need to do well in this job. I want to make money so I can move out and be on my own. I need to get on with my life. You know that."

"It is not what I want for you, Sarita. You are special. And I don't want you to carry the burden of living on your own with no support. No love. No happiness. Surely one cannot be happy alone. This is not the life Mama and I want for you," Papa said. "A young man is coming over a week from this Thursday. He is from the Gupta family. I have met him and his parents. Your mama knows them, as do your sisters. The matchmaker will be here, too. All are most fond of him and think he may be the one for you."

Sarita opened the door. She had removed all her makeup and stood in her nightshirt. She looked up at her father. She noticed the deep wrinkles in his forehead and his furry black unibrow. He smelled of cigars. His penchant for them caused her mother much pain, particularly because she suspected that it had led to the throat cancer he'd overcome ten years ago. He'd sworn off cigars, but they had crept back into his life. And no matter what his wife or three daughters said, no matter how hard they begged, he couldn't give them up.

"Papa, I have work to do on Thursdays—"

"No. Work does not come before this," Papa interrupted sharply. "I am not raising a son. You are my daughter. And I will not have this. You will be here that Thursday evening." He turned to walk away. "And you will act like a woman."

Sarita gritted her teeth. The night before she'd been so happy and now she felt like a schoolgirl, a prisoner in her own home. In that moment Sarita understood that when it came to the music she loved, the time for her was now or never. She would not let her father and "suitor night" ruin her future. Instead, she would at last sing in a competition that could fulfill her dream of being in a band, something she'd wanted so badly for years. She'd hidden her aspiration from her parents, who would never approve of that kind of life. But she'd worked all through college to pay for the voice lessons. She couldn't give up now.

She went to her room, shut the door, and pounded out a text to Damien saying that she would be at the club a week from Thursday.

BRYNNE

"Yes, she walked out of the restaurant last week. Left us all sitting there. I mean, I wouldn't consider that especially professional, would you?" Brynne munched on some almonds, which she carried in a tiny sack inside her fancy yellow clutch. She contemplated the cheese that was sitting on Leo's desk in the corner but noticed it had congealed. Leo sat back in his big leather chair, fidgeting with a couple of rubber bands. He was noticeably distressed, and that pleased Brynne.

"Kenzie left the dinner?" Leo didn't even look at Brynne, but she thought she was really getting through to him, that he would see what a complete disaster Kenzie Armstrong was, and how unprofessional and inappropriate she was for the track. "Yes, Leo. And I assume you know the story about her and the, well, the incident in New York. The thong," Brynne added.

He leaned forward, watching Brynne as she continued snacking on her almonds. She knew he'd respond to the thong.

"You don't know what happened?" Brynne tried to suppress her delight. She loved that she had the goods on Kenzie. She knew the information would destroy any positive thoughts he had about her.

He'd find the story comical and he'd repeat it a million times. She couldn't wait to show him the video, which was still on her phone. "She made a speech in New York about some movie she was publicizing, but unbeknownst to her, the back of her skirt got caught in her itty-bitty thong, and, well, it exposed her. Her derriere. To everyone. The whole audience."

Brynne stopped and took a sip of water, hiding a smile at Leo's rapt expression.

"Someone sent me the clip. Would you like to see it?" Brynne asked, but Leo closed his eyes and shook his head. "It was a few years ago. The video went viral, as they say." Brynne grabbed another couple of almonds, then folded the little plastic bag tightly and put it in her purse. "She's a disaster, Leo. You need to get rid of her. She might as well be a porn star."

Leo glared at Brynne. She waited for him to respond, but he didn't. Instead, he got up, thanked her for coming, and opened the door. But Brynne didn't move. She remained seated.

"Leo, do I need to remind you how many horses I have here? How much Tomlinson Industries pays you per month to keep them? Without them, I'm not even sure Grayson would continue."

Leo licked his lips and shifted on his feet. "Brynne, I appreciate that you train here. Of course."

Brynne, at five foot seven and in three-inch heels, towered over Leo, who was often mistaken for a jockey. She moved up alongside him and peered down as she delivered her parting shot.

"I'm warning you. Don't patronize me. You know who really runs this track. Me. I wouldn't mess with me if I were you. I'll be back here in a few days. And let me tell you, I don't want to see Kenzie Armstrong in that office. I don't want sluts who walk onstage flashing their buttocks at the audience. Grayson is much classier than that. Make sure she's gone."

Brynne spun dramatically and exited quickly. When she was out of sight, she heard Leo slam the door, which made her smile.

KENZIE

"Kenzie, please come in," Leo said through the intercom.

"Sure, Leo, on my way," Kenzie said. "Did you want to talk about the women's expo? I'm about to meet with Sarita and—"

"No," Leo interrupted. "Why the heck does Brynne Tomlinson hate you? And what's this about a thong? What in the world happened? She was just in here trashing you."

Kenzie's legs liquefied as she sank onto the chair opposite his desk. She didn't know what to say.

"Actually, Kenzie, I don't need an explanation. I don't care if you like to show your ass to a room full of folks. Doesn't really matter to me. What does matter is Brynne Tomlinson. Grayson is dying. I don't know if you've noticed. The commercial shoots and movie shoots we've had here recently aren't enough. We have to survive as a racing operation. This upcoming meet has to turn this place around. The last thing I want to think about is losing the Tomlinson horses. Keeping this place open year-round for training is essential, and I can't have her on my ass every second, demanding that I get rid of you. So figure something out. If you want to keep your job, you're gonna have to work with her."

Kenzie was heartsick. She struggled to gather her thoughts. She sat for another moment, and then when she realized Leo wasn't going to add anything more, she stood up and exited his office without saying a word.

She sat quietly at her desk for what seemed like an eternity. There was so much work to do, but it didn't matter. The only thing that mattered was Brynne Tomlinson. Why did this woman hate her so? Was she still angry that Leo hired her instead of Brynne's cousin? Couldn't she move on? Kenzie leaned back in her chair and thought about what she'd say to Brynne. After a moment she picked up the receiver and placed the call.

"What is it, Leo?" Brynne answered.

"Um, hi, it's Kenzie. Kenzie Arm—"

"Yes, I know who you are. What do you want? I thought Leo was calling me, from the Grayson caller ID on my phone. Oh, he must've asked you to call. Did he fire you?"

"Well, no. I was hoping you might give me a chance. You know, to maybe talk this out. Clearly we got off on the wrong foot, and I want to see if there's any way we might be able to—"

"No, there's not," Brynne interrupted. "I told Leo I wanted him to fire you. He needs to hire my cousin, who knows far more than you about advertising or whatever it is you do. Apparently he didn't get the message, so—"

"Look, please." Kenzie was practically begging. "Can't we please talk? I mean, we've never even had a conversation. It seems as if you want me fired for the sport of it." Kenzie waited but Brynne didn't respond. She wasn't sure if she'd already hung up. After a moment Kenzie continued. "Brynne, all I'm asking for is an opportunity for you to get to know me a bit. To hear what plans I have for the track. If after our meeting you still want me out, then fine."

There was a long pause.

"Fine. Tomorrow. Ten o'clock. Pissarro's." And the phone went dead.

Kenzie had come to the racetrack to get away from people like Brynne Tomlinson. She'd spent years healing. She just wanted to feel happy again. Life had improved. But now she had to convince Brynne Tomlinson to let her stay at the track.

It was times like these that made her think about the one person she missed so much. Her mom. The only one who'd understood. The one who'd listened. Her best friend. She missed her encouragement, her positive attitude, her unyielding support. She knew her mom would say that things would improve. And she'd end by saying, "Be strong. Believe in yourself." The words weren't unique, but Kenzie would give anything to hear them again.

And then the tears came. They trickled down her cheeks. She grabbed a tissue to wipe them away. She couldn't cry. Not at work.

"Be strong. Believe in yourself."

"Uh, is this not a good time?" Sarita asked as she peeked in the door.

Kenzie blew her nose and waved her inside. "You can come in."

Sarita had an armful of folders. She set them on Kenzie's desk and sat opposite her. "You okay?"

"First rule, never let them see you cry." Kenzie laughed as she tossed the tissue into the wastebasket under her desk.

"Sometimes one has to cry," Sarita said. "I want to apologize for being late this morning. Late night. But I have some good news. Word is getting out. Our social media profile is growing. Grayson has lots of new followers on both Facebook and Twitter, and I started an Instagram account and put great pictures of Grayson on there."

"That's good," mumbled Kenzie. She walked over to the window and looked out at the paddock.

"I'll have more information as—"

"It's okay," Kenzie interrupted, her eyes downcast.

"What's wrong?"

"Brynne." Kenzie wiped the back of her hand across her nose and sniffed softly, and then turned toward Sarita. "Leo said I have to make it work with her or I'm out. I'm meeting her tomorrow morning."

"Oh boy." Sarita walked over to Kenzie. They both stood silently admiring the paddock, which was being landscaped. Kenzie opened the sliding door onto the small patio, which had just one chair, and Sarita followed.

"So pretty out here, isn't it?" Kenzie asked.

"I love the smell of freshly cut grass," Sarita said. "But did you know that the scent is the lawn trying to save itself from injury just inflicted?"

"Really?" Kenzie turned toward Sarita. "No, I never knew that."

"Botany 101. Good to know, if you ever want to start a landscaping business."

"Don't tempt me," Kenzie said sarcastically.

Sarita walked to the chair and sat down while Kenzie continued to stare at the gardeners who were adjusting the automatic sprinklers in the middle of the paddock.

"Have you ever Googled yourself?" Sarita sat lazily on the chair and looked at Kenzie.

"Sure, why?" Kenzie asked, instantly tensing.

"You have quite an online presence. Lots of stories written about you."

Kenzie sighed. "Yes, I know."

"No, not about that. Not everything is about that!" Sarita stood.

Kenzie covered her eyes with a hand. "Oh great, so you know about that, too?"

"I learned about it when I first Googled you after my interview with Leo. But it meant nothing to me. It was obviously painful for you, and I certainly understand that. But more important, you were at the top of your game."

Kenzie lowered her hand and looked up to see Sarita's earnest expression.

"Almost every article I read referred to you as the consummate professional. And that hasn't changed. In the five weeks we've worked together, I've seen how talented you are. You just lost your way for a while. Lost your confidence. But you can get it back." Sarita moved closer to her and said softly, "You can turn this around."

Kenzie smiled. "*Confidence.* Yes, I remember that word. I remember once having had that."

"It's coming back." Sarita said tenderly. "Get a good night's sleep so you can face this—or rather *her*—in the morning."

Kenzie put her arm around Sarita. "Thank you. I appreciate that."

* * * * *

Even though Kenzie had arrived fifteen minutes early, Brynne was already seated when she walked onto Pissarro's patio the next morning. Kenzie pulled out the chair across from Brynne and sat down. Brynne sipped her latte and stared at her and then signaled for the waitress to bring Kenzie some coffee.

Kenzie was a wreck. Her nails were bitten to the quick, she'd somehow lost the middle button on her blouse between her apartment and the restaurant, and there was a big red blemish on her upper lip. A cold sore, no doubt. Despite planning a good night's sleep, she'd tossed and turned all night, worrying about this conversation. She was exhausted.

As soon as Kenzie's coffee arrived, Brynne told her how much she loved this place. It was private, quiet, and peaceful. She bragged about the dinner she'd had with Martin there just a few weeks ago to celebrate their anniversary. He had surprised her with a beautiful small yellow cake with white roses, her favorite. It had been such a romantic moment. He was so in love with her, even after nineteen years.

Kenzie knew Brynne was eager to share this information because she placed such a high value on marriage and family. The purpose was to make her feel insecure and inadequate. But Kenzie hoped to have a family someday, too. Although she didn't plan on sharing those personal thoughts with Brynne. She just wanted to get through their meeting with her job intact and was desperate to address the issue at hand.

"I think I should begin by saying I'm sorry." Kenzie placed her coffee cup in the saucer and noticed her hand was shaking. "I feel terrible that we got off on the wrong foot." She couldn't bring herself to look at Brynne.

"I appreciate that. But that's not what this is about."

Kenzie waited for her to say more. She knew Brynne would take her time.

"It's a personal thing," Brynne said as she glanced at two men sitting at the table next to them. "I just don't think you're the right person for the job. And then when I learned you were the one who walked off the stage, and then you bolted out of the restaurant—well, I just knew I was right. Grayson needs someone competent. You don't impress me as being . . . Well, you don't seem especially tough. You seem weak. And we need a strong executive at the track. Preferably a man. There are just certain jobs that require men. Like airline pilots or car salesmen. Would you fly on a commercial airliner flown by a woman? Or purchase a new car from one? It just doesn't seem right. I don't think women are properly suited for those positions."

Kenzie stared at her. Brynne was a relic from the past.

She took a beat and then sucked in a breath to speak. "I'm not weak," Kenzie said. "Yes, I was humiliated that day. But it was four years ago. My mother had died. I've had a lot of therapy in the ensuing years, and I discovered my reaction to the jeers and laughter was more about my inability to face my overwhelming grief, which I hadn't really dealt with. My mother was my only parent. I'm not asking for sympathy, Brynne. I just want you to know that I'm tougher than you may realize. I have a master's degree in marketing and succeeded in a highly competitive environment. I worked on that backstretch walking the ponies for years, and I didn't put up with crap from anyone. Not the horny guys, not the fractious horses. I'm plenty tough."

Brynne put her cup down but kept her hands around it.

"I don't mean to use my mom's death as an excuse," Kenzie continued. "It was a hard time, but I've managed to move on. I chose to be a hot-walker because at the time I didn't want to do much else. I didn't make any real money, but it kept me alive. Being around horses soothed me. I didn't ask to be head of marketing. But Leo had seen my résumé. He knew I had experience in that area and wanted me there, and now . . . Well, I'm enjoying it, and I think I can do a good job for Grayson."

A quiet, cool breeze came from the west. Kenzie could hear the rustling of the wind through the bushes around the patio.

"I understand you want to hold a women's expo at Grayson's on opening day in June," Brynne said. "I object to that more than anything. I think you're dumbing down the track and trying to make it into something it's not. No man would ever come up with that stupid idea. You know, women have a place. Frankly, it's the home. Maybe that sounds old-fashioned. But I honestly don't believe they belong in the positions that have traditionally been held by men. I especially don't like seeing them in the locker room, and surely not in the boardroom. I just think women need to, well, act more like women."

"Brynne, obviously, I disagree. However, I don't want to engage in feminist politics. I'm here to try to keep my job. I can assure you that I'm extremely competent and can handle the responsibilities of the position. We have a gigantic mall nearby and, as you know, Grayson is part of the Antelope Valley Festival and Alfalfa Fair. So we want to capitalize on that and create an event that might draw more fans to the races, particularly women. I don't know if it will work, but I want to try. I'm hoping to get your support," Kenzie said. Her heart was pounding. From Brynne's blank expression, she had no idea whether she'd made any headway with her.

"Would you consider yourself a feminist?" Brynne asked.

"If a feminist is someone who believes in equal rights, then yes. I guess I would. Why?"

Brynne just shrugged, took another sip of coffee, and asked the waiter to bring the check.

Neither spoke for a moment. It was an uncomfortable lull, which made Kenzie anxious. She picked at a cuticle and tugged at her ear. Was that it? Had she blown her only chance with Brynne? She tried to think of something else to say, but nothing came to mind. She peered at the men sitting next to them who were lost in conversation. When she looked at Brynne, she noticed she'd been staring at her.

"I think they're gay," Brynne whispered.

"What? Oh. Maybe," Kenzie said as she glanced at the men once again.

"So many men are gay now. A shame."

Kenzie wanted to roll her eyes but held back.

"Are you dating anyone? Other than Chase Fielding, of course?"

"No, I'm not," Kenzie lowered her eyes and sipped her coffee. "However, well . . ."

There was a pause. Kenzie closed her eyes, regretting that she'd offered more. She didn't mean to.

"Well what?" Brynne asked.

"Oh, it's nothing . . ." She set her cup in the saucer again.

"It's obviously something or you wouldn't have said anything," Brynne said. She leaned back in her chair, staring at Kenzie. "What is it?"

"Nothing, really."

"I don't believe you." Brynne leaned forward in her chair and placed her elbows on the small table. "Are you gay?"

"No, no, I'm not. That's not it." Kenzie took a deep breath. She surveyed the patio and saw that the men were getting up to leave. She felt Brynne's eyes on her, waiting for her to reveal some deep, dark secret. Maybe if she offered something personal it would connect them in some way. But it had to be something Brynne would appreciate. So Kenzie decided to go for it. "I know this may sound strange and I'm reluctant to share this," Kenzie said. "But . . . well, do you believe in psychics?"

"No. Not really." Brynne seemed immediately disappointed. She was apparently hoping for something far juicier. "I've never been to one. Why do you ask?"

"I don't believe in them, either. I think they're swindlers. But a strange thing happened. I found a ring on the beach. My friend's psychic told me it belongs to my future husband."

Brynne's eyes brightened for the first time.

"A jeweler looked at it and said it was a suffragette ring. But apparently it belongs to a man, which is rather interesting."

Brynne banged her cup on the saucer when she put it down. "Your future husband?"

"Yes." Kenzie smiled for the first time. "The psychic said he'll come into my life in the next six months."

The waitress brought Brynne the check, which Kenzie tried to take, but Brynne beat her to it. Brynne's entire demeanor had changed. Clearly this was the way to reach her. Time to up the ante.

Kenzie smiled, tossed her hair back, and sat up straight in her chair. "I'd like to believe it. It's a great fantasy. All I have to do is wait for some guy to enter my life, claim the ring, and marry me. Kind of like the magic slipper. A great fairy tale!" Kenzie looked at Brynne, who seemed mesmerized by Kenzie's animated presentation, smiling broadly. But within seconds her smile began to fade. Kenzie noticed that Brynne had been staring off to the side. Kenzie glanced in that direction but just noticed a few cars in the parking lot on the other side of the bushes that ringed the patio.

Then, just like that, Brynne got up, swung her bag over her shoulder, and started out of the patio toward the interior of the restaurant. Kenzie scrambled to follow. "Well, that's interesting," Brynne said as she led the way out.

"Interesting?" Kenzie was baffled. "Just interesting? Is that all you have to say?" She caught up with Brynne and gently grabbed her elbow. "Look, I need this job, Brynne. Can you stop for one second? I'm trying to make this work. I can't believe that I'm reduced to begging. I never had to . . . Maybe I should leave the track. Maybe it's not worth it. Maybe—"

"You're a pain in the ass, Kenzie," Brynne interrupted as she spun around to look at her. "Stay in the stupid job. I don't care anymore. This is a total waste of my time. I wish I hadn't agreed to meet you. Leo thinks you're better than my cousin. Fine. Let him suffer the consequences. Richard Grayson will fire him if the track doesn't improve. So let that be on your shoulders . . . You can let go of my arm now."

Kenzie took a deep breath and released her grip, not even realizing she'd been holding on to Brynne's arm. She didn't understand why Brynne was tense and agitated, when moments ago she'd seemed more relaxed and at ease. Kenzie had thought she was making some headway. But not anymore.

Brynne quickly turned on her heel and continued to march through the restaurant. Kenzie tried to keep up with her pace. She'd entered the main dining room and then suddenly came to an abrupt halt. Kenzie almost crashed right into her. Brynne took off her sunglasses. Only two tables were occupied inside. Brynne stopped and stared at one of them as Kenzie walked up alongside to see what had grabbed her attention.

On the other side of the restaurant, in the back corner, was Martin Tomlinson, his tongue in the mouth of another woman. Kenzie's body stiffened. She remembered him from their dinner. He wore the same distinctive yellow bow tie. It must've been his car in the parking lot that caught Brynne's eye. She expected Brynne would march right on over and raise hell, but she didn't. She just glared at them. Brynne turned around and looked at Kenzie. Kenzie averted her eyes, pretending she hadn't seen anything. Then, without so much as a good-bye, Brynne continued, unfazed, to the front of the restaurant and outside to the parking lot.

Kenzie watched as Brynne got into her car, looked back one more time at the restaurant, and then drove away.

* * * * *

"I noticed Del Mar got a great crowd with their Miss Cougar contest," Matt said as he tumbled into the chair across from Kenzie, who was seated at her desk later that day. "We gonna do that kind of thing here?"

"No. Why? Does that sound sexy and exciting to you?"

"Kinda." He smiled.

"Really?"

"Okay, I'm kidding. 'Cause I know that wasn't the reaction you were looking for."

"Well, maybe you're looking for someone who can teach you a thing or two?"

"Hmm, that could be interesting," Matt said as he flicked a piece of lint from his blue windbreaker. "So how was your breakfast with Brynne this morning?" He propped his right ankle on his left knee and clasped both hands behind his head. Kenzie noticed a few deep-set wrinkles on his left cheek, and that the bill of his black White Sox hat was worn and frayed. She liked that his dark-brown sideburns had bits of gray.

"Loads of fun," she smirked. "I guess Leo must've told you."

"Everyone knows everything here. You know that."

"I do. It's wonderful, isn't it?"

"Do I detect sarcasm?" he asked.

"Yes, you do."

"How was dinner last week? With your director boyfriend?"

Kenzie narrowed her eyes at him. "You're awfully interested in my personal life all of a sudden. It was fine."

"Really? I saw you leave. You didn't look happy. What happened?"

Kenzie got up from her desk and walked over to the window. She crossed her arms over her chest and stared outside.

"Nothing. Just wanted to go. And he's not my boyfriend." Kenzie turned around and looked at Matt. "Full of questions today, huh?" She reached for the sliding door and opened it slightly to let some air in. "Even though I enjoy talking to you, I'm not sure what I do is any of your business."

"Just curious is all." Matt blinked.

"You seemed pretty engaged in your conversation with your wife," Kenzie said without looking at Matt.

"Jealous?"

"Seriously?" Kenzie turned quickly toward him. She left the door ajar and walked over to the fridge behind her desk, grabbed two bottles of water, handed one to Matt, and opened hers. "Boy, you have a high opinion of yourself, don't you? And no, I'm not jealous. I'm not into married men."

Matt sat back in his chair and stared at her thoughtfully while he unfastened the bottle cap and drank a few sips.

"So what can I do for you? Do you need something? Tickets?" Kenzie asked as she sat at her desk.

"Am I getting on your nerves?" Matt smiled at her wryly.

"A little."

Matt took another sip of his water, then looked at his watch. "I think it's time for us to go out. It's six. Let's get some dinner."

Matt stood up and waited for Kenzie to do the same.

"Huh? Uh, no. I have a ton of work to do—"

"C'mon. Work can wait," he interrupted. Matt walked around the desk and took her by the elbow.

"No, really. Thank you. I'm going to work through dinner tonight. Have a lot to do here." She adjusted her computer screen and held off looking at him.

He stood awkwardly next to her desk. "I'm not married," he said after a pause.

"You're not?" Kenzie stopped what she was doing and looked up at Matt. He shifted his weight from one side to the other. "But you wear a ring."

"Yep, I still do."

Matt seemed to go from cocky to cautious in a split second. She wondered what happened to his marriage. Although their conversations had often been brief, she didn't ever remember him telling her about his wife.

"Are you asking me out on a date?" she asked hesitantly.

"No. I don't do dates."

"Well, I don't do hookups."

"I barely know what a hookup is." Matt laughed as he combed his fingers through his hair. "C'mon, this isn't a big deal. It's just dinner. I've wanted to ask you for a long time, and finally got up the courage. The least you could do is say yes and put me out of my misery. I'm sweating bullets."

Kenzie looked up at Matt and smiled. It *was* just dinner. Why not? She shut down her computer, grabbed her purse, and followed Matt out the door and into the parking lot, where he opened the passenger door and helped her into his truck.

He turned on sports radio. She was never into jocks or sports fans. In fact, she hardly knew anything about sports at all. She glanced at Matt, who had one hand on the wheel, the other resting on the window frame. He definitely had a sexy way about him. She didn't know what it was, but she liked his confident manner, and that he admitted he was nervous about asking her out.

She started thinking about what it might be like to kiss him. He had a really nice body. *Hmm.* While Matt listened to the baseball game, she recalled the time she'd seen him on the backstretch and noticed the waistband of his boxers sticking above his pants. She didn't want to look, but she couldn't help herself. Even though he wore virtually the same clothes every day—jeans, a white T-shirt, and a blue sweater under a black or blue windbreaker—she always thought he looked good. She remembered feeling a bit dizzy when she'd talked to him on the backstretch when Chase was scouting the location.

Could he . . . ? *Ack.* There it was again. That stupid prophecy from the psychic had entered her mind. It was making her crazy.

Matt made a sharp right turn into a small parking lot. "Going to Carmine's. One of my favorite places. Ever been?"

Kenzie unfastened her seat belt and looked at the old flickering sign above the restaurant, shaking her head. She'd never even heard of this place.

Carmine's was a cozy, dimly lit Italian hideaway featuring about eight tables, all with traditional red-and-white tablecloths and a drip candle in a wine bottle. Kenzie thought the place belonged in *The Sopranos.* The host escorted them to a small table for two in an alcove.

"This is really nice," Kenzie said as Matt pushed in her chair.

"My mother taught me well. Find a nice girl. Take her to a nice place." He sat down and opened his menu. "Wine?"

"Sure. Your mother sounds wonderful," Kenzie said with a pang.

"She's an attorney. Made partner and then built her own practice. Quite accomplished."

"Impressive. My mom taught high school English her entire adult life," Kenzie offered proudly.

"An equally noble profession," Matt said.

The waiter brought the wine and Kenzie watched Matt as he swirled his glass, took a sip, and then nodded to the maître d'.

"So how do you like the new job?" Matt sipped his wine.

"I like it. Just having a tough time with Brynne Tomlinson, but I think we came to an understanding."

"Meaning?"

"Meaning she won't insist that Leo fire me. At least for a while. Nice of her, huh?"

"That's absurd. Brynne is a frustrated lady who's living an unhappy life and looking for someone to blame." Matt opened his menu.

"What do you know about her?"

"Not much, other than that she seems miserable," he said.

Kenzie thought about her breakfast with Brynne and how she hadn't expressed any anger when she'd seen Martin with another woman. There was a silence as they both perused the menu, and when Kenzie looked up, she saw that Matt's eyes were on her.

She blushed slightly and then ordered dinner from the waiter, who offered them more wine, took their menus, and then quickly disappeared.

"Okay, you're not married." Kenzie relaxed back in her chair. "So who was the woman you were with at the restaurant the other night?"

"An old friend from college. I'd like to offer a great romantic story to make you jealous, but the fact is I'm not interested in her."

"Oh, I see . . . So you seem to think I'd be jealous seeing you with another woman," Kenzie said.

"Well, I'd hope so."

Kenzie leaned forward, took another sip of wine, and looked up at Matt. His clear blue eyes sparkled in the dark. She'd never really noticed how beautiful they were till now.

"I think you like me," he said, a hint of a smile turning up the corners of his mouth.

"Really?" Kenzie tilted her head. "Why would you say that?"

"I know when there's something there. And there is. You know, chemistry. I'm sure you've heard of it."

Kenzie felt her face flush again. She was sure it was the wine. She noticed that Matt's eyes were fixed on hers. His beautiful, soft blue eyes. Almost hypnotic. She wanted to look away, but she couldn't. For just a moment their eyes met, and then Kenzie averted hers. She'd never really seen Matt. Not this close. And not as a potential mate.

"You planned to take me out to dinner tonight, didn't you?" she said. "You had this reservation for us. How'd you know I'd go along?"

"I didn't." His lips were moist and upturned. "As you recall, it took a lot of coaxing to get you out of that office . . . I thought it was time. I wanted to get to know you. And frankly, when I saw that it might be heating up with that film director, I thought I'd better step it up."

Kenzie suppressed her smile as she scanned the small dining room and noticed that most of the tables were parties of two.

"This is a lovely place," Kenzie said as their dinner arrived.

"I'm glad you approve." Matt set down his glass but held his eyes on Kenzie's. "Look . . . I may appear cocky and tough, but the truth is I haven't been out with a woman in a long time. I'm rusty. Very new at this."

"Well, you seem to be doing a good job so far." She locked her eyes on his, then noticed a sheen of sweat on his forehead and decided to change the subject to ease the sexual tension that was building between them. "So I heard you were once a sportscaster. A famous one. Why a jock's agent?"

"Sorta fell into it." Matt began eating his meal. In between bites he offered up his past. "Not been doing it that long. Worked in film and stage production in my early years. But I loved the track, horses. My old man took me to Santa Anita when I was a kid. He had a terrible gambling habit, which I've been careful to avoid. But I really like the excitement, and I owned a few horses at one time, although it's an expensive hobby and a lousy business. Anyway, the station got sold, and when my contract was up it wasn't renewed. I hung around the tracks. One of my buddies was a jockey. He needed an agent, so we decided to work together."

"Turned out pretty well, because I know you represent the two highest-paid jockeys."

"Agents can only represent two jockeys, so why not have the best ones?" Matt leaned forward as he took a long sip of water.

"I hope they'll get some mounts at Grayson this season," she said.

"Oh, the jockeys will definitely be there. They like that place even though it's a rodeo. It reminds them of how they started out."

"So are you divorced?" Kenzie had been dying to ask the question.

"No." He paused for a moment and lowered his eyes. "My wife passed away. Two years ago. Ovarian cancer. A wicked disease. She went fast."

"I'm so sorry." Her tone was gentle and thoughtful. "I'm surprised I didn't know. We've been working together for four years. I can't believe no one told me."

"We were only married for two years, and at the time of her death we weren't living together." Matt put down his fork. He was speaking much more slowly now. Kenzie assumed he was feeling more at ease. "She asked me to leave. I was racked with guilt because I couldn't be the husband she wanted. Someone with a nine-to-five job who never traveled, or left the house at four a.m. to get mounts for jockeys. We just weren't right for each other. But I felt like I failed."

There was a long pause. Matt had stopped eating. He peered around the small dining room. She could tell he was still shaken by his wife's untimely death.

"It was rough," he said softly. "I haven't been able to take off my ring. I guess I still haven't gotten over it. I think the ring, well . . . it kinda makes me feel safe. Like I don't have to put myself out there again . . . kinda like what I'm doing now."

"I hardly think it was all your fault. There will be better times," she said.

"Yes." Matt offered a weak smile. "Better times."

They both took a sip of their wine and then planted their glasses on the table.

"What about you?" Matt asked. "You once told me you had a big-deal marketing job at a studio but then decided to walk horses in a circle."

"Well, yes, that's true," she said. "This isn't the career path I expected. But I'm okay. For now. This is where I want to be."

"For now?"

"Yes. I'm beginning to feel happy again. And that's what I want. I just want to be happy. I really like my job. I like the track. It's peaceful."

"It's not the high-powered position you used to hold at a studio. It doesn't come with tremendous pressure and anxiety. So you opted for something else. Something that wasn't so demanding."

Kenzie placed her fork on the plate and wiped her hands on the napkin. She was surprised at Matt's response. More insight than she expected from him.

"Some of that is true. There were other issues, too. Like my mom had just died and I never really dealt with it. I was busy. Moving fast. My work was my life. I should've slowed down. I should've spent more time with her. That's my biggest regret . . . that I didn't do enough for her . . . I just. I just . . ."

Kenzie drew a heavy sigh. Matt brought his hand under her chin and lifted it. He leaned forward, put his right hand behind her neck, brought her head closer to his, and then placed a gentle, warm kiss on her forehead.

"I understand. I do," he whispered, stroking the side of her neck with his thumb. His gaze remained steady on hers. "I've been there."

And then he kissed her again. This time on the mouth. It started out slow, but it was longer and deeper and so urgent that her insides roiled with arousal. When Kenzie came up for air, she felt dizzy and warm. She tasted the moisture of his lips on hers. Her fingers were entwined with his.

"That was nice," she said sweetly.

"It's hard to lose someone so close to you," Matt said so softly it was almost a whisper.

"My mom was my only family. My dad, well, I don't even know him, and my grandfather, whom I adored, died just one year before my mom," she said.

"That's a lot of loss for someone so young to handle. And you don't even know your dad?" Matt asked.

Kenzie shook her head. "Um, well, he was a sperm donor."

Matt raised one eyebrow.

"A lot of women used his sperm. He's a doctor. I have his full medical history, and I probably have tons of siblings, but he doesn't have a name. And he doesn't want to be found."

"Wow, well, let's hope you don't marry your brother," Matt said.

"You joke, but I definitely think about that."

"Well, my dad was not a doctor. He was from West Virginia and, believe it or not, he still lives there and manages a used car dealership. I don't think our fathers are related." Matt held on to Kenzie's hand and squeezed it a little tighter.

Kenzie gazed into Matt's eyes and said, "Ya know, you may have planned this evening, but I never dreamed I'd be here with you tonight, having such a good time. I'm glad you, well, kidnapped me!"

Matt leaned across the table, took her chin in his hands, and kissed her again softly. After a moment the waiter brought Matt the check.

"Please, let me pay half—"

"Next time," Matt interrupted. "This was my crime, and I'm going to pay for it."

After they finished dinner, Matt took her hand, and they walked slowly to his truck. He drove back to Grayson, which was quiet and dark. Everyone had gone home. Matt pulled his truck alongside Kenzie's.

"Thank you. I had a really good time," said Kenzie warmly.

"I'm glad. So did I. Would you like to do it again?"

"Yes. I'd definitely like to."

Matt unfastened his seat belt, brought his hand behind her neck, and drew her close. She felt the stubble of his beard against her cheek, and the softness of his lips on hers. She wanted this long, slow kiss to last forever.

"I have to go," she said drowsily.

"I know," Matt said.

She turned away from him and opened the door to let herself out.

Matt waited in the doorway as she got into her truck and started the engine. She glanced back at him, and he nodded and flashed a smile. She slowly pulled away and drove through the long parking lot till she came to the first stop sign. She reached for her phone to check her messages. It occurred to her that neither of them had done that the entire evening.

At that precise moment a text arrived. It was from Matt, inviting her to lunch the next day.

Kenzie's heart beat just a little faster.

GEMMA

"Oh my God, he could be the one!" Gemma sat high in her office chair, the phone pressed hard against her ear, her eyes wide and glowing.

"Figured you'd say that," Kenzie said. "But you're missing one thing: He has to be the owner of the ring. Remember? That's what your great fortune-teller said. And I wore the ring yesterday and Matt wasn't like, 'Wow, that's my ring you're wearing.'"

"Oh, good point." Gemma eased back into her chair, stretched her legs out under her desk, and gazed out her office window, which had a clear view of the picnic tables outside the commissary where a few employees were having lunch. "Hmm, well that could be a problem."

"That we're even discussing this is crazy," Kenzie sighed. "I really don't want to think that every single new guy I encounter might be my future husband. I just hate that Annalisa told me this."

"Don't speak ill of the dead," Gemma said.

"Fine. Anyway, how're things?"

"I discovered new information about Jeffrey, another favorite subject of yours. After I saw him at the pharmacy, I searched for more info about him." She sat up straight again. "His daughter, Scarlett, was featured in an article about high school freshman who volunteer at a local homeless shelter. She's working the food drive tomorrow, so I'm going. No one will know who I am. Seems like the perfect opportunity to see who Scarlett is, and maybe I'll run into my father again. I'll tell Peter I have a doctor's appointment, grab some canned goods, and be on my way."

"Oh, Gem," Kenzie said, "do you really think that's a good idea?"

"I can't stop thinking about him." Gemma's shoulders dropped. "I wanted to hold on to the fantasy that he'd been stalking me as I had him. After hearing Mom's story I know it's not true. But I still want to meet him. I need to find a way into his life."

"Gemma!" Peter King, Gemma's boss, shouted to her from his office. "Where's my schedule for tomorrow?"

"Oh, Peter wants something," Gemma said to Kenzie. "I'd better go."

"I don't know if you should pursue this, Gem. It sounds a little dicey."

"I need to do this, Kenz." Gemma pressed her lips together. "I just do."

"Okay, it's your life. Just be careful," Kenzie said.

"I will." Gemma hung up. "Coming, Peter."

Peter was in his office playing *Candy Crush* on the computer. Gemma didn't mind working for him. He was a nice enough guy but really lazy. If it weren't for her keen eye, he would never have any scripts in development. He'd say, "The two of us are a team." Right. If they were really a team, then why wasn't she also a producer? And why did she get paid a tenth of what he made?

Peter's father was a highly successful talent agent. He'd made sure that his son had a long-term producing deal at a studio. It certainly provided job security for Peter, despite how little he seemed to do. But Gemma had far more drive than he did.

The two of them sat in adjacent spaces—Peter in an office and Gemma in the adjoining reception area. Communication flowed easily as they explored ideas that could be adapted for films. Gemma longed to be a producer or an executive at a studio and hoped one day that Peter would either promote her or recommend her for a higher position elsewhere.

"Uh, hellooo? Is anyone there?" Peter asked.

"Was working on something," Gemma said as she approached the archway into Peter's office. She handed him a note card. "Here's your schedule for tomorrow. Anything else?"

"You seem distracted. Is everything okay?"

"Just browsing the Internet for new ideas," Gemma lied.

"Great. See if you can find something that will play in China," he said. "That's what the studio wants. I don't even know what that would be. I guess like *Transformers* or something."

Peter was so out of it. Gemma could do his job blindfolded. She'd been an assistant to three other producers already, doing the same thing over and over. She'd find the idea, give it to her boss, and he'd produce the film. She'd receive no credit, no money—just a thank-you. She'd been stuck in this position for too long. She hoped Annalisa was right and that somehow she'd get a promotion.

"I'll look for some more ideas like that," Gemma said as she stood in the archway separating their offices. "In the meantime, I'll be in after lunch tomorrow. I have a doctor's appointment in the morning."

"Okay," Peter mumbled.

Gemma smiled and returned to her desk.

* * * * *

Gemma was the third person in line at the homeless shelter the next morning. She clutched a sack of groceries filled generously with canned goods for their monthly food drive. Two young women sat at a table just beyond the entrance to the building. As she approached them she lifted her chin to appear confident.

"Hi, I have a bag to drop off." Gemma addressed a young woman whose name tag said *Scarlett* and then licked her lips. "Where would you like me to put it?"

"Awesome," Scarlett said. "Thank you for coming today." She shook Gemma's hand and took the bag from her. Gemma was speaking to her half sister, whose voice was light and breezy. Scarlett had beautiful white teeth; long, straight dark hair; and big blue eyes. But not green like her father's.

Their father's.

"Let me get you a receipt." Scarlett had a charming lilt to her voice.

"That's okay. I don't need one," Gemma said as she watched Scarlett set the sack in the corner with several other bags filled with grocery items.

"We give everyone receipts. We kind of have to."

"Okay. Sure." Gemma stood awkwardly next to the table as Scarlett wrote out a receipt. She wrote slowly, making sure every letter was legible. Gemma's eyes darted about, watching as others gathered nearby waiting to make their donations. Many were mothers with children. A few teenagers, apparently friends of Scarlett's, showed her photos on their phones and texts they'd just received. Scarlett smiled sweetly but was focused on completing the receipt.

"I'm writing a receipt for the lady," Scarlett said to her friend. "I can't look at your stuff now, but I will in a minute." And then she looked up at Gemma. "Here you go. Thank you for coming today."

Gemma was just some lady. But she wasn't. She wanted to tell her right then and there, *I'm your sister!* But she couldn't. She had to be discreet.

"You're welcome. Oh, and what's your name?" Gemma asked, to keep her cover.

"Scarlett. Thank you again."

Gemma waited for Scarlett to ask her name, but she didn't. The line had grown, and now about twenty people stood behind her. She wanted to say more, but she had to move along.

As Gemma exited the building, she surveyed the street to see if Jeffrey was there. He wasn't. Maybe he'd pick Scarlett up later. She figured she'd take the gamble. Her car was parked across the street. She got in and waited like a cop on a stakeout.

She focused on her phone so she wouldn't look suspicious sitting in her car. An hour passed. The wait seemed interminable. But then a black Range Rover drove up to the building. The tinted windows made it hard to see who was driving. Gemma strained to get a good look. She remembered the SUV from the pharmacy because it had a red decal on its fender. But when the door opened it wasn't Jeffrey. Instead, a heavyset woman appeared. She was wearing a white uniform and sneakers. Gemma figured it was a housekeeper or nanny who had come to pick up Scarlett.

She peered at the entrance to the shelter and saw Scarlett emerge and dash toward the car, her backpack bouncing on her back. If Gemma wanted to do anything more, she had to do it then. And just like that, without thinking, she jumped out of the car and raced across the street.

"Oh, Scarlett, hey, uh, do you have a moment?" Gemma was out of breath. Scarlett seemed startled. The nanny was standing by the Range Rover with her keys in one hand, signaling to Scarlett to hurry up with the other, as she was double-parked.

"Um, yes?" Scarlett paused and crossed her arms over her chest.

"I just . . . well, I think what you're doing is great. And I wondered . . . well, I wondered if maybe . . . if maybe I could help? Is there anything I can do to support you here? To help the homeless, that is."

Scarlett offered a slow smile. Gemma thought she was relieved that she wasn't about to kidnap her.

"Sure."

"Well, when is your next thing? Um, your next event, or whatever this is called?"

"Tomorrow. We're doing this again. You want to help us write receipts? 'Cause Olivia can't come on Saturdays."

"Sure. Tomorrow. Saturday. Same time. Okay, sure." Gemma was relieved. She'd made contact. Scarlett raced to the SUV and got in, and she and the woman drove away.

Gemma's hands were trembling. If only she could say something. She couldn't—not yet—but she had a good feeling about everything, despite her mother's warnings.

* * * * *

The next day Gemma sat next to Scarlett at the table. When there was no line, they talked about movies and their mutual addiction to *Swing Copters*, the video game they played on their iPhones. It also turned out they'd both been to the recent Bastille concert, sitting within a row of each other. And they both loved the TV show *Girls* and could name the song at the end of each episode since the series began.

Gemma couldn't believe how many interests they shared. But then, they were sisters. Of course they'd have many things in common.

They sat at the table for hours, talking and laughing and greeting the folks who arrived to donate goods. They had so much fun together that Gemma completely lost track of time.

When she looked up to greet the next donor, she saw Jeffrey standing right smack in front of her. He'd been watching them.

Gemma felt her throat constrict. He was within inches of her. She couldn't stop blinking. She wanted to say something, but the words were stuck in her throat.

"Daddy! Hi, great. You're here. Oh, it's time to go. Okay, I'm ready." Scarlett jumped out of her seat, grabbed her backpack, and started to leave. "Oh, this is Gemma. This is my dad. Gemma's helping us out. She's been great."

Gemma didn't move. The blood drained from her face. She just stared into his green eyes. He extended his hand, which she took in hers.

"Hi, Jeffrey Kahn. Good to meet you, Gemma. Are you a volunteer at the shelter?"

Gemma nodded, unable to utter a word.

"Well, good, we'll see you again, then." Jeffrey let go of her hand and helped Scarlett put on her backpack.

"See ya, Gemma!" Scarlett shouted. "Was fun today." Gemma nodded as she watched them move swiftly out the door and toward Jeffrey's car. Scarlett got into the backseat behind the driver. Jeffrey was about to get inside, but Scarlett rolled down her window to get her father's attention.

"Dad, can we invite Gemma to join us for dinner sometime?" Gemma had started walking down the front steps of the building toward her car, which was parked on the street. She couldn't help but hear their conversation, with the two of them only a few feet away from her now.

Jeffrey stopped, then turned around and looked at Gemma, whose hand was in her purse fiddling for her keys while pretending she had no interest in their conversation.

"Sure, okay," he told Scarlett. "Hey, Gemma!" Jeffrey shouted. "Why don't you join our family a week from Wednesday? We're preparing dinner for the shelter at six thirty. Would you like to help?"

"Say yes!" Scarlett yelled from the car's back window. "Please!"

"Sure, okay, sure," Gemma said, though she was rather *un*sure. She stopped for a moment to acknowledge them, then nodded and said, "That would be nice. A week from Wednesday. Dinner. With the family."

She got into her car, sat for a moment, and took a deep breath. Gemma didn't even realize what she'd said till they had gone. Then she repeated the words. "Dinner. With the family." Of course, it was her family. All she needed was the courage to tell them.

SARITA

"You look tired," Kenzie said to Sarita. They were getting ready to leave the office for the day.

"Oh, I'm all right. Just have a lot on my plate," Sarita sighed.

"Other than work? Like what?"

"Oh just stuff, you know." Sarita shoved some files into her backpack and hoped that would satisfy Kenzie's curiosity.

"You're so secretive, sometimes I wonder if you have a whole other life." Kenzie laughed.

Sarita was startled. She stared at Kenzie, who was clearing items off her desk. For a moment she wondered if Kenzie knew about her other identity, something she'd worked hard to keep hidden.

"Other life? No, just busy. I have a boyfriend. We go out a lot." Sarita shrugged. "Just stuff," she repeated.

"Well, I hope it's at least fun," Kenzie said. "I've got to get going, but by the way, you're doing a great job. I'll see ya tomorrow." Kenzie grabbed her bag and took off down the stairs to the parking lot. "Make sure to double-lock the door when you leave."

Sarita waited until Kenzie, the last person in the building, had left the office before she changed clothes. She had it all worked out.

First she locked Kenzie's door, then ran to the bathroom, kicked off her jeans, and threw on her skirt, leggings, boots, and shredded gold top. And then the wig. She stuffed her other clothes into a bag and then sneaked down the back stairway, which led directly to the parking lot. She slid into her car, looked around to make sure no one saw her, then pulled out her cell phone and called her father.

"Papa, I'm so sorry, but it seems we have another late night at work. I can't get home in time for dinner."

There was silence on the other end. She gritted her teeth and took a deep breath. She'd anticipated this response but was prepared to go head-to-head. She had rehearsed what she would say numerous times over the past ten days. She would not give in.

"That's not acceptable, Sarita. You are to be home. Your mother has gone to the trouble of preparing a sumptuous meal, and the Guptas and the matchmaker are on their way over. Please do not bring shame upon our family."

"I'm very sorry, Papa, but my job—"

"Your job can wait!" he shouted. "It is nothing but a job. Nothing. It is not your life. Your life is family. We are about family. Do you hear me? I won't hear about this job anymore. No more. You will be here. There is to be no discussion."

Sarita's lips trembled. She'd known the conversation would play out like this. She'd expected nothing less. She was nearly in tears but pulled herself together, took a couple of deep breaths, and told her father that she was sorry. She couldn't be there.

"You will be home. I hope you understand what I'm saying," he said.

"I do," she said softly.

And then he hung up. She sat a few minutes, thinking about the call. She closed her eyes. She imagined her mother running around, making sure the family home looked presentable for their guests. Her mom wanted to impress the young man's family. She pictured the matchmaker, who would be appalled when she didn't show up. She thought about the next morning, when Sarita would see her parents, and how rough it would be. But she would not be deterred. Her heart was set on that competition, and nothing would deny her this opportunity.

She took a few more breaths, put the car in gear, and drove off to the club.

As she approached the club entrance, Damien appeared. He could tell that she was anxious. He knew what tonight meant to her. She'd worked hard for this opportunity and wanted it badly. She offered a soft smile, then collapsed into his arms.

"I made it," she whispered.

Damien held her and kissed the top of her head. She peered up into his deep-brown eyes and brushed her thumb against his cheek. Then she brought his face to hers and kissed him passionately.

"Hey," Levi Evans said, "sorry to ruin this moment, lovebirds, but Sarita's on in four."

"I'm ready," Sarita said. She and Damien found a seat at a table up front.

The club was in an old strip mall. There was just a simple index card taped to the door, with "Deathrock Bar" in red lettering. An intimidating bouncer stood at the entrance. Inside, the walls were painted red and black. There were candles everywhere and a few chandeliers. A small stage and an even smaller dance floor. The place reeked of cigarettes, cinnamon, and patchouli. Several folks were wearing the popular whiteface makeup, Victorian corsets, top hats, and black lace, while others simply showed up in dirty old jeans and grungy T-shirts. When the bands were on break, the two big TV screens featured videos of the Cure, Bauhaus, and Sisters of Mercy.

Sarita sank into her chair and drank her beer. She had let go of the stress she'd felt following her conversation with her father. Damien kept his arm around her and held her close. She enjoyed his warm embrace and doting manner. She leaned back in her chair, closed her eyes, and quietly rehearsed the song she'd be singing in minutes.

Levi ran onstage and pointed to Sarita, motioning for her to come up. Sarita sipped her beer and then walked onto the stage. She began singing "Amazing" by Johnette Napolitano. At first Sarita held the microphone close to her lips. She sang slowly, letting the emotion register on her face. And then, as the music escalated, so did her voice, and she could feel it send a chill through the room. Tonight her voice had the timbre and tone of Adele's husky sound.

Every time she glanced at Damien, he was staring at her. He hung on every note and watched her every move. She cradled the mic, closed her eyes, and sang the last few bars. And then there was an ovation. Everyone jumped out of their seats and applauded. She was that good and she knew it. Sarita smiled at the audience, then placed the microphone back in its stand and returned to her table.

"You were great, baby!" Damien shouted as Sarita approached. He handed her a beer.

As Sarita sat down, she recalled the first time she'd attended a Goth event. It was at a club in lower Manhattan, near where she went to school. A girlfriend had taken her there. Sarita wasn't sure it was for her, but the community embraced her, and she'd felt accepted quickly. It was warm and comforting, the people friendly and caring. They encouraged her singing, and she became a fixture in that community. It had become her new family. When she moved back home, she heard about Deathrock Bar. Its ambience was similar, and over time she made new friends and became a part of that community as well. The Goth culture provided a safe place for her to grow and experience a life much different from the one she had known in Desert View. This was where she belonged.

Sarita listened carefully as several others sang their hearts out, hoping they'd get the opportunity to be the lead singer in Moody

Gray's new band. She prayed her performance was good enough to earn her a spot among the five semifinalists. And then Levi made his way onto the stage to make the announcement.

Sarita had made the cut.

"Yes!" Damien shouted along with the others who were cheering her on as well.

She couldn't believe her good fortune. Fans came over and high-fived her. She was beaming. The idea that she had a shot at becoming the lead singer in the Witches of Skeletal Symphony was beyond exciting. Damien grabbed them both a beer and they toasted her success.

Now it was late and most everyone had left the club. Sarita was starting to fade. As she rested comfortably in Damien's arms, she closed her eyes and thought about how happy she was. She was enjoying her life. She felt Damien's hands on her back and a soft kiss on her head. She was warm and cozy.

If only she weren't so tired. But her double life was taking its toll. Although she worked hard to keep them separate, doing so left her exhausted. Sarita and Damien were the last ones to leave the club. Damien walked Sarita to her car, which was parked on the street. He kissed her good-bye and waited for her to start the engine before he moved on. But Sarita's car wouldn't start.

"Oh no," Sarita cried. "What am I'm going to do? It's so late."

"I'll call a tow truck and get it to my mechanic," Damien said as he punched numbers into his phone.

Sarita yawned as she got out of the car and sat on the curb. She lowered her head to her hands and rubbed her eyes. "I can't believe this night. It was so great and now this."

"Hey, it'll be okay." Damien sat down beside her and held her head against his chest as he repeated the address to the operator.

"And I almost forgot that I ditched the big matchmaking dinner tonight. They must be out of their minds."

"You'll have your own place soon," Damien said as he kissed the top of her head.

"My father's impossible. You don't know. He'll be screaming his head off tomorrow morning, telling me what an ungrateful daughter I am."

Damien stood up and put his phone in his pocket. "The driver will be here in about an hour." He reached for her hand to help her up from the curb. "I'll take you home and then meet him back here."

Sarita looked up at him. "Oh, Damien, I'm so sorry. No, you don't have to do that."

"It's okay."

Sarita closed her eyes and pulled her knees to her chest, circling them with her arms. Damien watched as she rocked back and forth. "You know you can live with me," he said.

"I know." She looked up at him. "I just want to live on my own first. I want to have that opportunity. None of my sisters got to do that. Are you okay with that?"

"I am," Damien said as he sat down beside her on the curb. "I understand, and I don't want to push you into something that's not right."

Sarita brushed her hand across his cheek and kissed him on the lips. "Have I told you how wonderful you are? You're amazing."

Damien stroked the side of her cheek with his thumb. "C'mon, let's go." After a moment he helped her up and they slowly walked across the street, got into his car, and drove to Sarita's home.

Her house was pitch-black. Just the porch light was on. Damien parked a few doors away and turned off the engine.

"Why don't you enter through the front door. No one's up. I can't imagine anyone will see you," Damien said.

"I can't risk it. It's easier for me to climb into the attic. Its on the other side of the house, so they can't hear me," she said. "Except

I forgot to leave the portable ladder outside. I'll have to use the aluminum one that's at the back of the house."

Damien sighed. "All right, but let me help you."

They got out of the car and walked to the back of the house to retrieve the ladder. Damien set it up so that it was securely fastened to the attic window.

"Okay, all set," he said quietly. "Text me when you're inside."

"Of course. I'll walk you to the porch." Sarita took his hand as they moved to the front of the house and stepped onto the shaded entryway. "Thank you again for everything tonight," Sarita whispered. "I love you so much."

"I love you, too. You're tired." Damien took her in his arms and kissed her. "But you had a wonderful night. Proud of you. Get some rest."

And then there was a loud clatter that nearly stopped her heart. The aluminum ladder had dislodged from the attic window, banging to the ground. Within seconds every light in the house was on.

And just as suddenly, the front door opened and there was Papa staring at them.

Sarita could imagine what her father was thinking when he saw a man with a green Mohawk, spiked leather choker, torn leather jacket, and fingerless gloves embracing her on their porch. The second Papa came into view, Damien instinctively stepped away, but it was too late. Papa slowly raised his right arm, which held a handgun aimed at Damien's head.

"Papa, no. It's me. It's Sarita!" Sarita screamed as she ripped off her red wig. Surely he recognized her. Papa stared at this person who claimed to be his daughter, but he didn't look convinced. Sarita knew she looked nothing like his daughter. "Papa, please put the gun down. It's me . . . This is . . . this is my boyfriend . . . Damien."

Papa squinted, confused. Mama now stood at his side. Both in their dressing gowns, they seemed stunned, speechless, and frightened. Papa's gun was still pointed at Damien, who was petrified.

"Papa, please put the gun down," Sarita cried again.

He must have recognized her voice, and he did as she asked.

"I'm sorry, Mr. Mahajan," Damien said. "We didn't mean any harm . . . I . . . Uh, maybe I should go . . . Sarita . . ."

"You should . . . please . . . Please go. Don't worry . . ."

"Okay." Damien backed away. "Please be safe and let me know if . . ."

Sarita knew he was frightened. Who wouldn't be, having had a gun pointed at his head?

"It's okay," she said softly. "I'll be okay . . . I'll see you later."

Damien turned reluctantly and ran to his car.

"I didn't mean to wake you," Sarita said to her parents once she heard Damien's car pull away. No one said a word. Papa opened the door wider so Sarita could enter their home. She began to sob. "I'm sorry, Papa." The heavy black makeup she'd applied earlier had seeped into her eyes and trickled down her nose.

Papa held the gun at his side. All was eerily quiet. Her father closed the front door, but both he and Mama remained huddled in the doorway, staring at a person who claimed to be their daughter. Sarita waited silently for whatever would come next.

Mama didn't make a sound, holding her hand over her mouth in horror. Sarita knew they were shocked. What in the world was she doing, and why was she dressed like that? They'd never understand.

"I don't know who you are anymore," Papa whispered. "You have dishonored us." Papa turned around and walked slowly toward the staircase down the hall. Her mother followed. Sarita watched as they solemnly climbed the stairs to their bedroom. She heard their door close, and then the house became still, quiet, and engulfed in darkness.

BRYNNE

Brynne Tomlinson was satisfied that the simple breakfast was perfectly displayed on the richly grained rosewood buffet table in her dining room, where she and Martin would eat alone.

The Tomlinson home in Bel-Air was perched high atop an upper hill, with breathtaking views that extended from the Los Angeles Basin to Catalina Island. The newly renovated eighteen-million-dollar estate sat on one and a half acres. In addition to a glistening mosaic glass-tile pool, it included a dance studio, gym, hair salon, and home theater. Brynne had spent three years on this masterpiece, overseeing the design, which boasted a grand staircase at the entry, soaring ceilings, gorgeous moldings, and walls of French windows that opened onto terraces with golf course views. She created a luxurious three-thousand-foot master suite handcrafted in mahogany, along with a children's wing with four bedrooms, more than enough space for her twins. Three housekeepers, a laundress, head chef, cook, and five security personnel kept the home running.

Brynne never considered being an interior decorator. She never thought she had the talent. But when the renovation was complete, *Architectural Digest* had asked to photograph some of the rooms.

"Brynne, dear, while you're up, would you mind bringing me a bit more marmalade for my toast?" Martin asked, without looking away from his iPad, which sat next to his coffee cup on the table. Martin was a creature of habit. Every morning that Brynne could remember, he'd enjoyed a slice of toast, a dab of orange marmalade, one poached egg, two pieces of bacon, and a cup of steaming-hot black coffee.

Martin and Brynne had met at Ole Miss and never looked back. It was as if they'd been separated at birth and reintroduced at freshman orientation. Unlike their friends, they'd enjoyed a perfect nineteen-year marriage. Other than a few minor bumps here and there, it was nothing short of blissful. But, of course, Brynne would not have it any other way.

"Certainly, darling," Brynne said as she collected the marmalade from the credenza and handed it to Martin. As if it were a scene out of *Downton Abbey*, a uniformed waiter appeared, offered more coffee, and replenished the marmalade supply.

Brynne sat next to Martin, took out her phone, and glanced at her emails. She wasn't her usual self this morning, but Martin didn't seem to notice. She had an upset stomach and hadn't slept well the past few nights. She couldn't stop thinking about what she'd seen at breakfast last week with Kenzie. She wanted to pretend it hadn't been Martin at the corner table in Pissarro's—the same restaurant where they'd celebrated their anniversary. She wanted to believe there was some great reason why another woman had his tongue in her mouth. The thought distracted her all day every day. Whatever was going on with Martin and this hussy, slut, home wrecker, whatever she was, it wouldn't disrupt her marriage and the life Brynne had worked so hard to maintain. She would find the willpower to put it out of her mind like it had never happened.

But it annoyed her that she'd had to witness the scene. If it hadn't been for breakfast with that awful Kenzie, she never would've known about it. Kenzie Armstrong was like a water cannon of bad luck, spraying it everywhere she went. But now Brynne absolutely had to find out who that slut was. Who the heck was messing with her husband?

"Are you going to the office later today?" Brynne asked softly.

"Mmmm," Martin replied, ignoring the interruption. His eyes were glued to his iPad. He loved that toy. Brynne thought he loved it more than his family, as he spent every waking minute with it.

"I may meet Patty at Pissarro's today." Brynne purposely mentioned the name of the restaurant. She hoped it would provoke a reaction, but Martin didn't flinch. It was as if she'd said it looked like rain.

"Okay, well, I guess I'll see you at dinner?" Brynne asked.

"Yep. I'll be home later." Martin stopped reading and looked at his watch. "Around eight, maybe nine. I may take a ride to the Seal Beach office and see what the staff's doing down there. I'll let you know." He smiled as he grabbed his iPad, tossed the last bit of toast into his mouth, and exited the room. Brynne remained seated and wondered how long it had been since Martin had given her a kiss when he went off to work.

Brynne's phone rang in her hand while she climbed the long staircase to her bedroom. "Hi, Mother. I'm doing fine. How are you?" Brynne dragged herself up the stairs lethargically. "Happy living in LA? Better than the storms up north, huh?"

Brynne entered her bedroom, across the hall from Martin's. She gazed out the window at his Ferrari, which was headed down the driveway.

"Yes, the girls are fine. Back at school. Miss them terribly, but I text them every day to make sure they're keeping up with their schoolwork," Brynne said without a single suggestion that, no, things were not fine. That in fact she'd recently witnessed her husband's tongue buried deep inside another woman's mouth. But no big deal. Admitting that things weren't fine wasn't the Southern way adopted by this Northern California girl. Appearances were terribly important, and it was imperative to remain positive. Besides, negativity only caused wrinkles. When their conversation concluded, Brynne said she'd stop by in the next few days.

Martin had inadvertently dropped the clue she'd been seeking this morning. Seal Beach. Tomlinson Industries had an office there, and the other woman might be a coworker. Everyone knew about marriages that were broken up by work-related affairs. These damn career women were really ruining it for everyone. First they abandoned their children, and then they had sex with their colleagues.

Brynne sat at her computer and found the website for Tomlinson Industries' Seal Beach office. She scrolled through the staff bios until she came across a photo of a woman with that distinguishing flourish she remembered so well: a diamond in her nose. Brynne stared at the photo of Marcella Gomez, who was young and attractive. It was she. The woman with the diamond in her left nostril who had welcomed Martin's tongue—and God knew what else—into her mouth.

Brynne continued searching for more information about Marcella Gomez. And then she came across an address for a recent Tomlinson Industries Seal Beach staff picnic that was held at the home of the human resources manager, who happened to be Marcella Gomez. Brynne couldn't believe her good fortune. She scribbled the address onto a Post-it, stuffed it into her pocket, ran into her closet, changed into jeans and a sweater—an outfit she'd never wear except to spy on her husband's mistress—raced down the staircase, out the door, and into her car.

As Brynne drove down the long, winding driveway, she wondered what had happened. What did she do wrong? Why would Martin consider having an affair? An *affair*. The word sent shivers up her spine. It made her so frantic she decided to stop at a Starbucks for some hot tea to calm her down.

As she waited in the long line, she thought about her first date with Martin at Ole Miss. She'd sneaked him into her dorm and let him feel her up. She thought she'd gone way too far, but then the next night they went further. She smiled recalling his voracious appetite for sex. Where they did it, how many times, and how many ways. But no matter how much sex they had, it was never enough for Martin. He was insatiable.

In their early years sex was just constant. Martin couldn't get enough. Every single night he demanded they try something new. Something clever and wonderful that would titillate him.

After the twins were born, Brynne just couldn't satisfy him the way he wanted. She was exhausted from taking care of two little babies with just one night nurse and a housekeeper. She was left with the bulk of the work during the day. It wasn't until she got a full-time nanny that she could breathe again.

Then Martin got a prescription for Viagra, and all hell broke loose. The man was a maniac. He sure didn't need Viagra, for heaven's sake.

Within a month or so Brynne was back to having sex every twenty-four hours. Martin was glowing. He was a brand-new guy, having erections every two seconds. In order to satisfy his drive, they became regular customers at the Pleasure Chest, a boutique that carried a wide variety of sex toys. Although Brynne would arrive wearing big dark sunglasses, trying to hide her identity, the clerks greeted Martin and her as if they were family. She prayed they'd never run into anyone they knew, but she was hardly concerned, as most of her friends weren't even having sex.

Then, about six years ago, Martin discovered Internet porn. Her salvation.

He would crank his shank for hours, rarely leaving the computer in his office across the hall from their bedroom. Brynne was thrilled. She thanked Bill Gates every day for bringing sanity back into her life. Martin was so obsessed with Internet porn that it became better than the real thing. But that was not good for Brynne. No matter what she tried, Martin preferred masturbating to pornographic video clips, webcams, and images. He no longer needed her to satisfy his sexual appetite. He spent so much time in his office that he began sleeping there, too. Brynne had had enough. She decided to just enlarge his office and make it into his own master suite. Shortly thereafter Martin, along with Madame Palm and her five daughters, moved in. And sex with Brynne came to a screeching halt.

But now things were different. Apparently, Martin's obsession with Internet porn had waned, because he had his tongue in another woman's mouth, and that was not good. Brynne would have to introduce sex back into their lives.

"Brynne!" Kenzie was suddenly standing right next to her. She pointed to the table beside them. "This is my friend Gemma Haskins. Would you like to join us?"

Brynne was horrified. She hadn't a drop of makeup on and wasn't prepared to see anyone here. And certainly not Kenzie, of all people. Had she not been lost in her thoughts, she would've seen Kenzie and hightailed out before she was discovered. She was furious with herself. But it was too late.

"No, thank you." Brynne pursed her lips and stared straight ahead. "I'm just getting some tea and will be on my way." She adjusted her dark sunglasses to keep her eyes well hidden.

"Nice to meet you." Gemma stood and reached out to shake Brynne's hand. "I've heard so much about you."

"I'm sure it was all positive," Brynne said. She glanced quickly at Gemma, and then continued to focus on the clerk about to take her order.

"But of course." Gemma offered a wide grin.

Brynne was next in line. Her escape couldn't come fast enough. She ordered hot tea and demanded that it arrive instantly, as she had no time to spare. And then, with keys in hand, she grabbed the piping-hot cup and quickly headed for the exit.

Kenzie and Gemma wished her a good day, but Brynne flew out the door, pretending not to hear them.

Marcella's home address was affixed to the visor so Brynne could see it. She tore onto the freeway, drove a short distance, then turned down the exit ramp and headed west in search of Westbury Avenue. She slowed down as she approached the street, which featured small cottage-like homes and cars parked haphazardly on front lawns. There were makeshift carports and aluminum trash cans on the aprons.

And then her phone rang. It was Martin. She pulled over and greeted him with a vibrant hello.

"Brynne, do you remember the date of the Bel-Air Black-and-White Ball?" Martin was businesslike. Brynne could tell he was in a hurry.

"Uh, yes. I believe it's one month from tomorrow night, why?" Brynne bit the inside of her lip. "We're still going, right?"

"I was thinking of taking a business trip that weekend, but I'll postpone it. We'll go." Brynne sighed deeply.

"Heard from the girls today?" Martin asked.

"We Skyped earlier. Marianne has a cold, but not to worry. Of course, I do." Brynne started to relax. "Brianne told me to give them some space. Can you imagine?"

"Okay, good. Busy. Gotta go. Have a good day."

"Oh, okay, honey." For a moment Brynne thought Martin might be interested in a longer conversation, but that hadn't occurred in a long time. She should've known. "Yes, I know you have to go. Talk to you later." After she hung up she took a deep breath, then put both hands on the wheel, sat up straight, and pulled back onto the street. It was useless to hang around there. Things were fine. Martin was making arrangements to go to the ball a month out. He obviously didn't plan on leaving her. She could return home.

But just as she began to pull away from the curb, she thought she noticed Martin's Ferrari parked farther up the street. She squinted to see the license plate, which read *TI*, for Tomlinson Industries. So it *was* his car. His gorgeous two-hundred-thousand-dollar Ferrari was parallel parked between an old Honda and a pickup truck. She glanced once more at Marcella Gomez's address and discovered it was just up the block.

Brynne didn't move. Should she get out of the car and walk up the street? What was he doing there? Working? Having sex?

She decided to wait. She had always trusted Martin and never dreamed for one second that he'd have an affair. Was this his first? She thought about other women he'd worked with. Was he having affairs with them, too?

Men rarely left their wives for their mistresses. The mistresses got the crumbs—that was what she'd always heard. Martin would never leave her. She kept telling herself that. Never.

A half hour passed. She felt dirty and foolish sitting in her car, terrified someone might sprint out of one of these hovels and rob her. She wanted to get out of this seedy neighborhood.

She would work on rebuilding her marriage. She would stop at the Pleasure Chest and see if any new gizmos had come in. She hadn't been there in years. Maybe she could find something provocative that would get Martin out of his room and back into her bed. Her job was to please her man, and somehow she had failed.

Just as she was about to leave, Martin emerged from the house up the block and walked toward his car. Brynne sat up straight, leaned over the steering wheel, and watched intently. And then came Marcella. Brynne squinted to get a better look. Marcella wore tight jeans and a low-cut bright-red sweater that barely contained her breasts, which were bouncing up and down. Martin reached for Marcella's hand as they walked to his car. He opened the passenger door for her. She gave him a peck on the cheek and got inside. Then he walked around the car, opened his door, slipped into the driver's seat, and quickly sped away.

Brynne felt like she'd been kicked in the gut. She hadn't moved. Her eyes were fixed on the now-empty parking spot.

Despite Martin's request, she was not having a good day.

KENZIE

Kenzie picked at her takeout salad, looked at her ring, and then at the business card Harriet Fuller, the jeweler, had given her. The name on the card was Jasmine Ray, the department head of Women's Studies at UCLA.

"Wait," Sarita said. "So the fortune-teller said your ring, which the jeweler thought once belonged to a suffragette, now belongs to your future husband? And then she dropped dead?" She laughed. "I'm sorry, but what a crazy story."

"I know," Kenzie said. "But that's what happened."

"So within six months—no, I guess five now—you're going to meet your future husband. Well, that's pretty interesting."

"It's ridiculous. Yet I'm embarrassed to say that I can't stop thinking about it."

Sitting on the opposite side of Kenzie's desk, Sarita lifted herself up and tucked one leg under her. "Well, my mother's sister, Aunt Anju, was devoted to the Indian guru Sathya Sai Baba, who was a spiritual healer and also offered prophecies." Sarita unwrapped her tuna sandwich and placed it on top of the brown bag it came in. "She couldn't leave the house without consulting him. Then one day she had a miscarriage. She scolded the guru for not alerting her to this misfortune. Instead of admitting that he was a fraud, he blamed her for not taking better care of herself. That ended her fascination with her so-called spirituality."

"I'm not saying I necessarily believe what this psychic said." Kenzie was defensive. She sat back in her chair. "That's why I called this woman Jasmine Ray to learn a little more about the ring. I guess it would be pretty cool if it really was worn by a suffragette."

Sarita smiled broadly. "I think you want to believe the psychic."

"I'm just curious about the ring," she argued. "I'm meeting Jasmine tomorrow at her home."

"It's pretty, by the way." Sarita admired the ring. "I'll be interested to know how it got into the hands of some guy who is going to marry you, though." She giggled, then gulped down the rest of her sandwich, took some of the papers off Kenzie's desk, and put them in her backpack. "I'm going to call the editor and see how he's doing on the promotional video. Hoping to see an edited version soon."

"Good, let me know if you need any help," Kenzie said as she swiveled her chair toward her computer and began working.

"Hey, Kenzie," Glenn Winkler said. He waltzed into her office without even knocking just as Sarita had exited.

Glenn enjoyed his job at Grayson. Although he was hired as Leo's assistant, he seemed to believe that both he and Leo held the same position. Whatever Leo did, wherever he went, so did Glenn. Leo was enamored with Glenn's Harvard education and lineage. He loved that Glenn was a direct descendant of President William Howard Taft. No one like that had ever worked at Grayson. Leo enjoyed hearing Glenn's family stories, half of which Kenzie swore he made up. But Glenn knew how to work Leo. It almost seemed as if Leo thought that by hanging around Glenn, he'd pick up some of his assistant's social status.

Kenzie wasn't terribly impressed with Glenn. Considering he'd graduated from a top Ivy League college and had all sorts of fancy credentials, she expected him to be, well, smart. It wasn't that he didn't know the players on every sports team, or didn't understand theoretical and experimental condensed matter physics, but he just lacked common sense. Maybe they didn't teach that at Harvard. Or if they did, Glenn missed that class.

Kenzie hated his smug attitude, his grand sense of entitlement. He never waited to be invited to meetings or even asked if he could attend. He just showed up, and no one ever asked him to leave. He was always in her face. Asking questions. Snooping around. She didn't trust him.

Glenn slipped into the chair across from her desk. "Need anything?" He leaned back, balancing the chair on just two legs. Kenzie prayed the chair would tip over. She needed a good laugh. But Glenn was able to balance the chair expertly, which was a metaphor for his life.

"Nope," she said. "Sarita and I are working on the event for opening day. But if I need some help, you bet I'll come calling." Her answer was an invitation for Glenn to leave, but he didn't take the hint.

"Oh, good. Well, so what else is going on?"

Kenzie stopped and turned toward him. "Like what? What do you mean?"

"Like your love life. You have one, right?" Glenn smirked.

"I'm not sure it's any of your business."

"Oh, c'mon, Kenzo. You're a great-looking gal. I can't imagine you aren't getting laid." In normal business operations, this was sexual harassment and grounds for firing. But those rules didn't seem to apply at Grayson. There was no human resources department. No one to enforce standards. Far different from her past corporate life, when this kind of language would never have been tolerated.

Telling Leo would only further Glenn's rise, as misogynistic behavior wasn't condemned, so it was up to Kenzie to enforce whatever rules she could.

"Glenn, are you confused about your position here? I don't believe you do much but ingratiate yourself with Leo. So let's get a few things straight. First, my name is Kenzie. Not Kenzo. And second, mind your own business. In fact, don't you have some work to do? How come you're not with Leo? Doesn't he need someone to hand him the toilet paper?"

"Go out with me," Glenn said as he continued to balance the chair on its back two legs and swing back and forth.

"Don't be absurd."

"C'mon, be my cougar. I've never gone out with an older chick."

"I'm not even going to dignify that with a response. I have work to do, and you need to find some." Kenzie got up from her chair, walked around her desk, and parked his chair back down. After a moment Glenn got up to leave.

"So you think I could be the one? For you?"

Kenzie stood at the door. "What do you mean, the one for me?"

"I could be your future husband. Lemme see the ring," Glenn said.

Him, too? How did Glenn know about the prophecy?

"My great-great-grandmother was a suffragette. So maybe that ring belongs to her? Then it would also belong to me. Never know." Glenn offered a wide grin, then sauntered out the door.

Kenzie stepped back to her desk and collapsed into her chair. Everyone knew?

Oh . . . Brynne. Of course Brynne would share this with the entire world.

Even if Glenn's great-great-grandmother was really a suffragette, Kenzie would still find him revolting. There was no way Glenn would ever be the one.

* * * * *

Kenzie and Matt had seen each other several times over the past ten days. They'd spoken on the phone often, sometimes late into the night. They'd pick up breakfast and sit in one of the boxes at the track, watching the Thoroughbreds train. Later they'd hang out in Kenzie's office watching live horse racing from Santa Anita, Belmont Park, Gulfstream Park, and other racetracks around the country on TV. They shared an affinity for old movies, board games, and even country-western music. Kenzie grew more interested in sports, while Matt became addicted to *House Hunters International*, one of Kenzie's favorite TV shows. Whatever there was between them was certainly growing.

Matt had invited her to meet him at his favorite restaurant, and Kenzie had been looking forward to it. She pulled up to the valet stand, got her ticket, and entered Craig's.

She could tell from the crowded entryway that this was a popular place. Scanning the dark room with its comfortable blue-leather booths and chestnut walls, she spotted Matt having a conversation with Joe Harper, Josh Rubinstein, and Craig Dado, who ran Del Mar racetrack. Matt said his good-byes, then nodded to Kenzie, grabbed his beer, and quickly made his way over to her.

"Hey." Matt wrapped his arm around her back and kissed her lightly on the cheek. "You made great time."

"I did. When I texted you earlier I thought I'd be late due to traffic, but it cleared up."

Matt introduced Kenzie to Craig Susser, the owner of the restaurant, who offered her a drink and then escorted them to a booth nearby. As soon as they sat down, the waiter appeared with Kenzie's glass of wine.

"Thank you," she said.

When they were settled in the booth, Matt lifted his glass to her. "I know this is a long way from the track, but I think you might like it here. Good to get out of Palmdale now and then."

"It sure is. I'm happy to be here . . . with you." She clinked his glass.

"So all going well at Grayson?" Matt asked.

"Oh, the usual craziness. I don't think it would interest you that much."

"Why not?" he asked. "I'm very interested in you. In case you haven't noticed."

"Yes, actually, I've noticed and I like it." Her face lit up when her eyes met his. "I'm trying to coordinate one event with a lot of folks who have other agendas. That's the biggest obstacle—getting folks to work together."

"It's always about the people. And attitudes."

Kenzie took a sip of wine and felt her shoulders relax while she leaned back into the booth.

"You did it before," Matt said.

"It was a long time ago. Another life." Kenzie sighed. Her other life was still a sore subject. A chapter that had both good and bad memories.

The waiter rattled off the specials and then took their orders.

"Do you ever think about it? That other life? Want to go back?" Matt asked.

"Yes, I think about it. But no, I don't want to go back, at least not yet." Kenzie held on to her glass for a moment and then took another sip of wine. She hadn't told Matt the details of that day onstage four years ago. It wasn't something she wanted to relive. Every time she thought of it, her stomach would get tied in knots. But Matt was easygoing and nonjudgmental. She certainly felt safe with him. Maybe it was time to tell him. "Something happened. Something that was . . . Well, it was . . . humiliating. I felt tremendous shame. And I didn't know how to handle it, so I handled it badly."

Kenzie set her glass on the table and took a deep breath. Matt waited for her to continue. "Anyway, I'm sure it'll sound like it was no big deal. But it was . . . at least to me."

"What was it?"

"My mom had just died. I was incredibly nervous. I didn't really deserve the job I had. I mean, I really wasn't ready for it." She paused to clear her throat. "I made a speech. A big one. And right before I went onstage, I stopped at the restroom, and I guess . . . Well, it was so embarrassing, but I guess I didn't get my skirt all the way down, and well . . . Even now I have the hardest time saying what happened." She rubbed her forehead and bit her lip. "I froze midspeech. And then, well, I just walked off the stage. It was pretty awful."

Matt put his arm around her, drew her close, and kissed her lightly on the cheek. "You don't have to go on. It's in the past. I'm sure it was upsetting for you."

Kenzie loved the way she felt when Matt threaded his arm around her. Her whole body just melted. She enjoyed the sound of his voice and loved how he looked deep into her eyes. She sat for a moment taking it all in. It had been a long time since she'd had a romantic relationship.

The last one was just after college. John Rosenbaum, a guy she'd met at a party. They had lived together and lasted about a year. Since then it had been a series of dates, or more often hookups. Kenzie was guarded. Her mother wondered if this was a trait she shared with her dad, because her mom was the opposite—far more trusting and eager to open her heart.

But Kenzie was wary of men. She didn't trust them completely. She'd invest in them and then they'd reject her, one way or another. Whether it was her own father who had never wanted to know her, or her beloved grandfather who'd died on her, or the boyfriends who left her for other women. It took time for her to open up.

But she was starting to get there with Matt. She'd missed having someone at her side, someone who was genuinely interested in what she had to say. Someone who was patient and kind. She enjoyed Matt's sense of humor and sharp wit. He was challenging and yet thoughtful. Slowly but surely her defenses were starting to break down.

"I guess it sounds stupid, but I wasn't able to shrug it off. My friend Gemma kept saying it wasn't a big deal. That I was making too much of it. She said the paparazzi have captured moments much worse and published those photos online and in magazines. But those are people in the public eye. Celebrities. I wasn't that. I was the consummate professional who lived for perfection. I wouldn't tolerate any mishaps. I was a control freak living in an uptight corporate world. So to have that happen . . . Well, for me it was career suicide. I was devastated."

"Did you get fired?" Matt asked softly.

"No. But my boss knew I wasn't functioning at the level they needed. So we agreed that I should take a month's leave. But that wasn't long enough. They needed to go on and so did I, so I quit shortly thereafter."

The waiter brought out their dinners. Kenzie took another sip of wine. Her face was hot, yet she felt cold. She draped her sweater over her shoulders.

"I have a good job now." Kenzie was eager to change the subject. "I like it. I'm doing well."

"The demands aren't as great," Matt said as he poured ketchup on his hamburger. "It's certainly not the kind of pressure you were under before. But I understand you were building a career, and then it kind of went awry."

"Yup, that's kind of what happened," she said.

Matt smiled and with his free hand tucked a lock of her hair behind her ear. Then he brushed his finger along her cheek. She leaned into his chest as he wrapped his arm around her shoulders. He took a forkful of his baked potato and fed it to her. She eased back into his arm and chewed slowly, thinking it was remarkable that a baked potato could be so delicious. Her body tingled all over. She couldn't remember ever feeling this content and happy.

"I really enjoy being with you, Kenzie. I'm glad I summoned the courage to invite you to dinner."

"I only wish you'd done it sooner," Kenzie said. "I feel like we have to make up for lost time."

"We'll have plenty of time to be together." Matt rubbed her shoulder. Kenzie closed her eyes to savor the moment. She took a deep breath and leaned in closer to Matt.

When they'd finished dinner and were heading for the exit, Craig, the owner, held the door open and invited them back again soon.

"Before we get our cars, wanna take a walk? It's a nice night," Matt said as he wrapped an arm around Kenzie.

"Sure. It would probably help to work off some of that great chocolate pizza I couldn't resist." She laughed.

"Yeah, me too."

They strolled down Melrose, then turned left. Matt's arm was still draped around Kenzie's shoulders, her arm behind his waist, the two of them talking now and then but mostly relaxing in each other's company.

"I haven't been on this side of town in so long," she mused.

"Me either, but I keep a place here."

"Really? You do? Where?"

"Oh just two blocks over." Matt pointed to his right. "Down that street. It's just a one-room apartment on the second floor. I used it when Hollywood Park was open so I didn't have to drive all the way back to Palmdale."

"I'd love to see it sometime," Kenzie said as she buttoned her sweater. The night was getting cooler.

"Well, sure . . . But it's not a big deal." Matt used his left hand to pull at his collar. "Could use some fixing up. Probably needs a woman's touch."

"Well, when you're ready to show me, I'd be happy to take a look. And don't worry, I'm not going to give you a grade."

They walked arm in arm for two blocks till they came to what looked like a small apartment building. Matt nodded toward an outside white-stucco staircase.

"That's it. Upstairs. Wanna take a look?"

"Sure," Kenzie said.

"Okay, like I said, I don't want to raise expectations," Matt said as they hiked up the stairs. He opened the door. "It's just a room really."

Kenzie looked up at the high vaulted white ceiling and down at the hardwood floor. There was a big brown desk with stacks of paper, some pens, and a small lamp that leaned against a big picture window with a white curtain drawn to one side. A small bathroom was at the back, and a fireplace on the opposite wall. A long white couch and small cherrywood coffee table were in the center. Matt had described it well. It was sparse but practical.

"Wow, it's like the North Pole in here." Kenzie wrapped her sweater around her body as if she'd just entered a freezer.

Matt set the thermostat on high and then turned on the gas fireplace. Kenzie stood right in front of it. Within an instant she felt the warmth. Matt sat down on the couch and stretched his legs onto the coffee table.

"This is pretty nice," she said. "But, uh, you're missing a bed." She shared a look with Matt.

"I'm sitting on it. It opens up into one. Like I said, it's no-frills." Matt raised his arm and gestured for her to come sit on the couch next to him. He helped her take off her sweater, which she tossed onto the coffee table and then slipped back into his arms. They sat quietly without saying a word, gazing at the fireplace.

"I really believe you bring out the best in me. And I hope I do that for you, too." Matt kissed the top of her head. "I don't believe I've ever enjoyed being with anyone as much as I do you."

"I love hearing that. I feel the same way." Kenzie rested her head against Matt's chest. She could feel his heart pumping wildly.

"I love you, Kenzie. I do," Matt muttered.

Kenzie was filled with desire. It was the first time she'd heard Matt say those words. She closed her eyes and leaned in closer to him. And then he tilted her head up, brought his lips to hers, and began kissing her lightly at first, then longer and deeper. She breathed in his scent and felt the roughness of his stubble against her cheek and the heat of his body on hers. Her heart raced as his left hand unbuttoned her silk blouse and pushed it off her shoulders. She felt his gaze as he unfastened her belt and slowly unzipped her jeans, and she sighed as the back of his fingers brushed against her bare skin and then slid gently beneath the lace trim of her panties.

"I think about you all the time." Matt's voice was low and smooth, his lips close to Kenzie's ear. "It makes me want you more and more." She closed her eyes, parted her legs, and felt the softness of his lips as they grazed down her neck.

"I love you, too, Matt. I do," said Kenzie breathlessly.

The fire cast a warm glow on Matt's chiseled jawline. Cradled in his arms, Kenzie felt safe, secure, and desired.

* * * * *

The next morning, when Kenzie woke up in her apartment, she'd almost forgotten about her appointment with Jasmine Ray. She hadn't gotten home till very late last night. The memory made her glow all over.

She threw on some clothes and raced out the door. During her drive she thought of nothing but her night with Matt, going over every detail of their lovemaking. She wanted to live it all over again. She recalled his broad grin and blue eyes that sparkled in the moonlight, the way his fingertips felt as they danced across her skin, and how his eyes studied every inch of her, sending twinges of excitement through her body. She was so caught up in the memory that she almost missed her exit.

And yet there it was again—that nagging thought that Matt might not be the one. That this relationship would somehow fail because Annalisa predicted a different outcome. Try as she might, she couldn't get the stupid prophecy out of her mind. Maybe Matt was a necessary relationship. Someone to prepare her for the real one to come—the man who would someday be her lifelong partner. Her future husband.

She wished so badly that Matt owned the ring, even though she knew it was crazy to think this way. If only fantasies came true.

She reached Jasmine's modest home, at the end of a dirt road nestled deep inside Topanga Canyon but perched on a hill with a beautiful view of the Pacific Ocean.

She drove her car right up to the front door, got out, and knocked.

Jasmine Ray was an elderly woman with silvery white hair collected at the back of her neck in a neat ponytail. She wore a blue-and-white striped T-shirt, faded jeans, and red flip-flops. She was lean, her movements spry. When Kenzie identified herself, Jasmine welcomed her with open arms.

"Oh, I'm so glad you came. And so eager to take a look at that ring," Jasmine said. "Come inside, my dear. Have a seat right here at my kitchen table."

Kenzie sat, took off her ring, and set it on the table while Jasmine grabbed her eyeglasses off the kitchen counter. "You described it well on the phone." Jasmine said. She held the ring up to the light and inspected it inside and out. She turned it around several times and looked closely at the inside of the ring.

"Oh dear, I didn't even offer you anything to drink. What can I get you?" Jasmine put the ring on the counter and rushed to the refrigerator. "I have water and soda. I'd offer you more, but I haven't had a moment to get to the market. My daughter's coming by later. Maybe I should ask her to pick up something for us?"

"Oh no, please don't worry. I'm fine, Jasmine. Thank you for meeting with me. I'm just curious about this ring. Well . . ." She laughed, embarrassed. "A psychic told me it belongs to my future husband. Sounds crazy, I know. And why would a man own a suffragette ring anyway?" She wondered if Jasmine might know the answer.

"Well, I don't know," Jasmine said as she retrieved the ring and returned to the kitchen table to sit across from Kenzie. "But this ring looks just like the ones worn by the suffragettes who worked on the passage of the Nineteenth Amendment. The rings were all made with three semiprecious stones: an amethyst, a pearl, and a peridot. There were a limited number made."

Jasmine inspected the ring again, this time more closely. "I think it might've belonged to Minnie Fisher Cunningham."

"Who was she?"

"Well, she was a suffragette and politician. But the reason I think this ring might've belonged to her is because of this." Jasmine pointed to a microscopic inscription on the bottom inside portion of the ring. "Can you make out those two letters?" Kenzie craned her neck to see what Jasmine was referring to. She could barely see them. "Here." Jasmine reached for a magnifying glass that was sitting in a mug on her kitchen table and handed it to Kenzie. "Take a look at it through this magnifying glass. I believe those letters are *J* and *J*. But I'm sure your eyes are better than mine."

Kenzie looked at the ring through the magnifying glass and held the ring up even higher. She squinted. "Wait, I think you're right. Yes, *J* and *J*. I do see them."

Kenzie handed the magnifier back to Jasmine, who examined the ring again. "I believe the *J*s stand for Josie and Jimsey, two orphaned children Minnie and her husband, B. J. Cunningham, adopted. So I would guess if it's a real ring from that time, it might in fact be hers."

"Wow. I never even noticed the initials. What else do you know about Minnie Cunningham?"

"Well, she was the first woman from Texas to run for the United States Senate. And then she ran for governor. She was never elected to office, but she paved the way for future generations. I'd be darn proud to wear that ring."

Kenzie held the ring in her hand and gazed at it.

"You know, Minnie and other women like her at that time inspired each other to fight for change. They developed deep friendships and sacrificed plenty in order to gain the right to vote," Jasmine said.

Kenzie had certainly heard about Susan B. Anthony and Elizabeth Cady Stanton, both tireless champions for women's rights, but she'd not heard about Minnie Fisher Cunningham and her accomplishments. Suddenly the ring had far greater significance.

Jasmine took an album from her bookshelf in the den and brought it to the kitchen table. She showed Kenzie photographs of Minnie and other suffragettes. Kenzie was fascinated. She asked a lot of questions, which Jasmine was only too happy to answer.

She learned about the suffragists and their steadfast devotion to one another and how they worked together toward their common goal.

Kenzie and Jasmine were so absorbed in the materials that neither had paid attention to the knocking at the door until suddenly they heard a voice.

"Mother? Are you there? Mother?"

"Yes, dear. Come in," Jasmine said, and then whispered to Kenzie, "My daughter."

"Oh, well, I'll be going then," Kenzie said. "This was great. Thank you so much for taking the time."

"Of course, my dear. But you don't have to leave." Jasmine raised her voice. "Go ahead, the door is open, come on in."

"Mother, the door's jammed. I think the lock needs to be fixed."

"Oh dear. Well, I'll have to get that done. Just push hard," Jasmine said as the door opened. "Kenzie, dear, this is my daughter."

Kenzie turned around and almost fainted.

"Brynne?"

GEMMA

Gemma was the first to arrive at the homeless shelter. The past twelve days had been excruciating. She couldn't wait to be with Jeffrey and his family. *Her family.* She sat in her car until she saw the black Range Rover. Jeffrey and Scarlett jumped out, then Dylan, a young boy about ten, and Emily, their mother. Gemma knew their faces because she'd seen photos of Dylan's soccer games, Scarlett's swimming meets, and Emily's five sisters on Facebook and Instagram. She felt as if she knew them all. The one she knew the least was Jeffrey, who had no social media presence.

Gemma watched as they unloaded their SUV and brought out what looked like a feast. Gemma was inspired by their generosity and goodwill. They seemed like such a lovely family. She took a deep breath and opened her car door. Scarlett wore a big smile and waved when she saw Gemma step out of the car.

"Hey, Gemma, good to see you," Jeffrey said when he saw her emerge. He carried a few trays into the shelter, then into the kitchen, where Emily and Dylan had already begun to set up. They would serve their home-cooked meal in the dining hall.

"Gemma, this is my wife, Emily, and son, Dylan," Jeffrey said when he entered the kitchen with Gemma following close behind. Emily stepped forward and shook Gemma's hand. Dylan ignored her.

Jeffrey placed the trays on a counter as the rest of the family went to work. It was obvious they had done this several times before. Everyone had a job. Scarlett set the cupcakes she'd baked on a platter, and Dylan unpacked the soft drinks. Emily warmed the meal in the oven to make sure everything was hot when it was served.

Gemma wasn't quite sure what to do. She leaned against a counter but found she was in the way, as everyone was moving about so quickly and purposefully. They all knew what to do—except her.

"Want to set the tables?" Jeffrey asked as he looked at Gemma.

"Sure," she said. But she didn't know where anything was stored. She scurried about looking in the cupboards. Then Jeffrey pulled out place mats and napkins from a drawer while Emily reached for a stack of white plates and handed them to Gemma. She took everything into the dining room and set the tables.

The folks who lived in this small temporary shelter entered the dining room. Their faces were drawn and weathered. Jeffrey took the meat loaf out of the oven while Emily grabbed a few serving dishes, and Scarlett and Dylan placed all the desserts on the buffet table. Gemma thought they were the perfect family, a family she wanted to be part of. Jeffrey brushed something off Scarlett's sweater and gave her a big hug. It was such a loving gesture. She hoped someday he would do the same for her.

"Hon, are you almost done?" Jeffrey asked. Emily set the dinner on the table in the dining room. The guests' faces lit up. Several of them thanked Jeffrey and Emily. Then Scarlett and Dylan brought out water and soft drinks. Gemma stood to the side and smiled as everyone sat down to eat.

The entire family settled in the archway between the kitchen and dining room. The folks thanked them for a marvelous dinner. Jeffrey, standing right between Gemma and Emily, draped his arms across their shoulders, and Gemma took a quick selfie and texted it to Kenzie.

"Girls, you did a great job. Gemma, nice to have you with us tonight," Jeffrey said.

Gemma smiled at her father. She felt the love, the connection, and didn't want this evening to end.

"Okay, gang, so how about we all get some pizza?" he asked.

"Sure, let's get this place cleaned up, and then we'll go," Emily said. As she went to the kitchen, she shouted to Gemma to join them as well.

Gemma wasn't sure about that plan because suddenly reality crept in. As much as she had enjoyed her evening with them, this was not her family. She felt like an interloper, like she didn't really belong. She knew she'd continue to feel that way until she revealed herself and they learned the truth about her. She wondered if they'd welcome her with open arms. She desperately wanted that to happen.

Life would've been different had Jeffrey been part of hers. She couldn't understand why he'd rejected her in such a big way. His hostile feelings toward her mother also bothered her. Maybe her mother was exaggerating. Maybe the story wasn't entirely true. Maybe over the years her mother's resentment had grown, and the story had as well. There had to be another side. Jeffrey's side. She longed to hear what he had to say. Because this Jeffrey seemed the opposite of the one her mom described. He was far more caring and generous.

Her phone buzzed. *So that's him and the family?* Kenzie texted.

Gemma moved off to the side and typed her response. *Yup.*

Does he know who you are yet?

Nope. Have to figure out how and when to tell him. Gemma typed quickly, with one eye on the keyboard and the other surveying the room to make sure no one was asking for her.

Nice-looking. Especially Scarlett. You doing okay? Kenzie asked.

Conflicted. Had a good time but turned down dinner with them tonight.

Take it slow - ball's in your court. You are my family and I love you!

Gemma smiled as she put her phone back in her pocket and walked into the kitchen. She thanked Emily for the invitation and suggested they have dinner another time.

Jeffrey grabbed a sponge and wiped the kitchen counter as Emily gathered things they'd brought and stuffed them into a plastic bag. They were ready to leave. Gemma walked toward the exit to haul the trash outside and then felt a hand on her shoulder.

"Gemma," Jeffrey said. It wasn't a question. It felt more like a command. Gemma stiffened. She stopped, then spun around. Her gaze met his. There they were—his eyes. Her eyes. The same green eyes. How could he not notice? She looked up at him and noticed a tiny scar on the tip of his nose. She saw bits of gray in his otherwise flawless deep-brown beard.

"Yes?" Gemma asked. Her voice cracked, and her mouth was so dry she wished she had remembered her mouth spray.

"I . . .Well, I just wondered," he said. "Didn't you say you worked at this shelter? Isn't that how you know Scarlett?" Jeffrey reached for Gemma's trash bag and swung it over his shoulder, then placed his other arm behind the small of her back and moved with her toward the exit.

"Well," Gemma said, "I worked here a while ago. But I met Scarlett when I brought some canned goods for her food drive." She hoped the half lie she'd come up with would appease Jeffrey's curiosity. She couldn't stand all the deception and longed for the day she could tell him the truth. She looked at Jeffrey again as he tossed the bag into a bin. He brushed off his hands, thanked her for helping out that evening, and then joined the others in the SUV.

As the Range Rover started to pull away, Scarlett opened her window and asked Gemma again if she wanted to join them for pizza. Gemma smiled sweetly and said she'd take a rain check. Then she heard Jeffrey say, loudly enough for her to hear, that Gemma had a life, but he hoped she would come to dinner with them soon.

As they sped off, Gemma opened the door to her car, started the engine, turned up the music, and drove home.

SARITA

Sarita sat quietly at the dining room table, contemplating her breakfast.

Other than meeting for lunch during the past week, she and Damien had hardly seen each other. Damien told Sarita that he was surprised to hear that her parents never spoke of what had happened that night. He didn't understand their narrow-minded approach, their lack of curiosity or interest in who Sarita really was. But Sarita liked it that way. She didn't want to discuss anything with them. It was easier just to go on as they always had. She'd take her meals, sleep, and go to work. Life continued as if nothing had happened.

But this day was different.

"Mama can take you to work, or you can continue taking the bus till your car is fixed," Papa said as he buttered his toast, his eyes focused on the task before him.

"The bus is fine." Sarita took a spoonful of oatmeal from the bowl in front of her.

"Mr. Gupta's family understood there was an emergency which prevented you from attending dinner. It's rescheduled for this evening. I will pick you up at work and bring you home," Papa said, "so you will be on time."

Sarita didn't acknowledge him. Her job was of utmost importance right now. That was her ticket out. The more money she saved, the sooner she could leave. She checked her phone for the time, then hurried through her meal so she could catch the bus.

Her commute took much longer now, almost an hour on the bus from her home to Grayson. It gave her plenty of time to think.

Once she arrived at the racetrack, she Googled Rahul Gupta, whom she would meet later that evening.

"According to LinkedIn, Rahul is director of sales for Gupta Imports," Sarita said to Damien on the phone later that day. "Of course that's what he'd do. He did what was expected of him. Works in the family business."

"Sounds perfect for you," Damien said.

"His company's based in Mumbai, and he travels there a great deal." She ate the second half of her chicken salad sandwich at her desk, as dinner would be later than usual. "I kind of feel sorry for him. This meeting is such a waste of time."

"You'll get through it. You know what you want in life. You're strong and confident. I can't imagine he won't fall head over heels for you."

"I doubt that." She laughed. "I'm hardly the kind of woman he wants."

"Then it's his loss," Damien said. "And I couldn't be happier. More important, how're you doing there?"

"Hanging in." She sighed. "It's just better for me to live at home and try to keep the peace. But I miss seeing you."

"And I miss you, too. I'll come by your office tomorrow for lunch. I just couldn't get away today."

"That's okay. I understand," she said. "I'm sorry we can't see each other at night. I just can't risk it right now."

"We'll meet at lunch," he said.

"And if I can possibly sneak away, you know I will."

"I don't want you doing that. Let things calm down a bit. You know I'm here for you. And always will be."

"I love you, Damien," she whispered. "Thank you for being so patient."

"I love you, too. We'll make it work."

When Sarita hung up she turned around and was startled to see Kenzie standing at the edge of her cubicle.

"Are you working two jobs?" Kenzie asked.

"No, not at all," said Sarita uneasily. "Why do you ask?"

"Well, let's see." Kenzie leaned up against the wall inside Sarita's tiny workspace. "Yesterday you were sound asleep at your desk. Today you're wearing shoes that don't match, and I found this in the ladies' room." Kenzie pulled a red wig out from behind her. "Unless Leo or Glenn is a tranny, I don't know what this was doing in there, especially since I found it next to your backpack." Kenzie produced Sarita's backpack and set it on the floor. "You never impressed me as being a party girl, but maybe I don't know you well."

Sarita was exhausted. She was tired of the secrets, sneaking around, the long hours, and pretending to be someone else all the time.

"It's not exactly another job," she said. "It's . . . well . . . it's another *life*."

"And what kind of life would that be?" Kenzie asked. "Wanna tell me about it?"

"Okay." Sarita got up from her chair, picked up her backpack, and slid her arms through the straps. "But my car's still in the shop, so my father's picking me up soon. I was going to wait outside for him."

"How about I come wait with you?" Kenzie asked.

"That'd be great." Sarita felt the tension in her muscles relax.

Kenzie and Sarita sat on the white brick wall by the parking lot in front of Grayson Downs. As the sun began to set over the San Gabriel Mountains, Kenzie listened intently as Sarita offered the details surrounding her double life. She was so glad to tell Kenzie everything. When she was done she let out a huge breath.

When Mr. Mahajan arrived, Sarita hugged Kenzie, then threw her bag into the backseat and joined her father in the front. Her father drove them home, but neither spoke a word. When she entered her home, she saw the traditional Indian garb lying across the back of the sofa. She took the garments to her room and changed clothes.

Sarita took a selfie in the sari and texted it to Damien.

Sexy girl, he texted back. *Trying to make me jealous?*

Sarita texted a smiling emoji.

At precisely eight o'clock, the doorbell rang. Sarita had watched her two older sisters go through this many times, and now it was her turn. She felt like a trained dog. Dressed as if she were attending an Indian wedding, in an embroidered gold sari, she met the Guptas and the matchmaker at the door. Then they all took their seats at the dining room table. Mama served dinner, while Sarita poured tea and then took her place across from Rahul.

"My daughter, Sarita, just returned from university," Papa announced.

The Guptas sat quietly as they ate their dinner. Sarita thought the situation was stilted and strange—forced conversation between two families that adhered to ancient traditions.

"And what did you study?" Mr. Gupta asked.

"I majored in English," Sarita said. She watched her father, whose hands were clenched in his lap. Sarita knew her parents were holding their collective breaths, hoping she wouldn't humiliate them.

"Did you enjoy your time on the East Coast?" Mr. Gupta continued. "Were you happy to return home?"

"Yes and yes." Sarita offered as little information as possible while she enjoyed her mother's delicious *biryani*, a traditional savory rice dish.

Papa changed the subject and spoke about a lecture he'd attended about the current Mumbai economy and how it had affected his business and others. This created lively conversation that involved Rahul as well, and Sarita was relieved to sit back and enjoy the rest of her dinner while they talked shop.

She used the time to daydream about Damien. She thought about the fun they'd shared. Like the time she hung her key chain on his earlobe, and then he grabbed her red wig, threw it over his green Mohawk, and danced to the beat of his favorite band while making pancakes and bacon for her in his kitchen. She loved his silliness and uninhibited disposition. Damien had such a good sense of self, and was a remarkably supportive and understanding boyfriend. She wondered how long he'd put up with the constraints on their relationship.

Just before dessert Papa suggested that Sarita and Rahul have a few moments alone, and he ushered them into his study off the dining room. Sarita entered while Rahul stayed behind to talk with his father, Papa, and the matchmaker. Sarita closed the door to the study, took a seat, and eavesdropped on their conversation.

"An arranged marriage is part of our tradition," Papa said. "Now that Sarita is back with her family, this is what she will pursue. She will obey. She's a good girl and will make a good wife."

Sarita reached in her bra, took out her cell phone, and called Damien on FaceTime.

"I miss you, baby," she whispered when she saw his face.

"Me too," he said. "Any chance you can sneak out of there?"

"I can't. Not now," she said faintly. "But I'm thinking of you. Are you thinking of me?"

"All the time," he said softly.

"Are you thinking of this?"

Sarita glanced at the door, which she knew could open at any time, and quickly lowered her midriff top, unfastened her bra, and exposed her breasts. "Papa thinks I'm a good girl and will make a good wife. What do you think?"

"Mmmm . . ." Damien raised his eyebrows. "I think you're amazing . . . But I think you're good at most anything . . ."

BRYNNE

"Jasmine's your mother? Seriously?" Kenzie asked as Brynne hopped into her car, which was parked outside her mother's home. Just as she started the engine, Kenzie sneaked in next to her.

"What're you doing?" Brynne asked.

"I'm waiting for my answer."

Brynne didn't move. She looked blankly in front of her. Kenzie sat quietly.

"Fine. You win. Yes. She is," she said. "Now get out of the car. I want to be home before Martin—"

"Brynne, what kind of world do you live in?" Kenzie interrupted. She turned toward her. "This isn't about winning or losing. This isn't a game. I just had a wonderful conversation with your mother, who you somehow neglected to mention was a renowned expert on gender issues."

"So?"

"So why wouldn't you mention that?"

"Why should I?"

"Are you ashamed of her?"

"Of course not," Brynne said. "And may I remind you that I'm not the one who is ashamed of anything. I didn't expose myself to an audience and then rush off a stage. I've had the right kind of life."

"Really?" Kenzie asked. "Are you suggesting that I should want your life? Lest you forget, we left the restaurant together and caught your husband, Martin, well . . . you know . . . Doesn't appear that things are going all that well in your life. I'm sorry, but why would I want to be married to a man who cheats on me? And why would I want to hide the fact that my mother was a scholar? Do you realize how lucky you are to even have your mother . . ." Kenzie's voice was shaking. "Alive? And well?"

Brynne turned off the ignition. She took a cigarette from her purse and lit it. She took a long puff, opened the window, dangled the cigarette over the side, and gazed at the shrubbery that lined the driveway. Kenzie fanned the smoke away with contempt.

"It's a long story that I don't care to go into or, frankly, share with you."

Brynne hated that Kenzie knew. That she was the one to see Martin with Marcella that day in the restaurant. Such a humiliating incident. And now she was rubbing it in her face. She hated how bold and determined Kenzie was. Brynne had to assert herself and make sure Kenzie knew who was in charge. "You know I could still get you fired."

"For what? For not kowtowing to you? For not being what you want me to be? Do you honestly think I can't get another job now? I have skills. I have experience. I have a résumé. What do you have? What've you done?"

"I'm a wife and mother. Something far more important than anything you've accomplished in your life."

"If you're so good at it, then why was Martin making out with another woman in the restaurant?"

"That's a low blow. You don't have to be so rough on me," Brynne said as she took another puff.

"You're kidding, right? You're asking me to lay off, when you've been trying to get me fired?" Kenzie asked.

Both sat silently for a moment, looking out their respective windows.

"I just want to say that your mother is lovely," Kenzie said quietly. "You're lucky she's alive. I wish I had mine right now."

"It's a terrible thing to lose your mother, I know—"

"No, you don't know, Brynne," Kenzie interrupted. "You can't know until you experience it. And as much as we don't get along, I don't wish that on anyone, not even you. You can't know what it does to your life, to your self, to lose your mother. The person who brought you into this world. The person who was always in your corner. The person who will always love you, no matter what."

Brynne was shaken by Kenzie's outburst. She'd really not seen this side of her. She thought about her own daughters and what it would be like for them to lose her. How would they ever go on without her? The idea of losing her own mother was equally devastating. Despite their differences, Brynne loved Jasmine. She thought about what it would've been like to lose Jasmine when she was in her twenties. How much her mother would've missed out on. She never would've known Brianne and Marianne or Brynne's life today.

Brynne just wished her mother were . . . different.

"My mother was . . . Well, she wasn't the kind of mother I wanted. She was in love with her job," Brynne said.

Kenzie looked sharply at Brynne, whose eyes were focused on the healthy and vibrant bushes of colorful bougainvillea. "I couldn't compete. She wanted to change the world. I wanted her to be the mother I saw on TV. I wanted her to bake cookies and be a Scout leader. But she didn't. She wanted to join protests and attend women's meetings. My father couldn't stand it, nor could I. He moved out. Married the perfect wife, the mother I wanted but who didn't want me. And then my younger sister died of a grand mal seizure, and my mother became even more estranged from me. She wanted me to be like her, and I wanted to be anything but her."

Brynne looked toward a young girl who was settled in a shallow sandbox on the front lawn next door. She was playing alone with a truck, hauling sand to the other side of the box.

"I got into Ole Miss and never looked back. I'm living my life. Not hers."

"You became a Southern woman, accent and all, even though you were born and raised in Northern California, home of the women's movement. How ironic."

Brynne lowered her window, blew out a long trail of smoke, and then threw the butt out the window.

"Aren't you going to step on that? We're in a burn area," Kenzie said.

"It'll be fine."

Kenzie jumped out of the car, ran to the driver's side, and crushed the butt with her shoe. Brynne watched in amazement.

"It would've burned itself out," Brynne said.

"And what if it didn't?" Kenzie said as she returned to the passenger seat.

Brynne sat still as she admired the hedges and then noticed that the tulips were in bloom. Her mother had recently taken up gardening, and it was clear she was great at that, too. Whatever she set out to do, she did with fierce determination. Brynne thought about how strong her mother really was. She'd lost her husband to another woman and then cared for and suffered the loss of her disabled daughter, and yet recovered, finding a new career and then becoming a renowned expert in her field.

"Are you going to leave Martin?" Kenzie asked softly.

"Of course not," Brynne said as she watched the girl in the sandbox play with the truck. "Never. I'm committed to this marriage. And I know he is, too, despite what you saw. He is."

"How do you know he won't leave?"

"He won't. He needs to keep his marriage intact. If for nothing else, then for appearances."

"Appearances?" Kenzie asked. She rolled her eyes.

"I know what you're thinking," Brynne said.

"Really? What?" Kenzie brushed her finger across the mahogany console between them.

"You think I'm a fool to stay with him. But you don't know what it's like being divorced. I saw what happened to my mother. I've seen what happens to other women. They lose their money, their social status. And worse, they fly coach."

"Do you really like your life, Brynne?"

Brynne thought for a moment. "Nothing is going to change. I will make sure of that," she said.

"What are you so afraid of? Are you afraid to be on your own? To explore who you really are?"

"What do you mean? I know who I really am. You're looking at her."

"You're not that happy. I can see it in your eyes, and I hear it in your voice," Kenzie said. "I saw it at that restaurant. And I'm seeing it here today. And your mother did all right, despite the divorce. You don't dislike your mother. You admire her."

Brynne stared out her window. The little girl loaded the truck full of sand and made several deliveries to the other side of the sandbox. She had successfully sculpted a sand castle.

"That little girl is me," Brynne said, her voice quivering slightly as they both looked at the child. "She wants to move out of her mother's home into a castle."

"She's a little girl. You're not. That was who you were. Once. But you know what's going to happen to that castle. It's going to get washed away, because sand castles don't last."

Brynne's eyes filled unexpectedly with tears as she continued to stare at the little girl.

There was a silence.

"I need your help with the women's expo at the track," Kenzie said

"Are you blackmailing me?" Brynne asked. "Are you going to tell everyone about my marriage if I don't help you?"

"Not at all. I'm simply asking you to help me. Stop trying to bury me. Can we call a truce?"

Brynne contemplated Kenzie's request. She stared out the window, unable to look at Kenzie.

"Okay," she said after a long pause. "But I want you to know why." Brynne turned off the engine, sat up straight, and continued to stare in front of her. She held on to the steering wheel with both hands. "I know you haven't told anyone about that little incident we both witnessed at breakfast last week. It was a good piece of juicy gossip that would've spread like wildfire. If it had, I would've been embarrassed . . . And I, well . . . I want to thank you for not saying anything." Kenzie, who had been staring at Brynne, turned away and looked out the passenger window. Brynne added, "I'm not saying we're going to be best friends or anything . . . I'm just saying I appreciate that."

Neither said a thing, just looked out their respective windows.

"And by the way, my life will not change," Brynne said. "Martin isn't leaving. I'm not leaving. Do you understand?"

"I admire your tenacity," Kenzie said as she turned and looked at Brynne again.

Brynne bit down on her lip, and it started to bleed. Kenzie reached across the console and took her hand. "I will help you, and you're going to help me," she said softly. "It's what women do, Brynne. They help each other. It's what we're going to do."

"I don't need any help." Brynne's voice was flat.

"We all can use some help at one time or another." Kenzie smiled.

Brynne said nothing. She didn't believe women could help one another. That didn't seem possible. She competed with women for men, for pageant crowns, and for tennis trophies. The idea that women would truly support one another was an alien concept. She didn't trust them. However, Kenzie seemed different from the women she'd come to know.

"Brynne!" Jasmine shouted from the front porch.

Brynne looked up the second she heard her name, and when she realized her hand was still in Kenzie's, she yanked it back instantly.

"Oh, Kenzie," Jasmine called. "You're still here, good. You forgot your ring. I didn't want you to leave without it."

Kenzie leaped out of the car. Jasmine met her on the walkway and gave her the ring.

"Can you imagine if you lost this?" Jasmine laughed.

"Is that the ring you told me about?" Brynne shouted from her car. "The one that belongs—"

"Yes," Kenzie interrupted, "to my future husband."

Brynne looked at Kenzie, who was standing with Jasmine, and smiled. "Well, then we'd better find him."

KENZIE

Kenzie was excited about meeting Matt for dinner at Craig's again. They had gone there a few times, and it was becoming their place. She leaned comfortably into Matt's shoulder as they sat in one of the big booths.

Matt turned his head and looked into her eyes. "I think you're getting to me."

She smiled. "Really? How so?"

"I haven't asked Craig to flip the channel on one of the bar's TVs so I can see basketball instead of the soccer game that's on now."

"Ah, that's a big sacrifice," she said. "Especially because we always seem to have a table with a clear view of one of those TVs."

"Yes, that happens magically."

"I see. I guess you prefer my warm and cuddly personality to tonight's game. I'm flattered," she said.

"I prefer being with you over anything else," he said. "Anytime. Even though I don't know that I'd call you warm and cuddly."

Kenzie pulled away from his grasp. "What does that mean?"

"Hey, you don't open up all that easily. Takes time to get to know you. I've had to do some gentle probing, but I'm getting there." He pulled her back toward him and kissed her softly on the head. "But I see why. You've had some tough times. Maybe a little more than one should at your age. But things are looking bright. You've got me now."

"Really? I've got you. How great is that?"

"I'd say it's pretty great," Matt teased.

"I agree." Kenzie cozied up next to him. "I'm pretty happy."

As the waiter walked by with a tray full of entrées, Kenzie inhaled the familiar aroma of charred steak.

"Just pretty happy?" he said after a moment.

"No, I'm happy. Really. I love being with you." Kenzie looked down and straightened the napkin on her lap.

"Uh-oh, I feel a cool breeze coming my way. What's going on?"

Kenzie couldn't believe Matt knew her that well already. They'd been seeing each other for almost two months. She was extremely happy with him—but that was the problem. She didn't want to tell him about the stupid ring. It was ridiculous. Matt would laugh, and she'd feel foolish. She had to put it out of her mind, but now Matt, like a dog with a bone, wouldn't give up.

"I'm waiting. Something's up. What is it?" Kenzie could feel Matt's leg shaking beneath the table.

"Nothing. Really. Everything's good." She smiled, trying to hide her anxiety.

The silence felt heavy as they both focused on the waiter who had just arrived with their entrées.

Maybe she should tell him. Just get it out there. Put it on the table and see what happened. Maybe she'd get the surprise of her life, and Matt would say, "Yeah, by the way, that ring sure looks familiar. In fact, I believe it's my great-great-grandmother Minnie's.

How the heck did you get it?" Kenzie laughed to herself at the absurdity, yet hoped that a crazy thing like that would come true.

"I had a really strange thing happen a couple months ago," she said. She lifted her fork, then set it down. "It was about this ring, the one that I'm wearing." Kenzie showed it to him. She glanced up at him to see if it registered in any way, if he showed some sign of recognition. "Does it look familiar?"

"Nope. Should it?" Matt asked, and continued eating.

"No, of course not." She laughed nervously, lifting her fork again to begin eating. "But, well, I know this sounds absurd, but I'm going to tell you anyway . . . Gemma's psychic told me it belonged to my future husband, and that he would enter my life within six months."

"Well, that's interesting. Do you believe in psychics?" Matt took a sip of water.

"Not at all," she said.

"Then it doesn't mean much, does it?"

"Guess not." Kenzie shrugged. She continued eating, deciding not to say more. She wondered if Matt had already known about the ring. If everyone knew everything at the track, maybe he knew this, too. Maybe that was why it seemed to be no big deal to him.

The two of them ate in silence for a while. Then Matt set his fork down and took a long sip of wine.

"Speaking of rings, I wonder if you noticed I no longer wear mine."

Kenzie smiled. "I *have* noticed. You haven't worn it in some time."

"I don't know why I held on to it for so long."

"It provided protection. It said, 'I'm not available.'"

"True," he said, raising his eyebrows.

"I think when you suffer big losses in your life, it's harder to turn the corner and recover. The grief is overwhelming. Losing your wife, even though you were already separated, is tragic. I can see why you were reluctant to go back on the market, as it were. It's hard to get out there and try again when the thought of loving someone and then losing them is still raw."

"You've helped me a lot." He put his fork down, took her hand, and kissed it. "I never thought I'd love someone again. Or find someone to love me. My world has color in it now. It had been gray for an awfully long time."

Kenzie leaned over and kissed Matt on the lips. "I feel the same way. I love you. I tell you that often and I mean it . . . It's almost scary how much . . . Having you in my life has made me feel alive again."

"And, I'm a lucky guy." Matt pulled her close. "To have you in my life. I'm grateful for every day we have together, and I love you more than you'll ever know. The fact that I can tell you that shows how comfortable I am with you."

The waiter approached to offer them dessert.

"Wanna share some chocolate bread pudding?" Matt asked.

"Of course. Are you kidding? I love that dessert!"

"Well, good . . . then bring it on." Matt continued holding Kenzie in his arms.

"It means a lot that you can express your feelings for me," Kenzie said. "It's hard to do that sometimes, but it feels nice to hear."

"I think we trust each other, and that's important in building a relationship."

"It is," Kenzie said. "I still struggle with being able to say what I feel. I guess we're all afraid of saying something and then being attacked."

There was a silence.

"I'm glad you said that, 'cause, well, there's something I want to talk to you about. And I'm kinda afraid to discuss it." Kenzie looked up at Matt and noticed his lips were tighter than usual. "I haven't wanted to broach this . . . and I don't know if it's the right time . . ."

"What? What is it?" Her eyebrows pulled together. She could tell from his voice that he was anxious. Matt sat up straight and released Kenzie from his embrace.

He coughed and cleared his throat. "I'm going to try to explain it as best I can."

"Okay . . ." Kenzie picked at a cuticle under the table.

"You know what happened? To you in New York?"

Kenzie nodded, feeling uneasy.

"Well, I um . . . well, I . . ."

"What?" she said nervously.

"I'm getting there. Give me a chance . . . I'm just kind of concerned about what you might think," he said.

"Well, whatever it is, I won't bite," Kenzie said, trying to ease the tension.

"Well, okay then." Matt used his napkin to wipe his mouth, then took a sip of water. "I'm just gonna say it. Okay? There's . . . there's just no other way."

The waiter removed their dinner plates, and Kenzie sat quietly with her hands in her lap, waiting for Matt to get to the point.

"Remember that day in New York? When you spoke there?"

"Of course." Kenzie nodded. "How could I forget?"

"Well . . . I was there."

"You were there? That day?" Her eyes were wide with curiosity.

"I was." Matt nodded. "You see, I was the stage manager."

Kenzie grew very still. Matt took a breath and swiped a hand through his hair, waiting for her to say something.

"You were the stage manager who, uh, who pulled the skirt out of my thong . . . ? That guy? That was you?"

Matt closed his eyes and nodded.

"But how's that possible?" Kenzie couldn't believe it. "You're a jockey's agent."

"Not then," Matt said. "Remember I told you I'd worked in production early on in my career? Well, four years ago, when my contract was up at the station, I didn't know what to do. I was in New York meeting my agent. That afternoon I was supposed to meet a producer friend, but he was scrambling because his stage manager wasn't available for a gig the next morning. I'd done that work before, still had my union card, so I offered to help him out."

"Why didn't you tell me this? I told you what happened to me there and you never said anything."

"I know . . . I know . . ." Matt lowered his eyes. "Because, well, I wanted to, but . . . I don't know, I didn't want to hurt you . . . And I didn't know you as well as I do now . . . And, well, there was never a time . . . the right time. I tried . . . but I couldn't get there." He looked up at her. "I knew how upset you were by the whole event and how painful it was for you. I'm sorry . . . I should've told you before this."

Kenzie was floored. She didn't know what to say, how to respond.

"I heard the audience laughing, and I couldn't stand it. And I felt so . . . I just didn't know what to do. But I knew I had to do something. That's when I came onstage and plucked your skirt out of your . . . well, you know." Matt took a breath and reached for his wine.

Kenzie sat perfectly still. She lowered her eyes and stared at the chocolate bread pudding, which had just arrived. It would be delicious, but she wasn't hungry.

"That's pretty amazing," she said softly. "So you've known who I was ever since I started at Grayson."

Matt nodded. "It was my fault . . . I should've gone up there much faster . . . It was my mistake."

"What do you mean?" She cast her eyes on Matt.

"Well," he said as he shifted in his seat, "I let it go on too long. I was slow to react because, well, I was . . . well, I was laughing . . . with everyone else and—"

"You were *laughing*?"

"But only for a second." Matt bent forward and put his hand over his face. "I'm sorry. I really am." He took a deep breath, turned toward her, and held her chin. "I felt I had to tell you before we got too far along and—"

"Wait," Kenzie said. She looked him square in the eye. "You were laughing . . . *at me*?"

"I tried to find you. To apologize. But you'd already left," he said. "I felt terrible about what happened."

"Matt, I can't believe this." Kenzie leaned forward, placed her elbows on the table, and covered her face with her hands. "This whole thing. I mean, how could you laugh . . . and you were in charge. You should've done something right away."

"I know . . . I'm sorry. I really am," he said again, and averted his eyes.

Kenzie stared up at the TV behind the bar, trying to process the information Matt had dumped on her.

Matt reached for her arm. "Look, I made a mistake. But does that have to change things? Does it honestly change the way you feel about me? About us?"

"Yes," Kenzie said quickly. "It does."

Matt wiped the sweat from his brow.

After a moment Kenzie lifted her fork and picked at the chocolate bread pudding. Matt was still. A few seconds passed, and then Kenzie put her fork down. "I think we ought to take a break. I just don't feel good about us right now."

Matt's eyes widened. "Please don't let this come between us. I know it's upsetting. And I'm terribly sorry. I really am. I made a huge mistake."

They both sat for a moment in awkward silence.

"I think we should go." Kenzie eyed the exit. Without waiting for Matt's response, she took her purse and walked toward the door. By the time she got outside to the valet stand, he was beside her.

"I knew you'd be angry," Matt said. "It's why it took me so long to tell you. I understand you're upset. I would be, too. I just hope you'll find it in you to forgive me. Please . . . I love you, Kenzie. I really do."

Kenzie tipped the valet, got into her car, and sped away.

GEMMA

"Peter had a heart attack last night," Gemma told Kenzie when she answered the phone. She lit a cigarette while sitting on a bench outside the hospital.

"Oh my God! Is he going to be okay?" Kenzie asked from the other end.

"Not sure," Gemma said. "I'm waiting for an update from Peter's wife. He's in intensive care. I came here as soon as I could, but only family can visit him right now."

Gemma took a hit off her cigarette and stared at the hospital workers as they entered the building. There was a cool breeze. She wished she'd remembered to bring a sweater, but when Peter's wife had called early that morning, she'd taken off immediately for the hospital.

"I didn't realize how much I cared about Peter." Gemma took a long puff of her cigarette.

"I'm sorry, Gem. I know you like him. He's been a good boss."

Gemma blew out the smoke and said, "Ya know, I texted you last night to see if you wanted to get dinner but never heard back."

"Yeah, well, I was with Matt."

"Oh, that's nice," Gemma said.

"Not really," Kenzie said. "Turns out he was the stage manager in New York. You know, the one who came onstage and pulled my skirt out?"

"What? Are you joking?" Gemma asked. "How's that possible?"

"He told me last night."

"I thought he was a jockey's agent."

"He is. I'll fill you in later," Kenzie added quickly. "It's just not working. It doesn't feel right anymore. I told him I needed a break, but it's really over."

"That's too bad. I know you liked him. A lot."

"I did." Kenzie's tone was distant and cool. "But things don't always work out. I have to move on. Anyway, I hope Peter's okay. That's all that matters. Oh, and Gem, please stop smoking."

"Whoa . . . slow down. I know you too well, Kenz. Sounds like you're pretty upset. I can hear that cold, I-don't-care voice, which means you really *do* care, that you're hurting and dying inside."

Kenzie didn't respond.

"Look, call me if you want to talk about it. Matt seemed like a good person. I'm sorry it didn't work out. Maybe it's not over. At least not yet. I'll text you later and let you know about Peter," Gemma said as she took another drag on her cigarette.

Despite Kenzie's request, smoking was Gemma's go-to vice when things were rough, and right now they were. So many things had crossed her mind since she'd heard the news about Peter. She wondered how much damage the heart attack had done and whether he'd return to work soon. She thought about the good times they had together. Peter was easygoing and kind. He was different from Jeffrey, who was energetic, aggressive, and outgoing. When Jeffrey entered a room, people paid attention. He had presence. Peter was the opposite. He blended into the background. Jeffrey wasn't like that at all.

As she lit her third cigarette, waiting desperately for some good news about Peter, she received a text from Scarlett reminding her to come to her swim meet that day.

Over the past three weeks Gemma and Scarlett had spent a fair amount of time together. They'd gone shopping, had lunch, seen some movies. They'd developed a fondness for each other even though they were almost a generation apart. But Gemma didn't care. She enjoyed being with her sister.

It wasn't like Gemma to forget anything important, particularly when it came to Scarlett, but Peter's heart attack had deeply distressed her. In all the chaos she'd totally forgotten about the swim meet.

She finally received a text from Peter's wife. He was out of surgery. They'd implanted two stents in one of his arteries. He would be all right. Gemma was so relieved she almost broke down in tears. Peter's wife said Gemma could visit him the next day. Gemma sat for a while as the good news sank in. She took a deep breath, stamped out her cigarette, and smiled.

She could still make Scarlett's swim meet and was thrilled she'd been invited. Gemma wondered if Emily would be there or if she'd have Scarlett to herself. She hoped it would be just the two of them, and that afterward they could do something together. Because that's what sisters did. She couldn't wait for the day Scarlett would learn the truth.

* * * * *

Gemma entered the indoor swimming pavilion, and almost immediately her hair became limp and damp because the humidity in the aquatic center was overwhelming. The place was packed with parents, kids, and coaches waiting for the races.

Gemma knew Scarlett competed in the butterfly. She'd seen photos of her competitions and awards. Her room was probably filled with ribbons and trophies. Several young women on the starting blocks were adjusting their goggles and caps. Gemma hoped she hadn't missed Scarlett's race. A starter gun sounded, and then all six swimmers plunged into the pool. The crowd yelled and cheered them on. Gemma saw Scarlett approaching the starting blocks for the next race. *Whew.* Gemma realized she'd made it just in time.

Gemma looked around for Jeffrey or Emily, but she didn't see either. Just as the first race ended, she spotted Jeffrey walking through the door. He looked handsome in his freshly pressed blue jeans, white long-sleeved oxford shirt, and loafers. He noticed Scarlett immediately and waved. When Gemma raised her hand, Jeffrey nodded and walked over.

"Hey, Gemma, so great of you to come, especially since Emily has a bad virus," he said.

"Oh, I wouldn't miss it," Gemma said.

Jeffrey rolled up his sleeves and wiped his brow. There were no windows and just one set of doors in a corner. He didn't seem to know anyone, which Gemma found strange because the other parents did. Surely he'd gone to some of Scarlett's swim meets in the past. She figured he must know a few folks. But while the other parents were mingling, taking photos, and sharing stories, Jeffrey clung to his cell phone and scrolled through his emails. And while other parents moved closer to the starting blocks—with cameras ready and shouting final instructions to their kids—Jeffrey looked at his watch.

"It's great that you came to watch Scarlett swim." Gemma stepped closer to him, trying to make conversation. "I'm sure she's happy to have her dad here."

Jeffrey smiled but didn't respond. Gemma felt awkward. Had she said too much? Did he not want to talk? Should she give him more space? She longed for the moment she fantasized about, when she'd tell Jeffrey who she was and he would embrace her. He'd tell her how he regretted not knowing her all these years. He'd ask about her mom, and she'd lie and tell him how fond her mother was of him.

It was probably crazy to think this way, but she couldn't help it. Not being able to share the truth with him was starting to frustrate her. She wanted to tell him, but it was just never the right time. However, now they were alone. She'd rehearsed what she would say just in case the moment presented itself.

"I hope this doesn't go too long," Jeffrey said as he consulted his iPhone yet again. "It looks like I've got to get back to the office. Hopefully she'll be up and ready to go soon."

"Look, she's on the starting block," Gemma said.

"Oh, yeah, there she is. Didn't see her up there." Jeffrey barely looked up from his phone.

"I guess you're really busy." She hated competing with his phone for attention.

"Yep," Jeffrey said as he scrolled through his emails.

"So were you a swimmer?" Gemma asked.

"Nope. Not me or Emily."

"Oh. Well. Hmm." Gemma rubbed her forearms and glanced around the pool.

"Do you work? I mean other than helping out at the shelter," Jeffrey asked as he dialed a number and then held the phone to his ear, looking up at Gemma. She realized he knew almost nothing about her, and was eager to fill him in.

"Yes. Of course. I work with a movie producer," Gemma said. She never told anyone she was an assistant. She couldn't tell Jeffrey that, either. She wanted him to believe she was special. Someone more impressive.

"Sounds like a good job. Did you ask for time off today?"

"I have a flexible position," she lied. "And today, well, today wasn't busy."

"I wish I had light days." Jeffrey grinned for the first time. Gemma noticed the crow's feet around his eyes that became more prominent when he smiled. "I worry I'll give myself a heart attack."

"That won't happen. You're young," Gemma said. She would've said the same thing to Peter. And yet he was in the hospital recovering from a heart attack and only fifty, probably younger than Jeffrey.

"My dad died of a heart attack," Jeffrey said as he watched Scarlett and others adjust their caps and goggles.

"Oh, I'm so sorry."

"Years ago. I was in my twenties," Jeffrey said.

Gemma placed her left hand on her chest as if she were feeling the heart attack herself. She thought about her medical history and wondered if this information was included in the agreement he had with her mom. What other medical issues did he have?

Just then the gun sounded, and Scarlett leaped off the starting block into the water. "Oh, look, there she goes!" Gemma shouted as she peered above the crowd, trying to get a good look at her.

"Oh, yeah, great!" Jeffrey yelled along with the others.

Scarlett swam fast across the pool and finished the sprint in just under a minute. Jeffrey cheered when he saw that she'd come in fourth. He ran to the edge of the pool to congratulate her.

Gemma didn't want to interrupt this moment between Jeffrey and his daughter. *His other daughter*. It was their time. Scarlett sparkled with excitement. Gemma looked on and wondered what it would be like to have her dad, Jeffrey, applauding *her* efforts. She wanted him to be proud of her, too.

If only he could've been at her ballet recitals. Her mom had cheered her on. She was wonderful, but Gemma also remembered watching the fathers who held cameras, recording every moment. She'd always felt sad not having her father there. And that was just one memory. There were so many events in her life where she'd missed having a dad, where she truly felt that void. And now here he was. Would they ever be able to make up for lost time? And as much as she loved being with him now, would she ever really forgive him for turning his back on her?

Just as Gemma stepped away from the wall to go see Scarlett, who was now out of the water and drying herself off, she noticed that Jeffrey had dropped his phone on the ground when he'd rushed over to the pool. Just as she scooped it up and rubbed it against her pants to dry it off, a text came in from someone named Lauren. Gemma's eyes drifted down to the first line.

Darling, where are you? I'm waiting.

SARITA

Sarita thought the evening would never end. She sat on the ottoman in her father's study looking up at Rahul, who was leaning against the desk. He was so different from Damien, it almost made Sarita laugh. She noticed his narrow dark eyes and slicked-back hair, his prominent nose, and the black stubble around his chin. His white shirt and black tie seemed too big for his thin build. His black suit jacket hung loosely and didn't match his brown shoes. Sarita felt sorry for Rahul. His body was rigid and straight. He hadn't once cracked a smile. She wondered if he had a sense of humor.

"Your job sounds interesting. Do you like it?" asked Rahul.

"Yes, I do," she said, and wondered if there was more to this nice man.

"Do you think racetracks are a place for women? I never knew women worked there."

"Really?" Sarita couldn't help but laugh. "Of course women work at racetracks. Why wouldn't they?"

"Well, I just can't see you working there. Just doesn't seem like a place a woman would want to be." Rahul looked off in the distance and then focused on Papa's bookcase, which was filled to the brim with books and covered an entire wall of the small study.

Sarita stared up at him. "How do you feel about your wife working while raising kids? Is that something you'd be comfortable with?"

"Yeah, sure, it's okay." Rahul's eyes stayed focused on the bookcase as if he were looking for a particular title. "But not in the beginning. I think it's important for a mother to be with her children before they enroll in school."

Rahul continued to survey her father's study, with its classic quilted leather sofa, brown walls, traditional oak desk, and towering bookcase.

"I don't know if I feel the same way," Sarita said. "But I'm not sure if I want children at all. I want to start a career first."

Rahul fixed his intense gaze on her. "Does your father know this about you? I think he would be stunned if I were to tell him about this conversation."

"Trust me, nothing would surprise my father about me," Sarita laughed. "You sound like you're looking for a traditional wife. What do you plan to do with your life?"

"I work with my family. I'm in charge of regional sales for my grandfather's textile business."

"Is it what you always wanted to do?" Sarita asked.

"Of course. I've been working there my whole life. I really enjoy it. I hope to establish our brand in more countries around the globe."

"I assume you do a lot of traveling. Must be fun."

"Not really." Rahul shifted his weight from one foot to the other. "I'm not there to sightsee. I get in and out fast."

"Oh, that's too bad. I'd love to travel the world. I hope to do that soon," she said.

Rahul's arms were folded across his chest, as if to protect him from this scary young woman. He expressed little about himself and remained extremely serious and somewhat stilted. But Sarita didn't care. She'd heard enough. Rahul stared at Sarita, who knew she looked beautiful, calm, and feminine. It was obvious that she bewildered him. Then he lowered his arms and extended his hand to her. When she took it he asked if she was ready to return to the dining room.

When they entered they were greeted with smiling faces. But that changed quickly when everyone saw Rahul's serious expression. He walked over to Papa and shook his hand. "Mr. Mahajan, it was a pleasure meeting you and your family." Rahul looked at Sarita, who stood alongside him. "And of course, your lovely daughter, Sarita. But I have to be going now. Thank you again for a nice evening. We'll be in touch."

And with that Rahul's parents and the matchmaker followed him to the door. Sarita returned to the table, placed her napkin in her lap, and ate her dessert as her father walked them out.

"Time and time again you bring dishonor to our family," Papa roared as he returned to the table and sat down next to Sarita. His eyes were bulging and his hand was shaking. "Why? Have we not done enough for you? Have we not provided you with a good home? Education? What? What is it, Sarita? Where have we failed you?" Without uttering a word, Mama retrieved the dishes and took them to the kitchen.

"Why is family honor more important than individual freedom?" Sarita shot back.

Papa slammed his fist so hard on the table that a few glasses toppled. Sarita was surprised but didn't move. She kept her eyes focused on her plate and continued eating.

"What did you say to that boy? Why was he so eager to leave?"

"I said that I enjoy working and I'm not sure I want children. Was that such a terrible thing to say, Papa?" Sarita looked up for the first time. "He didn't like my answer. I also said that I plan to do a lot of traveling someday."

"I knew when we agreed to send you away to college that it wasn't wise. You could have easily attended a school nearby, like your sisters. It was a mistake. You convinced us it would be best. But you came back changed. I don't know who you are. You are not mine. You are a selfish woman. Not part of our family. Our world," Papa said. He sounded exasperated. "I believe we should send you back home. Back to New Delhi. Perhaps then you'll understand who you are, who *we* are."

"You mean to the place where a female medical student was abducted, raped, assaulted with an iron rod, and then left to die? You mean the place where women are murdered if they marry across caste or religious lines? Where oppression begins before birth, as female fetuses are routinely aborted? You mean that place? Is that where you want to send me now?"

Papa looked down at his empty plate as his wife returned, removed more dishes, and then walked back to the kitchen.

"We romanticize it, Papa. We enjoy the image of India as an industrious nation, full of ambitious wunderkinds. And parts of it are. The rising economy and beautiful films like *The Best Exotic Marigold Hotel*, which I know you loved, perpetuate that image. But, Papa, the country has not made any cultural change when it comes to women, even though the leader of the ruling party is a woman. Even though it once made Indira Gandhi the most powerful woman in the world. It's not the right place for me. It is not who I am."

Papa bowed his head. Sarita got up from her seat and moved next to her father.

"You can't force me to be who you want me to be," she said softly. "I am different from you. And from my sisters. I'm sorry if that disappoints you. I hope someday you'll accept me for who I am and not for what you always hoped I would be. You always told me to follow my dreams. But I'm beginning to think you meant your dreams, not mine."

Papa's eyes met hers, but he said nothing.

"I know you don't want to hear such negative things from your youngest daughter about your mother country," Sarita lowered her eyes. "But if I were to go there, I would not be any different. I would do as I wanted and once again you would be disappointed, as I'd only bring more shame to your family."

"Are you threatening me?" Papa asked.

"Of course not." She looked up at him. "I'm just telling you—"

"You are not telling me!" Papa rose from the chair and stood up straight. He stared down at Sarita. "Get your things and leave this instant."

Sarita just stared at him, confused and surprised.

"But, Papa, I have no place to go. I've been living at home, saving money so I can move out and—"

"You are done here. It's time for you to leave."

"Because we don't agree? Because we have different views on life? Because you want one thing and I another? I'm your daughter, Papa."

"You are not my daughter. I don't know who you are, Sarita. You want freedom? Take it. You want to be your own woman, as you say? Then go. Go now. I don't wish to see you here in the morning."

Sarita stiffened as Mama entered the room, having heard the argument escalate.

"Mohan, no," Mama said. "You cannot turn your daughter out of the house. She must stay, we will find a way—"

"She is to be gone by morning," Papa interrupted. He turned sharply and went upstairs.

"It's all right, Mama, I'll get my things." Sarita was shaken by his edict.

"Let me ask your sisters. I'm sure one of them can accommodate you," Mama said.

"No, Mama, it'll be all right. I'll find someplace."

Mama turned toward Sarita and held her.

"Are you going to move in with your boyfriend?" Mama asked.

Sarita was startled by her mother's question. No one had uttered a word about that evening. She wasn't sure where her mother stood.

"I d-don't know." Sarita's voice was trembling. "I wasn't ready to do that. I wanted a place of my own first. But maybe he'll take me in tonight."

"Be careful. Papa will never take you back if you live in sin. You know how he feels about that."

Sarita looked at her mother. "But I don't want to be taken back, Mama. I want to live my life. Not his." She stood for a moment, contemplating her circumstances. "He's throwing me out of his home." Mama wrapped her arms around Sarita, and Sarita buried her head on her mother's beautiful red-and-yellow sari, which she'd worn to welcome their guests. "I'm sorry I'm such a burden to you and Papa. I'm sorry for who I am."

Sarita started to cry. Her mother raised her daughter's chin so she could look into her eyes.

"Never be sorry for who you are," Mama said. "Never. You are a gifted, loving, wonderful person, my Sarita. And despite your father's behavior, he does love you. I know he does. You think about your life and what you want. And I mean what *you* want. I didn't get to choose, nor did your sisters. But you want to choose. You and your father have endured much. Give him time. It's been a rough couple of months. Let us all take some time."

Sarita held on to her mother. "Mama, thank you. Thank you for understanding."

Mama reached into her sari and pulled out a small wad of money.

"I grabbed this when I heard Papa would be sending you away. It's a thousand dollars in cash. I've been saving it in case any of my daughters should ever need it. You take it. Also, your car was returned this afternoon. It's fixed and parked on the street. Now go find yourself a place to stay. Maybe a hotel room for a while. It's time to move on, my daughter. Actually, you have already moved on. We are stifling you. You need to live your life, not ours."

Sarita moved from her mother's embrace and used the hem of her sari to wipe the few tears from her eyes. She tucked the money in her bra, hugged her mother, and then climbed the stairs to her bedroom. When Sarita reached the top, Mama raised her voice, "And don't forget your things in the attic!"

BRYNNE

Brynne checked her dark sunglasses to make sure they were securely fixed on her nose and then entered the Pleasure Chest. She lowered her head, grabbed a white basket, and walked stealthily through the aisles, glancing up now and then to make sure no one recognized her. She set out to find the crotchless lace thong she'd seen on the website, along with the candy bra advertised on the sign she'd seen when she entered the store. Once they were in her basket, she breezed down the aisle and tossed in a Hitachi Magic Wand, a porn flick, and one Jimmyjane pocket vibrator, and then marched quickly to the register. She was proud that she'd done her research ahead of time so she didn't have to linger in the store. She wanted to get in and out quickly.

Just as she was about to pay for the things, her phone rang. She was so startled that it dropped to the floor. When she retrieved it she saw Kenzie's face staring at her.

"Hi, Brynne. Do you have a moment?" Kenzie asked.

"Uh, no, not really," Brynne said softly as she pressed every key trying to get rid of Kenzie's face on the screen.

"Where are you?" Kenzie asked. "Is this a good time?"

"No, no, it's not." Brynne was flustered. She put her hand over the camera, hoping Kenzie couldn't see where she was.

"I called you on FaceTime because I want to show you some of our plans for opening day. We want to hear your thoughts," Kenzie said. "Sarita is with me."

"Hi, Brynne," Sarita said. "I think you have your hand over the camera. We're having a hard time seeing you."

"I can't do this now," Brynne shouted tersely as she paid the clerk in cash. She tossed the phone into her purse, gathered her purchases, and fled the store.

When she was safely outside she heard the muffled sounds of Kenzie and Sarita talking to each other in her purse, as she hadn't disconnected the call.

"I swear I saw a mannequin decked out in black leather and chains. Where the heck was she?" Sarita asked.

"Brynne? Are you there?" Kenzie asked. "I think she hung up. Let's try her later."

Brynne ran to her car, threw her bag under the seat, and hopped inside. She sat for a moment panting, trying to catch her breath. After a few moments she closed her eyes and began to relax.

She hadn't lost sight of her goal. She was on a mission. To keep Martin where he belonged. At home and back in her bedroom. At least she was able to get what she needed at the Pleasure Chest. Now she was ready.

Tonight would be the beginning of a new chapter in their lives.

* * * * *

"Oh, that was such a lovely evening," Brynne said as she and Martin waltzed into the entryway of their home after the Bel-Air Ball that night. "Loved seeing everyone. I can't believe it's so late."

Brynne followed her husband up the long staircase to his bedroom, her heart racing. She watched Martin emptying his pockets and preparing for bed. The crotchless lace thong and candy bra were so uncomfortable. She'd worn them all evening. She couldn't wait to have sex with Martin so she could take them off.

"Oh, darling, I meant to tell you that earlier today I used the American Express card and it was turned down." Brynne stood at his door. "I'll call them in the morning. I'm sure there was some mistake."

"There might be a problem," Martin said. He unfastened his gold cuff links and tore off his yellow bow tie and white tuxedo shirt as Brynne looked on.

"Okay, well, do you want to handle it, or shall I?" Brynne moved into the room and took a seat at the edge of his bed. She relished the time with Martin. They hadn't been alone in so long. Tonight was wonderful. She didn't want it to end.

"I'll handle it," Martin said as he stepped into the bathroom and closed the door.

"I saw Mother last week!" Brynne shouted. "She still hasn't gotten that screen door fixed. And I wish she'd wear her hearing aid. It wasn't till I yelled at the top of my lungs to open the door that she heard me." Brynne walked toward a full-length mirror and took off her earrings. She placed them in the side pocket of her red snakeskin bag, which hung off her shoulder. Martin exited his bathroom and adjusted his zipper. He connected his phone to the charger and looked at Brynne, who was now seated on the edge of his bed with her hands in her lap. She had perfect posture. Perfect nails. Perfect hair. Perfect makeup. She wanted to be absolutely perfect for Martin, especially tonight, the night she would break the pattern. The night they would once again sleep side by side.

Martin removed his pants, put on his robe and slippers, and sat down. "Come sit over here." Martin pointed to a chair across from him. A small black onyx coffee table was wedged between them. Martin propped his legs on the table and adjusted his robe. Brynne wondered if this was the time to part her legs and reveal her new underwear. She felt strange, inhibited . . . almost foolish, but she knew it was a surefire turn-on for Martin. He used to watch that scene in *Basic Instinct* over and over. It was all he talked about. It drove her insane, and not in a good way. But tonight she hoped to recapture those times back in the days when they had sex.

She hoped the candy bra was worth it, because her breasts were spilling out of it. The candy-coated disks were not meant for long-time wear, and they were cracking and falling apart.

Brynne glanced at Martin as she hiked her skirt up a little higher so it was well above her knees. She relaxed in her chair and slowly parted her legs. Just a little. She tried to recall exactly what Sharon Stone did, but it had been so long since she'd seen the movie. She couldn't remember.

"That American Express card has been canceled," Martin said.

"Oh." Brynne was surprised. She was so focused on her seduction that she'd forgotten about the credit card. "Is there something wrong?"

"Brynne, it's a lot more complicated than that." Martin took a deep breath. He coughed and then got up, grabbed a bottle of water from the small fridge next to the massive antique wood hutch. He lingered a bit. Brynne hoped he might be checking her out there . . . between her legs, but he wasn't, so she pulled them back together. He quickly returned to his chair. "Things have not been good at the company for a long time. I've kept it from you because I didn't want to alarm you. But it's bad."

"What do you mean, Martin? How bad?" Brynne didn't like his tone. She knew her husband well enough to sense that he was deeply troubled and anxious.

"I lost a lot. I've been trying to earn it back, but I made some bad decisions. I never really recovered from the stock market crash, the recession. I've been borrowing. A lot." Martin started coughing. Brynne knew it was bad, because Martin coughed when he was anxious. It made her nervous. "And, well, a lot of it's gone," Martin said. He gulped some water, coughed, and drank some more.

"Martin, I'm not sure I understand—"

"Brynne," Martin said, "we have about ten percent of what we used to have. The company's been operating in the red for some time now. I couldn't tell you. I was too embarrassed. I didn't want to do this to you and the girls, but I've failed you all. I'm terribly sorry." His voice cracked.

Brynne watched Martin, but he averted his eyes. He swept his hands through his hair repeatedly. His face was red, his jaw clenched. Brynne walked over to him, but he raised his hand. He didn't want her to comfort him. So she sat back down.

"It's my mistake," he said. His voice trembled. "I have to live with it, and unfortunately so do you. We have to sell the house. And the horses. We have to downsize."

"Martin. Oh my. I . . . I don't know what to say." Brynne was shocked. She sat very still, trying to absorb the information. Martin moved onto the edge of the coffee table a few inches from Brynne. She melted when she saw him move closer. She decided she would be upbeat. They would overcome this. They'd work together as a team. "Whatever we have to do. We'll . . . we'll work it out. We have each other. We're a family," she said softly.

She knew how difficult it was for him to admit such a failing. He was a proud man. So successful. This would just break him. He needed her, loved her. This was such a validation. She reached behind his neck, which was moist and warm, and pulled him close. She could only imagine the stress he was under. She brought his face toward hers. Then she brought her lips to his ear.

"It'll be okay, my sweet," she said softly. "All that matters is that I have you. Let's not think about this right now. Let's take a moment for us. To enjoy each other. I want to make you feel better. You still turn me on. Always have."

She parted her legs. Slowly at first. Then a little more. And more.

"I have something special for you, darling," she whispered softly. "Look, baby. Look what I have for you." She took his hand and placed it under her skirt and over her crotchless thong. Her eyes met his as she unzipped her jacket and revealed the candy bra. Much of the candy had cracked and fallen off. The bra provided little support for her breasts, which were round and full. One was almost completely exposed. She grabbed his free hand and held it to her breast. She'd never been sexually aggressive with Martin. She felt awkward and shy.

But she was determined to keep her man.

Martin took the bait. "I wasn't expecting this . . . I mean we haven't . . . Well, we haven't done anything in so long . . ." he said. He nuzzled at her breast while his fingers probed gently inside her. She moaned softly as his hand kept up a steady rhythm. She'd forgotten what it felt like to have him there. Inside. He took short breaths as he pushed her skirt higher and spread her legs wider. Then he knelt between her legs and used his tongue. Soon she was dripping with excitement. Then he grabbed her hand and placed it between her legs and urged her to pleasure herself.

"I wanna watch you do it. To yourself," he said as he stood up, unzipped his pants, and began masturbating.

"No, darling I want you, I want you—"

"No!" he barked. "Do it. Faster. Do it. I wanna watch you."

With her skirt at her waist and legs spread wide apart, Brynne did as Martin asked. She closed her eyes and moved her fingers rapidly. She would do anything to please him.

"Look at me while you're doing it. Show me. Don't close your eyes," Martin snapped.

"No, no . . ."

"Yes. Look at me, don't stop!" he shouted.

"No, I can't," she said. She suddenly began to feel self-conscious and embarrassed. His tone had become aggressive and callous.

"Brynne"—he was gasping—"look at me."

And then it was over.

Martin stopped abruptly. He zipped up his pants and turned away from her.

"I can't . . ." Martin was perspiring and out of breath. "I can't. I can't do this."

Brynne was confused. Maybe he couldn't get it up. He must not have taken his Viagra. She whispered that it would be okay, not to worry, there'd be other times. But Martin tightened his jaw, turned around, and told her to stop.

She pulled her skirt down, zipped up her jacket, and sat upright.

"There's one other thing," he said sharply. "This is hard for me to say to you. I'm sorry. I really am . . . but . . ."

And then his eyes filled with tears. He sat back down at the edge of the table, lowered his head to his hands, and sobbed. Brynne couldn't imagine what else could have happened. She waited and then watched as he got up, went to the bar above his small refrigerator, and poured himself a vodka. He drank it all at once.

Brynne stood up. She could hardly breathe. "What is it, Martin? What?"

"There's something else . . . well, some*one* else," he said as he turned toward her. "I've been seeing someone. For about two years. She's a career woman. And, well . . . well, we're in love."

Brynne froze. She met his eyes and then looked away fast. They stood in silence for a few moments. Martin grabbed his handkerchief and wiped away his tears, and then came toward her.

"In love?" Brynne's voice was shaking, and her body trembled. Her knees started to give way. Martin rushed to help her, but she pushed him away.

"I'm sorry, Brynne. I really am. I didn't know how and when to tell you. I've been trying to find the right time. I know it's a lot. I'm dreadfully sorry. I don't know what to say." Martin was breathless.

"You don't know what to say?" Brynne was in a state of disbelief. She had convinced herself that Marcella Gomez was just a sex toy. She never dreamed Martin was in love with her. "How am I supposed to react to this? Have you lost your mind?"

"Look, I didn't want to hurt you. And frankly, I was afraid," Martin said as he leaned against the wall between the seating area and the bed.

"Who is she?" Brynne began to scream. It had to be Marcella. But she wanted to hear him say it. "You're a married man. Does she not know that? Or have you lied to her, too? I want to hear her name. What's her name?" Brynne shouted.

"No, no, she knows I'm married," Martin said, his face buried in his hands. "And please stop shouting. You'll wake the staff and—"

"So you don't lie to her but to me?" she interrupted. "Your wife of nineteen years?"

Brynne grabbed a small lamp that sat on the vanity and hurled it across the room. It wasn't meant to hit Martin, but he was stunned. He rushed over and grabbed her arm, but she snatched it away.

"Don't touch me!" Brynne yelled. Her eyes were on fire. Her heart was beating out of her chest. She was filled with rage. Martin had never seen this side of her and clearly didn't expect it. He looked frightened. Brynne threw herself onto the bed and sobbed. "Get out of my house, you bastard. Get out! Get out! Get out! Now!" She slammed her fists into the mattress. Martin rushed to his closet and dressed. Then Brynne charged over to his dresser and yanked the drawers out, hurling his clothes all over the floor.

"Brynne, I'm sorry. I am. I really am. Please don't tell the girls yet. Please. Can we please just talk? Please. Just let me explain—"

"There's nothing to explain!" she screamed so loud she lost her voice. She began coughing and gagging. "We're done talking. You want to be with her? Go be with her. In her hellhole."

"Please, Brynne, just give me a chance to tell you everything," Martin pleaded.

"I don't want to hear more. I don't want to hear *everything*." She cried and coughed at the same time. "I saw you with her last month. I saw your tongue down her throat. I saw her in your car. I know her name. But it won't cross my lips." Brynne tore across the room and swept everything off Martin's shelves, desk, dresser, and mantel. Books, prescriptions, glasses, jewelry—all crashed to the floor. The room looked like a war zone. But Brynne wasn't finished. "I saw it all, you bastard. Now get out of my house before I call the police. I never want to see you again."

"Okay, I knew you'd be upset, but—"

"*Upset?* Really, Martin? You thought I'd be upset to hear that you lost our money and now you're leaving me and your family to be with your career woman?"

"It wasn't good, Brynne. For God's sake, we haven't slept in the same bed for years. You thought that by seducing me tonight it would change everything? We've grown apart. It's been over for a long time!" Martin shouted.

"I was holding on to . . . to our marriage," she cried. "I thought it was worth saving."

Martin grabbed whatever he could and rushed out the door. But Brynne got to her feet and went roaring after him. When he got into the car outside, she opened the passenger door.

"I did everything for you." Brynne was panting, exhausted and spent. "I created a perfect home. I gave you two perfect daughters. We had it all, Martin. We had it all. What the hell happened?"

"Maybe that's not what I wanted." Martin was sobbing. He started the ignition, his eyes red and swollen. "I fell in love with someone . . . someone I respect."

Brynne slammed the door and kicked the car repeatedly, then chased after it while she screamed obscenities at him. She tripped and collapsed on the side of the driveway. Her mascara had trickled down her cheeks, and she noticed a streak of blood on her arm and the side of her leg. She heard her housekeeper frantically rushing out of the house. Elena came to her side and helped her up.

"I'm okay, I'm okay." Brynne managed to get the words out. The two of them clung to each other as they returned to the house.

* * * * *

At nearly ten o'clock the next morning, just hours after Brynne and Martin had their hellacious fight, Brynne sat in front of her vanity looking at her puffy, bloodshot eyes. She brushed her hand against the bandage on the lower part of her arm, another reminder of the nightmare she'd endured. She was glad her daughters weren't living at home. She took a shower, dressed, and walked down the long stairway.

When she entered the dining room, she saw Martin from the back. He was sitting in his chair at the head of the table, eating breakfast with his iPad and phone. Stopping abruptly, she squinted to make sure she wasn't hallucinating. She looked around for Elena, her housekeeper, but didn't see her. She carefully crept into the dining room, her eyes glued to Martin, whose eyes were fixed on his iPad just like all the other times.

She walked up alongside him, gritted her teeth, and in her chilliest voice said, "What are you doing here?"

"I'm about to leave," Martin said as he quickly gathered his devices and threw them into his briefcase. "I just came to get some things. Elena said you were still sleeping, so I, well I thought—"

"Get out of here. Now," Brynne growled. Martin jumped out of his seat, took his briefcase, and headed for the door. Brynne followed.

Martin stood at the door and then turned just before he opened it.

"I'm sorry," he said softly.

"I'm not."

Brynne reached for the heavy thirteen-foot door and opened it as Martin passed through. Then she slammed it so hard the entire house shook. She walked back up the staircase, entered her bedroom, reached for her phone, and dialed a number.

"Mother?" she asked. "Are you there? I need . . . I need you."

KENZIE

"So you're living in a motel?" Kenzie asked. She and Sarita were walking back from the barns to their office.

"For now," Sarita said. "My plan was to save money so I could get my own apartment. May take just a little longer now." She followed Kenzie through the door to their office building and then up the stairs.

"Your dad sounds difficult, to say the least."

"He's a good man, just set in his ways," Sarita said. They entered Kenzie's office and sat opposite each other at the small coffee table in the corner. "I needed that walk. It was good."

"Me too." Kenzie stacked some materials to the side and then opened a large notebook.

"I noticed you barely said anything to Matt when we saw him on the backstretch," Sarita said.

"It's not working out." Kenzie thumbed through the notebook, her eyes fixed on its pages. "We haven't seen each other in over two weeks."

"Sorry to hear that."

"Let's get to work." Kenzie's tone was terse. She didn't want to think about Matt. But she couldn't *stop* thinking about him.

Maybe it didn't matter, because he wasn't the one. It wasn't his ring. As much as she didn't want to believe what Annalisa had said, the prophecy had a hold on her.

So later, when Matt walked into her office, Kenzie was less than enthused.

"Hey, Matt," Sarita said. He nodded back. "Um . . . I think I should . . . yes, I have to check on something. Why don't I come back in a bit?" Sarita didn't wait for a reply. She got up quickly, gathered her things, and left the office.

Matt leaned his left shoulder against the oak bookshelf next to the doorway. "Can I come in? Talk for just a second?"

Kenzie kept her eyes focused on the notebook and shrugged as Matt took a seat in the chair across from her. His presence ignited the same warm feelings she always had around him. But he'd deceived her. He wasn't truthful. How could she ever trust him?

"Look, I'm sorry. I don't know what else to say. We were having such a good time. Can't we move on and forget it—"

"I'm not sure I can do that," she interrupted.

Matt sat back in his chair and surveyed her office. She followed his eyes as they took in the room. She hadn't made it hers. No photos. No memorabilia. Nothing personal at all. It looked bare, like she'd just moved in. There was a sense of impermanence. She knew what he was thinking. That she was unable to plant roots. Unable to get close to people or become too invested in her work. She'd have the same thoughts if the office belonged to someone else.

"Why don't you have any artwork on the walls?" His gaze shifted back to Kenzie.

"I don't know. Never had time, I guess. Never really thought about it."

"Do you plan on staying here?"

"Of course. Why wouldn't I?" Their eyes met for an instant, but Kenzie averted hers quickly.

"I don't know," Matt said as he looked at the walls once more. "It feels temporary. Like you're just stopping by. Maybe you plan to go someplace else. Like back to the world you belong in, and try again."

She *was* afraid to embrace this job, but she was surprised that Matt knew it. She worried that if she did, it would be to the exclusion of everything else. She'd become an automaton again. A person with no life other than work. She didn't want to do that. If she had personal items, it would suggest that she was planting roots and embarking on another career here, and then it would hurt that much more if it all got snatched away again. It was better to leave the walls bare and stay detached.

"I'm happy here," Kenzie said with a cool resolve and then looked at Matt once again. "Did you come for a reason? Because I have a lot of work to do. And I think we kind of talked this through, don't you?"

"We all make mistakes," Matt said softly. "I obviously made one. I wish you'd forgive me." He paused. "I hope you'll think about us and the times we shared. We should be together, Kenzie." He got up slowly and walked over to her, whispering, "I miss you . . . But I don't want to fall in love with someone who is incapable of loving someone else."

"I'm capable of loving someone." Her voice was tight with emotion. "Someone I can trust and who wasn't laughing at my expense."

"It was only for a second," he said.

"I know. It was no big deal," she said.

"I didn't say it wasn't a big deal."

"To me it was a huge deal."

Matt paused and took a breath. "You know, I'm not so sure this is all about that anyway." Matt stood up and walked toward the door. "I think it might be about something entirely different."

"Oh really? What?" Kenzie turned to look up at him.

"I think you're terrified to commit to someone for fear they'll desert you. Like your mom. It's easier to find fault and hold a grudge than to take the plunge and experience a real loving relationship."

"Well, thank you, Dr. Phil," she smirked.

Matt swung the door open. "Maybe you should find the man who belongs to that ring. Maybe you'll have better luck with him." He exited without waiting for a response.

Kenzie propped her elbows on the table and held her head between her hands. How could he get to her like this? As much as she truly hated him for adding the line about the ring, she cared for him in a way that she'd never experienced before.

Matt understood her so well. She was deathly afraid of loving someone so completely. And that's what it would be with Matt. It still bothered her that he didn't own the ring. She wanted him to own it in the worst way. Because deep down she still wondered if Annalisa was right. She'd thought about it even more since she and Matt broke up. She was just two months shy of the six-month expiration. Would someone new come into her life in the next two months and be the one? It was hard to imagine that she could love anyone more than she had loved Matt.

"Hey, what's happening? You got everything set?" Leo asked as he burst into her office without knocking.

Kenzie sat up quickly. "All's going well, Leo. Sarita and I are on top of everything." She grabbed her notebook and a few folders and walked over to her desk.

"Good." He grabbed a handful of red licorice from Kenzie's plastic container and thrust several pieces into his mouth at one time. He walked to the window and stared at the empty paddock.

"Just a little over two months and we're on, baby. We're on," Leo mused, and then sighed deeply. His anxiety was palpable.

"We're going to have a great opening day. I just know it." Kenzie settled into her desk. "Biggest ever."

Leo said nothing and then left as quickly as he'd entered. On his way out he said, "Oh, Chase Fielding is here. Come see him when you can. He wants to talk to you about filming again."

Chase Fielding. She'd known he was off on location, and she hadn't given him a moment's thought after their dinner. But her job was making sure he got what he needed. Kenzie raked her fingers through her hair, took a swift breath, and hurried over to Leo's office, where Chase sat in the reception area. He stood up to greet her.

"Hey, how've you been?" Chase gave her a hug.

"Good, Chase, and you? Weren't you on location?"

"Yup. Was supposed to be five weeks, but we went over by three. Just returned. Anyway, I want to shoot some exteriors here before opening day. Was talking to Leo about it and he said I should arrange it with you."

"Sure, do you want me to talk to your location manager?" Kenzie was all business. "I think I still have his contact information."

"That'd be great," he said.

Chase paused before he continued. "You know, I wanted to call you after our dinner, but I had to leave the next day. I felt bad about how it ended."

"It's okay." She started picking at a cuticle. She didn't want this to become personal, as she had a job to do.

"Look, let me have my assistant talk to yours about the arrangements for the shoot. In the meantime, can I take you to lunch?"

"Well, first, I don't have an assistant." Kenzie laughed softly. "You're looking at her. And I don't take lunch. I usually eat at my desk."

179

"Would you like company?" Chase asked.

Chase seemed more focused, less frenzied. He spoke slowly and made eye contact. He wasn't fidgeting. He was lean and fit, his hair cropped shorter than the last time she'd seen him. "Okay, sure," she said and led him into her office. "I can only offer you some leftover chicken, though."

"I'm not hungry. I can always grab something later."

Chase stood by the door as she went to her refrigerator and pulled out a plastic box.

"Not the least bit appetizing." Kenzie scrunched up her nose as she opened the lid and showed Chase. "I'm not a great cook."

"It's okay." Chase smiled, then walked over to the sliding door and looked out onto the paddock. "Boy, what a beautiful sight."

"It is. I love it. I love watching the two-year-olds being schooled. Occasionally someone will even ride around and it just makes me smile," Kenzie said.

"I see why you traded your old life for this one. Nice and peaceful. Certainly not the insanity I deal with."

"Nope." Kenzie decided not to eat right then and put her chicken back in the fridge.

"Seeing anyone?" Chase continued to look outside.

"Well, I was. But not anymore," she said. No way Chase sensed the twinge of regret she felt.

Chase continued to stare out at the paddock. "I wanted to stop by, discuss the shoot," he said. "And . . . well, I wanted to see you. I wrapped a few days early, 'cause . . . well, my mom's in hospice."

Kenzie turned and gave him her full attention.

"I don't know how long this is going to go . . . I mean, last— well, you know." His gaze wandered over her face.

"I'm so sorry, Chase." Kenzie's eyes met his.

"I think it's really a matter of days."

"I'm so sorry," she said again. And of course, she knew what it was like. She walked over to the sliding door and put her hand gently on his back.

"Maybe that's why I wanted to see you." His eyes were downcast. "I don't know. I've never lost a parent. Or anyone really close to me. I knew you lost your mom and that you would understand."

Kenzie stood next to Chase as they watched two colts being led around the paddock by their grooms. Her eyes traveled to Matt, who was on the side talking to a female exercise rider who was about to go off to the track. Matt gave an affectionate tug at the rider's leg, which made Kenzie's heart twinge. He slapped the colt gently on its rear and walked behind him through the paddock and out toward the track.

"My mom was an obstetrician," Chase mused. "Way ahead of her time. She was the only woman in her graduating class. I don't think I ever appreciated how difficult that must've been." Kenzie watched Chase as he fiddled with his handkerchief and then stuck it back inside his jacket and looked at his watch. "I should go. I'm sorry to dump this on you. I just wanted to be with you. For some reason. Well, anyway . . ." Chase was fumbling for words. He walked across her office and reached for the door.

Kenzie didn't move, though she wondered if she should go over to him, put her arm around him, walk him out. But she didn't, and she didn't know why. Was she an uncaring ice queen, as Matt had suggested? Did she lack compassion? She wasn't sure why she didn't reach out to comfort this man who was suffering the kind of pain she'd once endured. Instead, she walked back to her desk as he opened the door to leave.

"I'm sorry, Chase," Kenzie said. "I'm sorry for what you're going through."

Chase turned toward her, nodded, and left.

Kenzie sat quietly at her desk. What was Chase trying to say? Why did he even come to Grayson? Was it really about filming something? Was he trying to reconnect with her?

Later that day, when Kenzie pulled her truck into a spot in front of her apartment, her phone rang.

"Hey, Chase, how're you doing?" Kenzie asked.

"She died," Chase said.

"I'm so sorry." Kenzie's voice cracked with emotion. She didn't mean for it to happen. It just did. And she was as surprised as Chase must have been when he heard it.

"I know it was probably strange today. I'm just having a rough time with this—"

"I understand. You don't have to apologize. Really," Kenzie interrupted. "Are you with people? You shouldn't be alone."

"I'm okay. I have siblings. We're all here. I'm just outside the hospice, taking a walk."

"I'm glad you're with each other. That's important."

"I'd been thinking of you since our dinner. I realized I wasn't the greatest of guys. I should've called you afterward. I'm really sorry about what happened that night. I want to apologize again. I wasn't considerate."

"It's okay, Chase. I've moved on."

She looked up at the leaves rustling through the trees and then peered across the street at a man walking four dogs, and was surprised by how orderly they were.

"Would you maybe like to try it again? Maybe go out another time?"

Kenzie didn't know what to say. She wasn't ready to go out with him or anyone else for that matter. She was still getting over Matt.

But what if Matt was the prelude to the real relationship? Possibly with Chase? It was clear Matt didn't own the ring, but she'd never worn it with Chase. She'd hardly worn it at all.

She'd often heard that real relationships came out of friend-ships. Her mother had told her that. She'd said it wasn't about lust. It wasn't about so-called chemistry. It came from shared experiences. And she and Chase certainly shared the experience of working in the same business and now the loss of their mothers.

"I don't know, Chase. I just broke up with someone and I'm still not ready. And besides, well, you just lost your mom. You need to be with your family."

"Well . . . okay, thank you for being there. Again, sorry to dump—"

"Just take care of yourself," Kenzie interrupted.

"I will. I'm going to her home to get some things. My sister wants to see if I can find an antique ring my mom used to wear. She's worried my mother lost it 'cause she hasn't seen it in years. It belonged to a famous woman, I can't remember her name. Anyway, I'm going to dig through her things and see if I can find it."

Kenzie swallowed hard. She opened her mouth as if to speak, but no sound emerged.

GEMMA

"Gemma, you've done a great job in Peter's absence." Stephen Strauss was the vice president of production at Fox Studios and the embodiment of the Hollywood executive. His hair was perfectly cropped against his head and he wore shiny black Gucci loafers, neatly pressed jeans, and a white oxford shirt with a blue Armani jacket. "I wonder if you might consider working on my team as a development executive. I have an opening and I noticed the ideas you brought Peter were quite wonderful. Though we haven't found something to work on together, I'm impressed with your commercial sensibilities."

Stephen leaned back in his chair, a pencil dangling from his mouth. He pulled it out every now and then as if it were an unlit cigarette. "Just so you know, I ran this by Peter, and he gave me his blessing and said you were more than ready to assume these duties. So what do you think? You haven't said a word."

Oh my God were the three words going through her head. It had been four months since Annalisa predicted she would get a promotion and here it was. She could not wait to dash out of there and call Kenzie.

"Oh, yes, of course. Of course I want it!" Gemma was beaming. "I'm just trying to calm down and be professional."

Stephen sprang from his seat, grabbed a file, and handed it to her. "Great. Here are the projects we have in development. A few are ready to go into production. Take a look at those first. I'd like you to stop by human resources so we can get the paperwork in order, and uh, let's say we start you the day after tomorrow, okay?"

"I'm ready!" Gemma was so stunned she could hardly think straight. Peter hadn't been back to the office yet. She'd been bored stiff.

"Thrilled to have you on board," Stephen added. "You've been working on the lot for a while, so you know plenty of folks here. As soon as we get things in order, we'll make the announcement and let her rip."

Gemma was more than ready. She was a studio executive. She'd worked for it and deserved it. She shook Stephen's hand, thanked him profusely, and promised to do a good job. She'd let it rip all right. She couldn't remember ever feeling this elated.

When she was far enough from the building, she crashed against a pole near some trash cans and sank to the ground. She closed her eyes, covered her mouth, and screamed loudly into her hands. After a moment she took out her phone and called Kenzie.

"Are you kidding me?" Kenzie howled. "Get out of here!"

"I can't even talk, I'm so happy," Gemma shrieked. "She said it. Annalisa said this would happen. Oh my God, it means you're next. It means you're gonna meet your husband."

"Let's enjoy your success and forget about Annalisa. She had nothing to do with this. You worked for this promotion. For years you thought no one noticed your good work, but they did. I'm so happy for you."

"I can't wait to tell—"

Gemma wanted to say *my dad*, but she stopped. Kenzie didn't like hearing about Jeffrey. She quickly recovered and said, "My mom."

"Your dad could care less. Forget him," Kenzie said, reading her mind. "But your mom raised you. Remember? Don't forget that. She didn't abandon you like Jeffrey. She'll be so proud of you. This is just so great. You're going to do so well."

While Kenzie offered more kudos, Gemma noticed a text from Scarlett, who invited her to join the family for dinner that evening. Gemma said yes immediately. She couldn't wait to tell them her great news. Jeffrey would be ecstatic. She would invite him to lunch, and she'd tell him everything. Then she'd ask him for advice.

"I've got to get to work," Kenzie said. "Enjoy this great time. Congrats!"

"We'll celebrate. On my new expense account!" Gemma shouted.

Scarlett texted the time and place for dinner. Gemma thought, what better way to toast her wonderful promotion than with her family?

She would tell her mother about the promotion, but not about dinner with Jeffrey and his family that evening. She didn't want to hear any more negative comments about her father. This wasn't something her mother would ever understand. She needed her father now. He'd guide her through the corporate maze, offer suggestions, and help her navigate the treacherous waters of senior management.

Her mother wouldn't have a clue. She never rose above bookkeeper and had just retired from that job of twenty years without a single promotion. Gemma loved her but never understood her mom's lack of ambition.

She'd stop at Saks, buy a new outfit, and get her makeup done. She was an executive now. She wanted to look the part. She couldn't wait for Jeffrey to see her tonight. He would be bowled over.

When Gemma arrived at the restaurant, Scarlett rushed to the entrance to greet her. She took her hand and walked Gemma to their table in the back of the room. Gemma was happy to see them all and couldn't wait to share her good news.

"I'm so glad you could come," Scarlett said loud enough for the other patrons to hear. "I want you to sit right next to me."

"Hi, Gemma, nice to see you," Emily said, barely looking up, her eyes focused on the menu.

Gemma sat down next to Scarlett and noticed Jeffrey and Dylan were engaged in their phones. They hadn't acknowledged her.

"Hey, Gemma's here," Emily said. "Can't you two look up for one minute and say hi?"

Dylan didn't move. Jeffrey leaned over and gave Gemma a perfunctory kiss on her head and went back to his phone. Now Scarlett was buried in hers as well. And then Emily's phone rang. Four for four.

Gemma sat quietly at the table and wondered if she should take out her phone, too. She sure didn't want to. She wanted to be with them but wondered if they wanted to be with her. She'd never seen them like this. She'd been there less than five minutes and each had split off into his or her own world. Maybe this was what being part of the family was *really* like. Maybe it was a good thing. The family felt so comfortable around her that they didn't feel the need to entertain her.

The waiter came by to take their orders. When he left, Gemma thought this was her chance. She'd tell them about her promotion before the texting duel started again.

"So I have some good news," she said. She looked around the table, but they were once again focused on their thumbs. Didn't they talk to each other? Weren't there rules about phones at dinner?

"What's that, Gemma? Your news?" Emily's eyes were fixed on her Facebook newsfeed.

"I got bumped up to the varsity soccer team," Dylan interrupted, completely focused on the game he was playing.

"That's great," Gemma said, trying to sound enthusiastic. She smiled broadly and looked around the table. Jeffrey was furiously pecking away at his keyboard. "So, um, I got a promotion."

Scarlett looked up, leaned over, and hugged Gemma. "Oh, that's great."

"Good for you." Emily glanced up at Gemma. "Will you be making more money at the shelter now?"

Gemma was taken aback. They'd gotten together several times over the past six weeks, but she realized that no one but Jeffrey knew what she did. They never asked. In fact, no one asked much about her at all. She was the girl from the shelter.

And then it occurred to her that they didn't even know her last name. Not once had she said it. If she had given her real last name, Haskins, Jeffrey would've known instantly who she was, and yet it never came up. She had already thought of a fake one but had never had to use it. It was amazing to her that they knew so little about her. She was just some woman named Gemma. She'd reluctantly begun to discover that they weren't the family she'd hoped they would be.

"Well, no," Gemma started to say. "I work in—"

"I've got to take this call. I'll be right back," Jeffrey interrupted as he put the phone to his ear and then headed for the entrance of the restaurant and out the door.

Gemma thought about the text message she'd seen on Jeffrey's phone at the swim meet. Was this call from Lauren, too? Was she waiting for him now? She hated her cynicism. Jeffrey wouldn't do that. She really wanted to believe he was a happy family man.

"It's really rude that Dad's always on the phone." Scarlett looked at Emily. "He didn't even ask how my field trip was today, Mom. I don't like it."

"I don't, either." Emily reached for Scarlett's hand and kissed it. "We need to talk about this. We should probably make a rule, no phones at dinner."

"He's a busy guy, moron," Dylan said without looking up from his phone. "He works hard so we can get great things. And go to great schools. Even though I hate school."

"Oh, don't say that. Things will get better. You made the soccer team," Emily said.

Emily, Scarlett, and Dylan talked about the video Dylan's school was making for some contest. Scarlett thought it was a stupid idea, which started an argument between her and Dylan. Their conversation escalated until Dylan called her a slut. Emily had enough. She grabbed his phone and put it in her purse. Dylan was furious and left the table. Then Jeffrey returned.

"Sorry, the wrong document got faxed this afternoon. I knew that temp didn't know what the heck she was doing. What's going on with Dylan?" He raked his hand through his hair and sat down.

"They had a fight," Emily said matter-of-factly. "I took his phone. He's pouting." Apparently this happened a lot, because Jeffrey just shrugged. Again, Gemma felt like an interloper. What the heck was she doing there anyway? And then Scarlett started whining.

"What's wrong?" Jeffrey glanced at Scarlett and put his phone beside his plate.

"Daddy. You're always on that thing. That phone. I hate it."

"Hey, I'm not on it now. Look, it's on the table."

"Turn it off," she said.

Jeffrey hesitated, and then he did.

"It's off. Happy?" Jeffrey clenched his jaw.

Gemma knew Jeffrey wasn't happy. In fact, she noticed he turned the phone back on when Scarlett wasn't looking and positioned it so he could see texts as they arrived.

"So, Gemma, you got a promotion?" Jeffery scooted his chair in closer to the table.

"Yes, I'm going to—"

"Why is she always with us?" Dylan had returned to his seat.

"Have you calmed down, young man?" Emily glared at him.

"Where's my phone? And why is *she* here all the time?" Dylan asked again as he stared at Gemma.

"Don't listen to him," Emily whispered to Gemma, trying to cover for Dylan's rude behavior.

"It's okay," Gemma said softly. But of course it wasn't okay. It upset her. She refolded the napkin in her lap.

"So you got a promotion. Great, proud of you," Jeffrey bit into his sandwich.

Finally. There it was. Recognition from her father. She'd known he'd be proud of her, and was pleased her promotion made him happy. Still, no one knew what it was for. But at this point Gemma hardly cared. She peered over at him, but his eyes were focused on his meal.

She was so sick of carrying the secret around. She wanted them to know who she was and why she hung around so much. She looked around the table. Everyone was eating. No one was talking. She wondered what kind of reaction they would have to her bombshell. A vibration came from Jeffrey's phone, which he quickly tossed into his pocket before anyone noticed.

"Where is that darn waiter? I want some fries." Jeffrey threw his napkin onto the chair, stood up, and darted across the restaurant.

Emily asked Dylan about homework. Then Scarlett took photos and Instagrammed them to her friends. She giggled when they texted her back and then sent them more.

Gemma was miserable. This was supposed to be a fun congratulatory meal with *her* family, who were supposed to be thrilled and excited for her. It was supposed to be a celebration. There'd be champagne and cake. Instead, it was a disaster.

Kenzie was right. She should be celebrating with her mother. What the heck was she thinking? She had to leave. Now. As Gemma looked around the table, she saw Emily talking on her phone, Dylan playing some sort of game, and Scarlett taking selfies. She realized that if she left, no one would even notice.

So she did.

She grabbed her bag and walked to the front of the restaurant. Surveying the room, she looked for Jeffrey but didn't see him. Then she glanced outside and saw him standing alone in the parking lot, smoking a cigarette. Ah, so that's what the agitation was about. He was a closet smoker. Well, so was she. Another thing they had in common.

She couldn't ask for a better opportunity.

This was it. The moment she'd been waiting for.

She quickened her pace and moved through the restaurant, then headed outside to where he was standing. But suddenly a car drove up alongside Jeffrey. He reached in the window and grabbed an envelope from the young female driver. Then he leaned down and kissed her on the lips. Gemma stopped dead in her tracks. The woman spotted Gemma, who was just a few feet behind Jeffrey. She glared at Gemma and then sped away.

"Lauren!" Jeffrey shouted. He turned around and saw Gemma. She didn't say a word. He put the envelope in his pocket, tossed his cigarette onto the sidewalk, and ground it hard with the heel of his shoe. He moved slowly toward her.

"Who's Lauren?" she asked.

"What do you want, Gemma?" Jeffrey sneered. His nostrils flared, his jaw tensed. He was almost growling at her. She had never seen him like this.

"Are you in love with me? Why are you hanging around all the time?"

Gemma felt sick. She wanted to tell him. But this wasn't the time. It wasn't the place. She wondered if that time and place would ever exist. When she didn't answer, Jeffrey turned and walked back to the restaurant.

Once he was out of sight, she ran to her car and raced out of the lot.

SARITA

"What's with the weirdos in your office?" Leo asked Kenzie over the intercom. "Is it Halloween or something?"

"Uh, Leo, why don't you come in here so you can meet them," Kenzie said.

He flew into her office in an instant. He'd clearly been waiting for an invitation, which was so unlike Leo, who usually just stormed in whenever he wanted.

"Leo, you know Sarita. And this is her boyfriend, Damien."

Sarita shifted uncomfortably under Leo's gaze. He'd never seen her with a white powdery face, heavy black makeup around her eyes, a red wig, nose ring, black shredded top, gold lamé short skirt, black tights, and army boots. He hadn't even begun to look at Damien. Sarita wasn't thrilled, but she and Kenzie had agreed it was time she revealed her true self.

"Glenn!" Leo shouted. "Get in here. It's Halloween in the middle of April!"

"Leo, really?" Kenzie rolled her eyes.

Glenn shot into Kenzie's office like a bullet. When Leo called, he ran.

"Oh, hey. Who is this?"

"It's Sarita," Sarita said.

"No? Really? You're in there?" Glenn asked. "Seriously? Wow. Great getup. Where you going? To some party?"

"You guys. You're being pretty insensitive," Kenzie said.

"It's no big deal," Sarita said. "This is who I really am. I know this 'getup' looks really silly to you, but it reflects the person I am inside. So I guess I'm kind of coming out in a way."

"Are you gay? Is that what you're saying?" asked Leo.

"No, Leo. She's not gay," said Kenzie. "She's Goth. And so is her boyfriend, Damien. And guess what, he's an account manager at Ernst & Young."

"No kidding," Glenn said. "Cool."

"Yeah, cool." Leo reached into Kenzie's refrigerator, grabbed a bottle of water, and tossed another to Glenn. "So are you gonna dress like that every day now? I mean, ya know I'm okay with it, but I don't know—the owners, trainers? They might think we're holding some kind of freak show up here."

"Don't worry, Leo," Sarita said. "Tonight we're going to a club where I'm performing. I don't have time to stop and change, so Kenzie thought it would be okay if I dressed in my full attire."

"Oh, well, isn't Kenzie wonderful," Leo smirked. "So good to know she's the one in charge."

"Leo, it's just for today," Kenzie sighed. "I didn't think it would be a big deal."

Leo gave a cocky wink. Sarita could tell he was relieved.

"Well, nice to meet all of you," Damien said. He'd clearly had enough. "Gotta get back to work. See ya later, babe."

"What do you mean, *performing*?" Glenn reclined in one of Kenzie's chairs.

"I sing with bands. Mostly at this one club, Deathrock Bar. It features a lot of Goth and New Wave music." Sarita tugged nervously on her nose ring.

"Wow, had no idea," Glenn offered a lackluster smile. "Good for you."

Leo couldn't keep his eyes off Sarita. She stood a few feet in front of him, and he just stared at her. His eyes ran up and down her body, taking in every detail.

"So, does that nose ring hurt? I mean, you had that pierced?" Leo grimaced. "That had to hurt."

Sarita felt uncomfortable being on display, almost like an animal in the zoo. Everyone was staring at her. Yet, she was relieved to be herself.

"Okay," Leo said. "This has been an interesting show. I don't really get it, but fine. I need you tootsies to stop playing around and get to work. We've got a big day coming up in six weeks." Leo started to leave, and Glenn jumped out of his seat and followed. As they exited Kenzie's office, Sarita's phone rang.

"Hi, Mama," Sarita said as she walked to the corner of the office so she wouldn't be heard.

"How are you, my dear? Are you still living at the motel?" Mama asked.

"Yes, Mama, you know I've been there almost a month. I'm fine, please don't worry about me." Sarita had texted her mom on a regular basis, but her mother never called at work. "Is everything all right?" Her mother remained silent. "Mama? Are you there?"

"Things are not all right, my sweetheart. Papa is in the hospital. He was rushed there last night. He couldn't breathe. Unfortunately, it seems his cancer has returned."

"What? Which hospital?" She paced nervously.

"Palmdale Regional." Mama's voice cracked when she uttered those words, as it was the same hospital where Papa had endured several rounds of chemo years ago. "Can you come by this evening and have dinner with me? Papa left an envelope he wanted me to give to you."

"Of course, Mama. Yes, I'll be there. And then I will go to the hospital with you."

There was a long pause.

"Mama? Are you still there?"

"Just for dinner, Sarita. We will meet for dinner. Your sisters and I will see him later . . . that is his wish."

Sarita almost dropped the phone. She tried so hard not to cry, but she couldn't hold it in. She shoved the phone into her back pocket.

"I couldn't help but overhear your conversation. Is your father in the hospital?" Kenzie asked as she handed Sarita a box of tissues.

Sarita nodded as she unhooked her nose ring, placed it in her pocket, and then blew her nose and wiped her tears. "His throat cancer returned."

"Oh, Sarita, I'm so sorry," Kenzie said. "Are you going to visit him?"

"No," she muttered. Her voice was barely audible. "He doesn't want to see me. My sisters and my mother will be with him." She stood helplessly in the middle of Kenzie's office.

"C'mon, let's step outside. Get a little air." Kenzie wrapped her arm around Sarita and opened the sliding door that led to the little patio that overlooked the grassy paddock. A groom was schooling a colt. Kenzie and Sarita watched as they sauntered by.

"There's something peaceful about watching horses," Kenzie said as she gazed at the colt a few yards away. "I don't know what it is. I just feel so bonded with them. It's almost spiritual. Maybe it's the mutual respect we have for one another. The kindness we share. Their insightful nature."

"I agree," Sarita said as she wiped the last of her tears from her cheek. "I love walking through the barns and visiting with them in their stalls. They have a calming effect."

"They do." Kenzie took a deep breath and blew it out slowly.

Neither said a thing as they contemplated the grounds.

"Thank you for urging me to let Leo and Glenn know who I really am," Sarita said. "It was time to stop hiding."

"I'm glad you told me about your other life, as you call it," Kenzie said. "There's nothing to be ashamed of. You should be proud of who you are, and that you're obviously a talented singer. That's impressive. Your dad just doesn't understand. He has different expectations."

"He sure does. He wants me to be a married woman," Sarita said. "Something I bet you know something about."

"Me?" Kenzie looked at her. "Why would you say that?"

"You know . . . the ring," said Sarita.

"I'm so sick of that ring." Kenzie shifted her gaze toward the paddock. "I rarely wear it. I love its history, but I can't stand the power it has over me."

"Think you want to get married someday?" Sarita asked.

"To the right guy, sure. What about you?"

"I don't know yet."

"It's okay—you're very young. You don't need to make that decision today."

Sarita smirked. Kenzie paused for a moment, then laughed. "Oh yeah. I forgot," Kenzie said. "You're going to be an old maid in a couple of years. What's that make me?"

Kenzie rubbed the back of Sarita's shoulder. They both watched the groom and colt as they walked around the ring one more time.

"My mother has an envelope for me," Sarita said "Something my father wanted me to have. She invited me over for dinner tonight. But I'm supposed to meet Damien at the club."

"I think the club can wait, don't you?" Kenzie asked.

"Yes, it can wait," Sarita said.

"Then you'd better get going. You don't want to be late for her." Sarita gathered her things and headed for the door.

"Hey, thanks, Kenzie. I really appreciate everything."

They hugged. Then Sarita left.

* * * * *

As soon as she walked into the house, Sarita realized how much she missed the pungent fragrance of her mom's cooking. The warm, sweet aroma of cinnamon and cloves wafted over her. She closed her eyes and inhaled.

"Mama, can I help you with anything?"

Mama looked up from the stove. At first she seemed startled. She wasn't used to seeing her youngest daughter dressed this way. Only once before—and late at night—had she seen Sarita in full Goth regalia.

"Sorry, Mama, I'm dressed like this because I was going to meet Damien at the club later. I hope it doesn't upset you too much," she said.

"It's fine, dear," she said. "Go ahead and set the table."

"And Papa? How is he?"

"He's on a ventilator and heavily sedated." Mamma tugged at the hem of her apron. "Hopefully he'll pull through so they can begin chemo."

Sarita placed the dishes on the table. Just the idea of her father so helpless, lying in the hospital unable to breathe on his own, was shocking. She couldn't believe how quickly this had happened. She remembered the last time she had sat at that table. She and her father had argued intensely. Now all was quiet. The house felt empty without him, yet it was full of his life—his books, cigars, artwork. She could feel him, smell him, and hear his voice. She fully expected him to walk through the door any minute. He was such a dominating figure in this otherwise all-female household, and she missed him, even though she knew he did not miss her attitude.

Sarita sat next to her father's place at the head of the table. Her mom set down a large platter of tandoori chicken, the fluffy, deep-fried bread called *bhatoora*, charred eggplant with ginger, onion, green chilies, and fresh tomatoes, and her mother's best dish, potatoes and peas in a tomato-based sauce. Sarita hadn't realized how much she enjoyed her mother's good cooking. She ate slowly, savoring every bite. They sat across from each other, but neither spoke. Sarita broke the silence.

"You'll go see Papa tonight at the hospital?"

"Yes," Mama said without looking up.

"Please say I asked about him."

"Of course."

Sarita knew her mother was deeply upset. It wasn't like her to be so still. She recalled the last time her father was in the hospital almost ten years ago, undergoing treatment for his cancer, and how devastating it had been for Mama, who had rarely been apart from her husband for most of their thirty-five-year marriage.

"Shall I move back into the house while Papa's in the hospital? So you have someone here with you?"

"That would be nice. I'd like that." Mama looked up and offered a faint smile.

"Then after dinner I will get my things and stay here until Papa returns."

There was a long pause.

"Can you tell him I'm sorry I brought shame onto his family? Please. Can you tell him that?" Sarita's anxiety grew as she watched her mother, whose expression hadn't changed. Her face was drawn, her eyes hollow and sad.

Mama looked down at her dinner but didn't respond.

"Mama. Please?"

Mama placed her fork next to her plate and folded her napkin. She left the table and returned with a sealed envelope addressed to Sarita.

"Papa asked me to give this to you." She handed it to Sarita. "He wrote it a few days ago."

"Do you know what it says?" she asked.

"I do not."

"Then I shall read it out loud, Mama, so you can hear it, too." Sarita took a long sip of water before she began to read aloud:

My dear one,

I'm sorry that we had words and that you have brought such shame to our family. I believe this is my fault. I did not provide you with a sound base. I did not have you study at the foot of an Indian master such as I did growing up in my native land. It is my wish that before we lose you completely, you spend some time in New Delhi with my sister, your aunt Bhutto, who will gladly provide room and board for a month so that you might experience my homeland in the home that belongs to the Mahajan family. It is my last hope for you, my dear one. Because I don't know how long I will be of this earth, my only wish is that my youngest daughter discovers the truth about her Hindu ancestry. I pray you will heed my words and follow the advice of your father and mother and spend the next few weeks in beautiful India. I shall welcome you upon your return. And not till then. Love, Papa

Sarita held the letter. She looked up and studied her mother, hoping for some reaction. But Mama looked down at her plate, then started to remove the dishes.

"Papa wants me to travel to India. Now. And he will not see me till I return." Sarita's body stiffened.

"I believe that's what he wrote." Mama took the leftovers to the kitchen and put them in plastic containers.

Sarita stood and followed Mama to the kitchen. "Mama, I can't," she said. "I can't leave now. I am doing so well in my job. I am happy where I am and with who I am. I know how much I disappoint Papa, but I just can't."

Mama worked furiously, putting everything away and making sure the leftovers were wrapped properly.

"I'm sorry Papa is ill. I just . . . I just don't want to travel to India, especially now." Sarita's hands were trembling, and her jaw tightened. She had reached her breaking point. "Have you nothing to say, Mama? Do you and Papa speak with one tongue?"

Sarita's voice was shaking as it escalated. She accidentally knocked a glass to the floor and it shattered into pieces.

Mama stopped. She looked at her youngest daughter with her matted black hair and strange, white, powdery face.

"Papa is extremely sick, Sarita. This is your life. You must choose your own path. I cannot decide for you."

Mama kneeled on the floor and picked up the tiny shards of glass, then cradled them in her apron and threw them into the trash. Sarita picked up the rest.

"I must go. Visiting hours will be over soon. Take some leftovers if you'd like," Mama said as she took off her apron. "And be careful, my little one. Be careful."

Mama leaned over and kissed Sarita on her forehead, and then ran to the living room, grabbed her bag, and left for the hospital.

BRYNNE

Brynne sat cross-legged, leaning against a tree in the parking lot of Grayson Downs. She wore an old pair of jeans, one earring, a necklace with the pendant facing the wrong way, and a pair of tan sneakers. She'd failed to notice that her gray T-shirt had several coffee stains or that she'd forgotten to wash her hair. And if only she could get rid of the blemish on the tip of her nose. She never had blemishes. Never. But life was different now.

"Oh my gosh, Brynne?" Kenzie jumped out of her truck carrying a cup of coffee in one hand and her purse in the other as she walked quickly toward her. "Where've you been? No one's heard from you in a month. I left messages, but you never responded." Brynne acknowledged her with a glance but didn't comment. Instead, she focused on her badly bitten nails. "What're you doing here? On the ground? You look terrible. What's going on?"

"My car won't start," she said matter-of-factly. "I'm waiting for the auto club. They'll be here in forty minutes or so."

"Um, well, okay, but you don't really seem—"

"Martin and I split up," she said.

"Oh no . . . I'm sorry." Kenzie edged closer to her.

"I've been to hell and back. I feel like I've reached the end."

"End? What do you mean?"

Brynne waved dismissively. "If I wanted to end it, why would I be sitting here? I'd be home taking pills. I thought about it, and pills seemed to be the best way. But I'm not going to do it, because then Martin would win. And he's not going to win."

"Well, that's good to know," Kenzie said. "Mind if I sit down?"

Brynne shrugged. Kenzie placed her bag on the ground and sat down next to Brynne. She offered her some coffee, but Brynne declined.

"But I'm not . . . I'm not really okay," Brynne said softly. She stared straight ahead, fighting back tears. "My home has been in foreclosure for nearly a year and I didn't even know it. Can you imagine? The bank took it. Martin didn't have the guts to tell me. I heard about it the day before the movers arrived. I was literally thrown out of my own house with no place to go. I'm in a hotel until I can get an apartment. Our money, the little we have left, is tied up in property. Martin is living with his girlfriend."

"You're in a hotel?" Kenzie raised her eyebrows.

"Holiday Inn in the Valley. Although I just put down a deposit for a furnished studio apartment nearby. By the way, I got a waitressing job at Mo's in Toluca Lake. I start in two weeks. I waited tables for one week in college. Figured I could do it again. If you come by, please leave a big tip."

"Waitressing?" Kenzie asked as she took a sip of coffee.

Brynne picked at the polish on her nails.

"That's not all." Brynne took a deep breath. "Before we married I foolishly signed a prenup, because Martin's family had a lot of money that they were not eager to share. Part of that agreement also states that I'm not entitled to anything Martin made during our marriage. Of course, Martin paid for my attorney to review the contract. Despite his objections I signed, because I was so in love.

I just never dreamed Martin would hold me to that thing. And I know . . . I know what you're going to say. I can't believe I did it, either. But honestly, I believed we'd be together. Forever. Perhaps I was naive, or maybe I just never wanted to believe otherwise. In any case, I was wrong. And I'm paying the price."

"You need an attorney," Kenzie said.

"Just hired one. Thank goodness the girls aren't home. I never dreamed I'd say that."

"Have you told them?" Kenzie asked.

"I've left messages for them to call me. They hate the phone. They only like to text. I told them it's important." Brynne sighed. "Martin always left this kind of thing to me. It will be a terribly painful conversation, to say the least."

"This is just awful," Kenzie said. "I'm so sorry. I don't know what to say."

"I'll be all right," Brynne said, trying to convince herself. "By the way, I secured some vendors for opening day."

Kenzie pressed her hand against her chest. "Thank you," she said. "I can't believe you did that, given what you've been through. That's so—"

"Hey, what're you gals doing out here?" Leo was carrying his briefcase. "Brynne? Is that you?"

"It's me, Leo." Brynne managed a weak smile.

"Whoa. What happened?"

"Martin left," Brynne said.

Glenn came up behind Leo. He stopped when he saw everyone staring at him.

"Is there a meeting?" Then he saw Brynne. "Oh, Mrs. Tomlinson, I—"

"Let's go, Glenn, got work to do," Leo interrupted. He grabbed Glenn's arm and ushered him away. Brynne was sure he was worried she might ask for money or a job or something that would make him uncomfortable, so he got out while the getting was good.

"I'm so sorry," Kenzie said again. "I know how much you wanted this marriage to work. It's terribly sad. And what Martin's done is despicable. But you're a tough woman. And you deserve much better than this. I know you don't believe it now, but change is good, and in the end you will be much better off."

"I don't know." Brynne's gaze was fixed on the ground. "You know what my mother told me? She said following a divorce a woman's income declines by an average of forty-one percent, close to twice the level of income loss that men experience. Interesting, huh?"

Kenzie shook her head.

"And I don't even have an income." Brynne glanced at Kenzie. "Anyway, I came to see my horses one last time before I sell them. Hoping I can afford to keep some, but who knows."

Kenzie stood up, dusted the back of her pants, then reached for her bag and coffee cup. "You're going to make it. You'll come back. Just takes time. Lean on your friends. Especially your girlfriends. We're here to help."

Brynne sat quietly for a moment.

"Do you want to come upstairs? Wait inside?"

"No, I'll be fine," Brynne said.

"Okay, well, I'm going to check on you later." Kenzie put her hand on Brynne's shoulder. "And don't be taking any pills."

Brynne managed a half smile and thanked her. Then Brynne watched as Kenzie walked toward the office building. Brynne stood but didn't even bother to brush off the leaves that had collected on her pants. She walked to her white Jaguar and hit the ignition, but the engine still wouldn't turn over. She sat in the driver's seat and just stared. Since she couldn't drive, she got out and began walking toward the barn.

Tomlinson Stables was emblazoned across the side of the structure. She traced the words with her hand and took a photo. Then she stopped at every stall and stroked and nuzzled each of her horses. There was one groom mixing oats. Brynne teared up. She knew this might be the last visit.

Martin had left them so deep in the hole that she wondered if she'd ever see financial daylight again. No home. No savings. No credit. No real job. She'd trusted him with so much, only to be left with so little.

In the last stall she found Eddie Pasghetti, her favorite horse. The one horse she did not want to part with because her daughters had named him. Eddie Pasghetti was six years old, and it was time to turn him out to stud. He'd had a fine racing career. He was all heart and now it was time he enjoyed retirement.

When she stepped into his stall, Eddie Pasghetti greeted her like an old friend. He snorted when she rubbed his nose. She remembered when he'd bucked wildly as a colt, but he had calmed down over the years. She rubbed the back of his ears and ran her hand over his beautiful, shiny chestnut coat. His body arched and his tail spun.

Brynne spent a few more minutes with the horse and then headed back to the parking lot so she could meet the tow truck. She kept checking her texts to see if her daughters had written back. She desperately wanted to talk to them but dreaded the conversation. She knew it would be hard on them. Life as they knew it was over.

Brynne would be there for her daughters. They rarely relied on Martin, who had little time for them. She would tell them what happened, even though Martin had asked that she not say anything yet.

She sent another text saying it was important that they speak as soon as possible. The girls had always responded when they lived at home. Annoyed, Brynne sent another text but still got nothing back. Suddenly frantic, she sent another and another, till finally they called.

Brynne stiffened when she answered. "I'm sorry to bother you at school," she said. "But something's happened. And I must tell you." She had worked herself into a frenzy and was hyperventilating. She opened her car door and sat in the driver's seat. "A month ago your father and I—"

"We already know," Marianne interrupted. "Dad texted us about it."

"He did? What did he say?" Brynne fanned her heated face.

"He left you for Marcella," Marianne said.

"Marcella? How . . . Do you know her?"

"I think he took her to lunch with us one time," Brianne said.

Brynne felt a lump in her throat. Martin had introduced his mistress to their daughters? And no one mentioned it? How could he? Thinking about it made her crazy with rage.

"Mom, we really can't talk," Brianne said. "We're in the cafeteria and have you on speaker, so it's kinda hard to hear. And I wanna get something to eat. But look, we're really sorry. You probably feel terrible. We wish we were there to give you a hug. Maybe we can talk later, when it's not so crazy."

"Yeah, really, Mom, so sorry," Marianne added.

There was a long pause. Brynne wanted to curl into a ball. "I wish you were here, too, and I really need you . . . But he took you to lunch with her?"

"Mom," Marianne said, "you had to know he was screwing her. I mean, c'mon, you knew he was doing his trainer a couple years ago, right? It's just who Dad is."

"His . . . *trainer*?" Brynne almost dropped the phone. No, she hadn't known. Apparently she was the last to know everything.

"What did you expect, Mother?" Brianne asked. "You weren't even sleeping in the same room. Like, how did you have sex?"

"Obviously they weren't having it, you idiot," Marianne interrupted. "Mom, you'll be okay. Just go shopping. You like that. It'll make you feel better."

Brynne sat in stunned silence.

"Hello? Are you still there? We can't hear you!" Brianne shouted.

Brynne wasn't expecting this kind of conversation from her angelic fourteen-year-old daughters, who had apparently turned thirty-five while she wasn't looking. How did they know these things? They talked about their father screwing his trainer like it was common knowledge. They were talking about sex as casually as they talked about gym class. This was a nightmare. Martin had warned her that they would become much more sophisticated living away at boarding school. He hadn't been much in favor of it, but Brynne had insisted. She wanted the best for them.

And now it seemed as if they had contempt for her. Somehow they blamed her for Martin's behavior. If she'd been a better mother, wife, lover, he might've stayed.

Deep down, she understood.

She had once had those same feelings.

It all came rushing back. Abandoned by her father, she blamed her mother. She attacked her mother unfairly, blaming her for his desire to be with other women.

"Mom," Marianne said, "we hate to go, but we kinda have to. I have volleyball practice and Brianne's rehearsing for a play. We love you and send you hugs! We'll talk later. Okay?"

"Sure, okay. Love you," Brynne whispered softly.

But they had already hung up.

KENZIE

"So who's it gonna be? Matt or Chase?" Leo said as he marched into Kenzie's office, cigar dangling from his lips. "I dig 'em both."

"What do you mean?" Kenzie swung her chair around and looked up at Leo.

"Oh, c'mon. Who's *the one*? We all wanna know, who's the guy? Who's gonna win the ring? It's like that bachelor show, right?" Leo laughed and plunged into the chair opposite Kenzie's desk. He leaned back and rested his feet on the desk.

"Neither. Okay? Got your answer?" Kenzie looked Leo squarely in the eye.

"Wait, is there someone else? Who?" Leo asked.

"No, there's not someone else. But it's really not any of your business, is it?"

"Hey, it isn't every day someone gets told the ring they have belongs to their future mate. I mean, you gotta want to know, don't you?"

Kenzie hated this conversation. She hated the ring. She hated that everyone knew this story. She wanted to fling the ring into the ocean. That was where it came from anyway. It had just floated ashore from some wreck a world away. So she might just do that. She couldn't stand the drama anymore.

She had tried to put the ring out of her mind because she didn't want to believe Annalisa's crazy prediction. And yet Gemma got a new job, out of the blue, just as Annalisa had predicted. Because the prediction came true for Gemma, it certainly could happen to Kenzie, too.

The good news was that Leo had the attention span of a gnat and was already out of his seat, moving toward the door.

"So when am I gonna see the video that's going on our website?" Leo said.

"Putting it up today. Exactly one month till opening day," Kenzie said.

"You like it?"

"Of course."

"Good," Leo said. "No pressure or anything. But if it doesn't work, you won't be the only one unemployed." Leo walked out and shut the door.

Kenzie closed her eyes. No pressure at all. She grabbed a couple of aspirin and water for her pounding headache. And then the door flew open.

"Can I come in?" Matt asked.

Kenzie was startled to see him. She nodded as she gulped down the pills.

"I haven't given up." He pulled a small vase of flowers from behind his back and presented it to her.

"Thanks. Sweet of you." Kenzie smiled, took the vase, and placed it on her desk. She had to admit that Matt's relentless desire to win her back was appealing. But her thoughts were elsewhere. Her back ached along with her head. She hoped the aspirin would kick in soon.

"So has the owner come forth?"

"This isn't the time, Matt." Kenzie was testy. She was focused on opening day. The last thing she wanted to discuss was the ring.

"Okay, well, I didn't come here to apologize again. I think I've done that enough," he said.

She was aware of Matt gazing at her as she leaned forward to inhale the scent of the flowers. She loved the pink roses' soft, delicious, and penetrating fragrance.

"I thought maybe we had a future," Matt continued. "But I guess not. I wish things hadn't turned out this way. I wish you'd give me another chance. But, well . . . I guess maybe I should leave you alone and, well . . . just wish you good luck with everything."

Matt turned around slowly, walked toward the door, and left.

Damn. Kenzie knew she was being too tough on Matt, but she couldn't help herself. She closed her eyes and smelled the flowers again. Why was she punishing him? This wasn't about him, it was about her. The ring. Her work. The anxiety of it all. The inevitable, onrushing, simultaneous crescendo. The stress was overwhelming. And she didn't know if she was equipped to handle it.

Then there was Chase. She hadn't heard from him after his mother had died. She should've called, made sure he was doing okay. Last time they'd spoken he was going to look for the ring his sister thought his mother might have lost. She was certain it was her ring. The ring she found. She had convinced herself that Chase was the one. But she told him she wasn't ready to go out with him. Would she ever be ready to see anyone while she still had feelings for Matt? Feelings she didn't want to address?

According to Annalisa's prophecy, she had one month left to meet her future husband. She regretted not going out with Chase. But she was afraid. Afraid she'd fall for him and then she'd be back to the life she once had. She didn't want to go there. But she didn't trust herself. She worried that being with Chase might work at first, but then she'd find herself married but unhappy.

Then, as if a lightbulb went off, she realized that meeting her future husband didn't necessarily mean she'd be happy. Many people married the wrong person and weren't happy and ultimately split up. Like Brynne, for example. Annalisa didn't say she'd be happy. She just said the ring belonged to her future husband. She suddenly realized that keeping the ring didn't ensure happiness. And that was the one thing Kenzie had wanted since the day she walked off that stage in New York. To be happy again. It didn't appear as if the ring was doing that for her. In fact, it had the opposite effect.

It was time to get rid of the ring. It was beautiful and Kenzie loved its history, but it had never been hers. It was simply a source of anxiety. Everyone knew about the ring and talked about it. With one month left in Annalisa's prediction, she decided she'd had enough and would part with it.

"It's up to ten thousand hits, and it's only been up one hour!" Sarita shouted as she flew into Kenzie's office later that day, carrying her open laptop. Glenn and Leo followed. Kenzie was confused.

"It's doing great," Glenn said. He moved alongside Kenzie and showed her the promotional video Sarita had just uploaded onto Grayson's website. "Look, Santa Anita, Del Mar, Belmont, Churchill Downs, and the *Daily Racing Form* already put the video on their websites. That's amazing. This thing's going viral."

Finally. Some good news.

"You must've sent this video to all of them," Glenn said with a twinkle in his eye. "Great idea. You *are* good at this!"

Sarita placed the laptop on Kenzie's coffee table. The four of them huddled around it and watched the ticker click off hits faster than a slot machine spins. She couldn't believe it.

"You made a talking horse?" Leo shouted. "We've got ourselves a regular Mr. Ed."

Kenzie knew Leo wasn't interested in details. It was nice that he trusted her, but this was his first glimpse of what she and Sarita had been working on the past few months. She'd begged him to watch a rough cut, but he only wanted to see the final product.

Kenzie sat with Sarita, Leo, and Glenn and watched the clip. It was a hidden-camera bit. Three unwitting young women approached a horse in its stall. One of them reached out to pet the horse, which obliged by placing its head on her shoulder and then nuzzled her ear. The women loved how friendly he was. And then he asked them to stroke his left ear. They jumped back and looked around to see who else was there, but there wasn't anyone. They were confused but curious. Then the horse asked for a carrot from the pail below. The women looked for the person providing the animal's voice. But it seemed to come directly from his mouth. Even his lips moved, as if he was speaking to them. They couldn't believe it. They fed him the carrot. He chewed, burped, and thanked them. They burst out laughing.

Two men and then an elderly couple with a child were next. Same reaction. Sarita, Leo, and Glenn were laughing hysterically. It was impossible to understand how the horse could talk. He seemed so lifelike. At the end of the thirty-second clip, the words *Grayson Downs Opens June 1—Be There* appeared on the screen.

Leo smacked Kenzie on the back so hard she almost fell off her chair.

She couldn't stop staring at the YouTube ticker. In just minutes the number of views had increased by a hundred. A talking horse, an old gag. But the world loved it. Just like they loved babies and dogs and UFOs, people loved seeing the talking horse.

Kenzie had asked the USC Robotics Research Lab if she could use their lifelike robotic horse for her video. The horse had been delivered to Grayson, and she and Sarita had planted a hidden camera in one of the barns to capture those candid moments.

Glenn, Sarita, and Leo were playing the video again and again. They'd dashed out of Kenzie's office and posted it on all their social media platforms.

Kenzie wanted to share the news with someone. And it wasn't Gemma. In her euphoria she realized Matt was the one she wanted to call. She walked to the sliding door and stared at the quiet and serene paddock. Matt would be thrilled for her. He was the most supportive man she'd ever known. He loved her very much. Yet, she'd been holding back, using his untruthfulness as an excuse simply because she knew he wasn't the owner of the ring.

But it went even deeper. She was afraid to let go, to enjoy true love for the first time, because if things didn't work out, or if Matt should die like her mom, the pain would be unbearable. She'd suffered that anguish before and didn't want to again. The thought of getting close to someone terrified her.

GEMMA

Gemma's hands were shaking so badly that she kept pressing the wrong digits on her office phone. She knew Jeffrey's number by heart, but the wrong number kept appearing.

She was hurt and disgusted by Jeffery's outburst outside the restaurant last month. She had to tell him who she was. It had gone on for too long. She was miserable and embarrassed that she hadn't found the opportunity. She always hoped there would be the right time. But it never came. Although she'd admit it to no one, she was worried he wouldn't accept her as his daughter. Deep down she believed that might be why she'd been putting off the conversation. It was no accident. She was enjoying the fantasy, living as if she was a friend of Scarlett's and becoming a part of Jeffrey's family that way. She worried how he'd react when he heard the truth.

It had been revolting to hear him ask if she might be into him. He was her father. She couldn't wait any longer. She had to tell him.

Gemma held the phone close to her ear and stared out the floor-to-ceiling window of her new office on the fourth floor, which offered a gorgeous view of the hills. She leaned back in her black-leather executive chair and stretched her long legs and brand-new pumps onto the ergonomic stool beneath her massive oak desk. While she waited for someone to answer, she raised her TV remote and switched the channel on one of her five TV screens.

Gemma was unsure whether Jeffrey would take her call. They hadn't seen or talked since their altercation outside the restaurant.

"Oh yes, I understand," she told Jeffrey's assistant. "Please tell him to return. It's important. Thank you."

Gemma hung up and waited.

She gazed out the window, thinking about how much she enjoyed the challenge and responsibility of her new position. Stephen, her boss, was extremely supportive. He trusted her. After a few weeks he'd increased her duties and added more responsibilities. She'd become his go-to person.

Writers, producers, and directors liked her confident, straight-forward manner. Her fan club was growing every day. Soon the most successful producers were asking to work with her. Her old boss, Peter, had recovered and returned to work, and she was thrilled to buy a project from him. Gemma was thriving and happy. Her life was almost perfect.

"Mr. Kahn's on the line," Adam, her assistant, spoke over the intercom.

She sat up straight, took a deep breath, and picked up the receiver.

"Hi, Jeffrey, thanks for returning my call."

"What do you want, Gemma?" Jeffrey's voice was stone cold. Gemma wasn't expecting a warm reception, but this was beyond frosty.

"I wondered if we could get together. Just one time. For lunch, maybe. Just us," she said. "I'm not in love with you. There's something else."

"What?"

"I'd rather not discuss it on the phone." She drew a long breath and continued. "I'd really like to meet in person. I know you're busy, but it's important."

Gemma bit her lip, waiting for him to respond.

"Okay, I have an opening tomorrow. One o'clock. The Palm. I'll make a reservation."

"Great. Thank you. I'll see you then," Gemma said as Jeffrey hung up.

Gemma was worried. She'd thought about this meeting for months. But she was unsure whether it would go well.

"Kenzie's calling on line two," Adam said through the intercom. "Do you want to talk to her?"

Gemma picked up the phone instantly. "Your timing's impeccable. I'm meeting him for lunch tomorrow. We just hung up."

"Well, he's finally going to know who you are. I pray it goes well," Kenzie said.

"Me too," Gemma said, taking a breath.

"Ya know," Kenzie said after a pause, "I've always been concerned about this. Worried that Jeffrey won't respond the way you want and that you might be hurt."

"It's possible," Gemma said. "But I need to do this."

"But what if—"

"I don't want fear to control my life," Gemma interrupted. "I want to work past it. If I don't try things, I'll never know." She took the handset off its base, walked over to the window, and peered down at the studio lot below. "Of course I want my father to embrace me. To love me. To accept me. But I know that may not happen. If he rejects me, I'll be upset, but I'll survive."

"But you'll feel terrible."

"Yes. But at least I'll know, Kenz." Gemma licked her lips. "I'll have closure. Sometimes we have to take risks. Sometimes things work out, and sometimes not. Once I knew he was my father, I wanted to go the distance."

There was a long pause as Gemma walked away from the window and returned to her desk.

"You gonna wish me luck?" asked Gemma softly.

"Yes, of course I wish you luck," Kenzie said warmly. "And you're right, Gem. Sometimes one has to take the leap. My mom used to say, 'No risk, no gain. No guts, no glory.' I'd forgotten about that till now. Jeffrey's darn lucky to have you as his daughter because you are a genuinely good person. I hope he realizes that and becomes some kind of presence in your life. I'll be thinking of you. Lemme know how it goes."

* * * * *

Gemma spent a long time primping before she left her office for lunch the next day. She'd brought three outfits to work and decided on a short, sleeveless blue dress, which looked lovely with her nude heels. As she drove from her office to the restaurant to meet Jeffrey, she called her mom from the car.

"This is it, Mom. He's going to learn who I really am today." Gemma checked her phone and noticed the time. "In fifteen minutes he's going to know the truth."

"Well, honey, I know this is something you've wanted for a long time. I worried all these years that you might discover the truth about your father. I hope when he meets the real you, he'll welcome you with open arms. I wish I could say that will probably happen, but I just don't know."

"I don't, either, but I appreciate your concern," Gemma said. "But, Mom, I've spent plenty of time with him and his family and gotten to know them all pretty well. I'm hoping for a good outcome." Gemma gritted her teeth as she made the turn onto the freeway. She wished just once her mother wouldn't dampen her spirit. Why couldn't she be more excited about this meeting? Was she still angry with Jeffrey? Why, after so many years? She should let it go. "I wish you'd be happy for once. Happy that I'm going to tell Jeffrey that I'm his daughter."

"I know this is important to you," her mom said. "But I'm your mother. And mothers worry. It's our job. And most of all, I don't want you to get hurt."

"Mom, I've gone over every scenario. I'm ready for him to embrace me with tears and excitement or reject me with anger and hostility. I've heard the stories about adoptees being shunned and turned away. I watch *Dateline*. I'm prepared either way . . . I just want you . . . I just want you to be supportive, okay?"

"I support you one hundred percent." Her voice was firm. "But more than that I want you to know that I love you. No matter what happens today, I want you to remember that, always."

"I know that, Mom." Gemma sighed as she turned into the parking lot at the restaurant. "I know that you love me, that you sacrificed so much to raise me by yourself. You did a great job and I love you so much for that," Gemma said. She hopped out of her car and handed the key to the valet. "I'm here. At the restaurant. I have to go now."

"Promise you'll call me when it's over," she said.

"I will, Mom, of course."

"Good luck, and I love you."

"Love you, too."

Gemma stepped into the restaurant just before one o'clock. Her hair was pulled back in a bun. Her green eyes were heavily made up to accentuate the color. The time was here, and she felt good. Once seated she ordered an iced tea and waited for Jeffrey to arrive.

Fifteen minutes passed. She checked her texts to make sure he hadn't been delayed and emailed her assistant to make sure he hadn't called. Then it was one thirty, and still no Jeffrey.

She wondered if he'd had an accident or lost her number. But he'd texted her before, so that didn't make sense. A half hour late to lunch was fine. She was okay with it. Even though she really wasn't. She didn't like it when anyone was late, especially since she was always punctual—a trait she clearly didn't get from him. He must've had an emergency.

At one forty-five Gemma saw Jeffrey enter the dining room. He sauntered through the restaurant, looking at every booth to see who was there. He stopped at one, shook a man's hand, exchanged a few words, and moved on. Gemma was surprised at how relaxed he seemed. He wasn't the least bit frenzied, as she would've been had she been forty-five minutes late to a lunch. She fully expected him to apologize profusely for his tardiness.

But he didn't.

Jeffrey took off his coat, rolled up his white shirtsleeves, and greeted Gemma with a handshake instead of the hug he'd given her in the past. He asked the hostess for a Coke and then grabbed a roll from the breadbasket.

"So what's up? Why'd you want to meet?" Jeffrey asked as he took a bite out of the roll and guzzled the Coke when it arrived. He set his phone on the table.

Gemma was startled by his bad manners. Wasn't he going to apologize for being late? She decided to ignore it. She hoped things would change once she got the words out.

"I was wondering if you could put your phone away for just a bit," she said. "I have something to tell you, and I don't want any interruptions."

"Well, I'm sorry," he said, "but we're preparing for trial and I have to be available. So I'll just leave it on the table and if it rings,

I have to answer." He checked it once more and then left it sitting by his water glass. "So what's this important conversation? Do you need money? Is that what you want?"

"No, it's nothing like that," she said. "I really don't know how to say this, even though I've rehearsed it many times." She took a breath. She hadn't thought it would be this difficult. She expected some preamble, like a discussion about his kids or her new job. But that wasn't going to happen. She didn't know how she could engage in such a delicate conversation when he seemed so detached and insensitive. "I don't know how to say this . . . and I'm worried about your reaction."

Jeffrey's eyes darted across the room as if looking for someone. He lingered on one table full of guys whose voices were heavy and loud. She could hear them talking about the Lakers game. It seemed that Jeffrey wasn't desperate to hear what she was about to say. She thought her dramatic buildup would have him begging for information, but he seemed indifferent. When he was done with the roll, he took a cracker from the basket and smothered it with butter. He wiped his hands on his napkin and drank more Coke. He called the waiter over and asked for some olive oil.

"So, um, do you want to hear what I have to say?" Gemma's forehead furrowed.

"I'm here."

"Well I'm . . . this is kind of hard for me. It's a big thing. A big deal . . ." Gemma took a deep breath. Her palms were sweating and her heart raced. She didn't think she'd be this nervous. But suddenly the floodgates opened and she could barely breathe. "I've been wanting . . . wanting to tell you this for a long time. But it had to be the right time. And, well, I . . . well I needed to be alone with you. Alone. And so here it is. Well, here it is. I'm . . . well . . . I'm your daughter."

Gemma stared at Jeffrey as he processed the information. But he offered no discernable response. He wasn't angry, sad, excited, happy—nothing. He wore a deadpan expression. In fact, he continued eating his cracker as if what she'd said had no significance. She wondered if he already knew. Gemma watched him carefully. He looked over at the other table again and offered a faint smile when one of the guys shouted that the Lakers should fire the coach. She couldn't stand it. Her stomach was in knots. She had to say something.

"You don't seem terribly surprised. Did you know this already?" Gemma asked.

"No," Jeffrey said. He took the menu from the waiter and ordered another Coke.

Jeffrey studied the menu. Gemma was cold. Her lips were trembling. She felt fidgety and jittery. She opened the menu and pretended to peruse it, but she wasn't hungry at all. She'd order something, but right now eating was the last thing on her mind. Of all the reactions she'd anticipated, indifference wasn't one of them.

When the waiter returned, Jeffrey ordered his meal, and then Gemma followed. But Jeffrey called the waiter back and asked how the hamburgers were prepared, and a further conversation ensued about whether their beef was grass fed.

Gemma wondered what was going on. So far she'd learned he didn't know she was his daughter but didn't seem to care. She guessed that was better than an angry response. He was probably stunned and needed some time.

"I know this is a big deal. I'm sure you need time to think about this and—"

"Not really," he interrupted. "I heard you. I don't like that you pretended to be someone else—that you played me and my family for fools. I took you at your word. That you were a volunteer at the shelter. You deceived us. And now I'm supposed to believe that you're my daughter?"

"Karen Haskins is my mother. You met her at a bachelor party, and she became pregnant. You took a paternity test. You and she had a contract—"

"One that was binding, last time I checked," he interrupted again. His brows bumped together as he scowled. "Did she not tell you I wanted nothing to do with you or her? Forever?"

Jeffrey's words sliced right through her. They were far more powerful than she could have imagined. It was one thing to read it and another to hear it. Her stomach dropped. Her body slumped back into the booth. Her mom was right. He was awful. Her mom knew him better than Gemma had realized.

Despite spending so much time with him, she'd never anticipated this reaction. He was rude and arrogant. She was sorry that they'd just ordered their meal. She felt stuck sitting there even though she knew she could get up and walk out anytime. But it was clear this would be her first and final meeting with her father. There would never be another time. Maybe by the end of the meal things would get better. Maybe he'd lighten up. Gemma, the eternal optimist, always looking for the silver lining, hoped for a better ending to what was so far a disgusting encounter.

"I know you wanted nothing to do with us," Gemma said softly. "I just thought, well, it's been a long time. Maybe things had changed. Maybe you felt differently now. I'm sorry I misled you. I didn't mean to, I wanted to tell you—"

"Time doesn't change anything," Jeffrey said. "So you're older. Big deal. Why does that make it any different? I made a decision years ago, and I expect the terms of that agreement to hold up."

Gemma felt the blood drain from her face. She could hardly breathe. Fortunately the food came quickly, and Jeffrey dug right in.

"Well," she said, "I don't think this could've gone worse. I knew this would be a shock to you, but I didn't expect you'd be this hostile. Perhaps over time you'll reconsider your position."

"Reconsider what, Gemma?" Jeffrey looked up from his plate. "What do you want me to reconsider? You? Do you want me to say, 'Hey, you're my daughter, I love you'? Or 'Cool, welcome to my family. We'll all get a pizza and celebrate. And let me put you in the will so everyone knows you're my daughter, too'? Is that what you want?"

The man had ice water in his veins. She'd never known anyone so bitter and hurtful. When she took one bite of food, she noticed Jeffrey's hands were shaking. His eating pattern had changed, too. He was manic, driving food into his mouth fast and furiously.

"I don't want your money, Jeffrey. I just wanted to know you. And I wanted you to know me. I'm not sure that you'll ever understand what it's like growing up without a father. I just wanted you to care . . . a little," Gemma said.

"Well, that's not going to happen. I have a family. Karen was a jerk. She let herself get pregnant and then insisted on having the baby." When he spoke, tiny fragments of food accidentally escaped from his mouth and landed on her plate. Some even got sprayed onto her silk dress. A souvenir from her great lunch that day. Jeffrey must've noticed, because he wiped his mouth on the napkin and then continued. She'd never seen him this angry. Never known this side of him. "I was pissed, frankly. It was wrong, and she knew it. It still infuriates me to think that she did that to me." Jeffrey picked up his phone and scrolled through his emails.

"Well, it's unfortunate that you feel that way. I was hoping you'd say . . . well, that you'd say something else." Gemma moved the food around on her plate but never managed to eat. "And just so you know, my mother is a great mom and I love her very much. She sacrificed a lot for me. Raised me on her own. Too bad you didn't really know her better."

Jeffrey put his phone in his pocket, asked for the check, and offered his card.

"I already paid," Gemma sighed.

"Oh, great, thanks. So are we done? And by the way, when I say done, I mean *done*—with me and my family. I don't think they cared much for you anyway, and like me, they wondered what the heck you were doing hanging around us when you should be living your own life."

"You're obviously angry," she said. By now she was shaking but trying to maintain a cool demeanor even though she was dying inside.

"And you wouldn't be? First being deceived and then blindsided like this?"

"I really enjoyed getting to know Scarlett," Gemma said, trying to change the subject. "She's wonderful. I'll miss her."

Gemma could barely hold back her tears. She lowered her head and stared at the napkin in her lap. Her salad was wilting, like her hair, her makeup, and everything else.

"I won't be coming by anymore," Gemma managed to say softly. She wasn't even sure Jeffrey heard her.

"Good." He sprang from the booth, grabbed his jacket, then turned around toward Gemma, who was slouched in the booth. "I'm sorry this isn't what you wanted. I wish you a good life."

Gemma didn't look up. She kept her eyes downcast and focused on her plate. When he was gone, she saw two tears fall onto the tablecloth. She couldn't keep them in. It was amazing she held them this long. The waiter swung by and asked if she needed anything. She shook her head.

Gemma signed the receipt, grabbed her purse, and headed for the exit.

The second she was safely inside her car, she began sobbing.

SARITA

"I think you should go to the hospital and see your dad," Kenzie said to Sarita, who was sitting in the chair on the other side of Kenzie's desk. "It doesn't matter what he said. If you want to see him, you should go."

Sarita reached for her backpack, which was on the ground next to her. "But he does not want to see me."

"That was two weeks ago, when he first went into the hospital." Kenzie's gaze landed softly on Sarita's eyes, and her voice was gentle. "It's time to go see him. You said he's gotten worse. It sounds like he may not make it. You must see him, Sarita. You have to. You need to say good- . . . Well, you need to go . . ."

"Okay," she said faintly. She wasn't convinced it was the right thing to do, but she did want to see him.

"Take as much time as you need," Kenzie said. Sarita stood, put on her backpack, and headed for the door.

"All right, but let me know if you need me to come back here to help with anything."

Kenzie got up from her chair and walked Sarita to the door. "Sarita, your father is seriously ill," she said. "Don't worry about work right now. We'll be fine. You need to be with him."

When she reached the door, Sarita turned and nodded to Gemma, who was sitting at the round table in Kenzie's office. "It was nice to meet you, Gemma. I'm sorry to hear about what happened with your dad at lunch the other day. It's his loss."

"That's so sweet, Sarita." Gemma moved over to the seat across from Kenzie's desk. "I appreciate that. It was a pleasure meeting you as well. And I'm glad you're going to the hospital to visit your dad. I hope he pulls through."

"Me too," Sarita said. She hugged Kenzie and then left her office.

* * * * *

Mohan Mahajan lay motionless in the ICU, tubes and IV lines attached to his body. Sarita's towering father, the one who set the rules and intimidated them all for so long, was helpless. Sarita walked in and placed a small vase of flowers she'd purchased at the hospital gift store on the table at the base of his bed. All she could hear was the steady rhythm of the ventilator pumping loudly. When she took his hand, his eyes slowly opened.

"Papa," she said softly, "I know you didn't want me to come. But I had to see you. You are my father. And I love you."

Papa lay still but didn't stop looking at her. He breathed heavily through the oxygen mask. She could tell he was deeply sedated. Mama told her he'd gotten better and had been off the ventilator and undergoing treatment for some time. But recently things had taken a bad turn and he was back in intensive care. Her sisters and mother had been at his side around the clock. Sarita was glad Kenzie insisted that she see him.

"I know you're disappointed in me, Papa. I know I didn't live up to your expectations. And I know you believe I've brought dishonor and shame to our family. I'm sorry I let you down."

Sarita was determined not to cry. She believed she had to be strong for her father. She knew he would never give her his blessing. He completely disapproved of everything she did. But she needed some kind of closure, some kind of discussion, even if it was one-sided. She watched as her father tried to reposition himself in the white sheets that enveloped his small and seemingly fragile body.

"Papa, is there anything I can do for you? Do you need a nurse?"

Papa shook his head and continued breathing steadily. The door opened and Mama approached.

"Oh, my darling," Mama whispered. She sounded surprised to see Sarita there. "I'm glad to see you." She rearranged the blanket slightly and placed the traditional Hindu prayer beads at the foot of her husband's bed. She leaned across Papa and kissed his forehead.

Sarita's throat constricted. She was scared. She'd never seen her father so weakened. She stood awkwardly shifting her weight from one foot to the other. Her hands were clenched, teeth chattering. The room was sterile and cold and smelled like bleach.

"Mohan," Mama said as she put another pillow under his head, "Sarita's come to make peace. She's come for your blessing."

Sarita was stunned. She started shaking her head.

"No, Mama, I would never expect that. No, it's okay. I know Papa is not happy with me. I don't want to upset him." Sarita's voice cracked.

Mama wrapped her arm around Sarita's shoulders and moved her gently toward the window so Papa could not hear their conversation.

"Do you remember the postcards Papa would send when you were away at camp in Maine?" Mama asked.

Sarita nodded.

"Do you remember the quotes he'd write on them? He had a library of books dedicated to quotations from the world's finest leaders. His favorite was Teddy Roosevelt's, which was, 'Believe you can and you're halfway there.'"

Sarita offered a weak smile as her mother continued.

"He only did that for you. His youngest daughter. The one he held in such high regard. And do you know why you were the special one?" Mama asked softly.

Sarita shook her head.

"Because you were the most like him. Stubborn. Obstinate. Opinionated. But also focused. And determined. Fiercely determined. Just like your father. And it's why the bar was set so high for you. Unlike your sisters, he expected more from you. You were the vessel to fulfill his unrealized dreams. You were his chosen one. But he applied too much pressure on you, and I told him as much many times."

She took Sarita's hand in hers, and after a pause she continued. "It is time, my darling. We need to let him go. He knows it, too. Papa and I are proud of the young woman you are. There is no shame in that. And I will not allow my daughter to feel her life must be lived under a black cloud, for you are a magnificent one. Your father had other ideas for you. But then you had ideas for yourself. And that is what makes you so special." Mama wiped a tear from her eye. "I've learned from you, my youngest one, that I must stand up for myself and for my daughters. I must ask for your forgiveness because I allowed it to go on too long."

"Oh, Mama, no, you—"

"But I did," she interrupted. "I was wrong."

Sarita took her mother's hand and kissed it. And then, after a beat, Mama went on to explain that Papa was in the final stages of cancer. It had returned with a vengeance. His body was ravaged. It could not stand any more treatment. The end was near. He would not be coming home. It wasn't as if Sarita didn't know. She did.

Sarita was impressed with her mother's strength, determination, and ability to deal with this tragic and desperate situation. She'd never seen this side of her, as her mother had lived in the shadow of her father. She had pitied her for her position in the world, for her subservient and agreeable nature, her willingness to go along with everything her father had wanted. But now she saw a different side. Mama was prepared to take over the helm. Sarita wondered if she had been there all along, if—even with her father's crazy edicts—her mother had always been the one quietly in charge.

Sarita gazed out the window at the street below, watching people going about their business, oblivious to her troubles. She knew that without Papa, things would be different. He was such a strong force in her life. Mama was right. Despite their differences, they were very much alike. They both had forceful, strong personalities.

Mama took Sarita's hand and placed it in Papa's. She moved back so Sarita could stand right next to her father.

"It's time you two put aside your differences," Mama said to both Papa and Sarita. "Sarita is a grown woman. She will make her own choices. Some we won't agree with. Papa and I have given you what you need in this world. And now you must find your way."

Sarita's mouth was so dry. She didn't know what to say. She hated seeing her father like this, frail, helpless, and sad. She gazed at his deep-brown eyes, which were half-closed. And then she felt him squeeze her hand.

She stood at his bedside for a while, just holding his hand. And then the words came to her. The words she had heard as a small child. She moved a chair next to his bed and continued to hold his hand. She began singing her father's favorite song, the song his mother sang to him when he was a boy. It was a Hindu lullaby that he'd sung to all his daughters when they were young children. The lullaby was about making one's way in life but never giving up on one's dreams. Sarita hadn't thought about that song till now. And it was stunning how she remembered all the words and the inflections, which she sang in his native tongue.

Sarita sang softly, her eyes closed, remembering the many times her father had sung these words to her. Mama reached for a tissue as she watched and listened to her daughter. She whispered that it was the voice of an angel.

Papa closed his eyes but never let go of Sarita's hand. Sarita thought she could make out a faint sound from her father, as if he was trying to hum along with her.

When Sarita hit the last note, she held it for as long as she could and brought the lullaby softly to a close. She lowered her eyes and saw her father's brimming with tears as he peered up at her.

"Papa," she whispered, "I listened to that song over and over. I recited the lyrics whenever I felt lonely or worried. I remembered you singing it to me when I was a young girl. You told me to never give up on my dream. Do you remember that?"

Papa closed his eyes.

"I did what you wanted. I never gave up on my dream. And my dream has been to be a singer. It's what I want. And I knew it the first day you sang this lullaby to me. I wanted to sing like you, Papa. I longed to have a beautiful voice like yours. I worked at it through the years, and now I'm about to get my first big break. I'm a finalist in a singing competition."

Sarita watched her father closely to see if there was any response.

"But later, Papa," she continued, "when it's the right time, I will go to India, just as you've asked. I will honor your wishes and learn about my ancestry. I will. For you, Papa. I will honor your wishes."

There was a long pause as Sarita held Papa's hand. Mama dabbed at her eyes to catch the tears before Papa noticed them. Sarita clung to her father's hand and searched his eyes for some kind of response.

He slowly closed his eyes and squeezed her hand. He held it for a long time. And then she noticed a faint smile as he opened and closed his eyes again. Sarita let out a sigh. She savored the warmth of his hand in hers. She didn't want to let go. Instead, she offered a gentle squeeze back.

As she gazed at him his smile faded and his hand fell from hers. Her mother moaned. And then she knew. He was gone. Sarita fell to her knees. She rested her head on his chest and cried uncontrollably.

Mama embraced her as their gut-wrenching sobs filled the room.

BRYNNE

Brynne had never been to Macy's. She shopped on Rodeo Drive in Beverly Hills, where the salespeople hustled to her the second she set foot in their stores.

Today was her fifth day working behind the linen counter on the third floor at the Macy's in the Fashion Center mall in the San Fernando Valley. She had a job. It was more money and far better than waitressing at Mo's, where she'd lasted two days.

She understood the world of sheets. She used to purchase the 100 percent Egyptian cotton sateen ones directly from Frette in Italy. Macy's had regular cotton sheets. And frankly, they seemed just fine. She'd slept on crappy linens at the hotel and now at the apartment but survived. No hives. No bed bugs. She was done with expensive sheets.

It had been a brutal two months, but Brynne was slowly coming back. Selling her horses had been the hardest part. But that money along with her new job gave her a fresh start. She was looking forward to a new life. She embraced her job and worked hard to become the best sales associate the department ever had. Brynne was sitting on the floor of the stockroom, rearranging the linens according to color, when a customer strolled inside looking for assistance.

"Hello? Ma'am? Is anyone there? I need some sheets for my son, who's going to college. I'll need several sets, as he throws them away instead of washing them. Kids today."

Brynne looked up and saw her friend Patty staring down at her. The second their eyes met, Brynne felt her stomach drop. What was her old friend Patty doing shopping at Macy's? Patty looked equally surprised to see Brynne on the floor of the stockroom.

"Brynne?" Patty asked. "What in God's name are you doing here? In Macy's? On the floor? In the Valley? Oh my gosh, you have a name tag. Do you? Are you work—no, you're not a salesgirl, are you? Are you working here? Oh my Lord."

Brynne stood up. She took a deep breath and held her head high, as if by doing so she'd gain some confidence. The last time she had seen Patty was at the dinner with Chase and Kenzie. Brynne had been on top of the world then. That was a different time, and yet not so long ago.

"Yes, Patty, I'm working here," Brynne said proudly as she brushed herself off and walked past her out of the storeroom and onto the floor. "And I'd be happy to show you some sheets for your son. Sam, right? You need a few sets?"

"Well, yes, that's why I'm here. At Macy's. I wanted some, well, some inexpensive sheets, since I have to buy a few. But first, I'm sorry," Patty said as she picked up her pace, following Brynne out of the storeroom. "I heard about you and Martin. And, well, I guess this happens. But you're working here? Things must be awfully bad," Patty said sympathetically. She then whispered so no one else could hear, "Do you need some money? I have a hundred-dollar bill. I took it out of Fred's wallet this morning. But I can always get more."

Brynne waved her away. "I don't need money, but thank you," Brynne said. "I'm making my own now, and I'm thrilled. It's about time, don't you think? I feel alive. I'm enjoying it here." Brynne wasn't completely convinced of this. But she sure wasn't going to let Patty take pity on her.

"But Brynne, you are a . . . well, you're a sales—"

"*Associate,* Patty. The words are *sales associate.*"

Patty just stared at her.

"So let me show you some sheets from our Martha Stewart Collection that would be perfect for your son," Brynne said as she moved toward the section. "And where did you say Sam is going to school?"

Patty followed as Brynne showed her a variety of sheets, extolling their virtues. She knew Patty wanted to know everything. Every detail about her fall from grace. But she would not reveal a thing.

* * * * *

When Brynne got home after work she tossed her purse onto the creaky breakfast table that came with her furnished apartment, and then kicked off her shoes and slid into bed without getting undressed. Leaving the Holiday Inn had been good, but to her this apartment was temporary housing, too. She couldn't wait to get out of there. The only personal item she'd put on display was a photo of her beautiful twin girls. She lay in bed and gazed at their picture, wondering how they were holding up, whether they were doing their schoolwork, getting enough sleep, and attending to their classes. She'd sent them more texts, but their responses were always brief: *We're good.* Or *We love you.* It wasn't nearly enough for Brynne. She was desperate to have a longer discussion with them about the impact of divorce.

Brynne and Martin rarely spoke, relying on email and text messages when they needed to exchange information. Although Brynne's days were busy and she enjoyed helping her customers, at night she was filled with sorrow. Thinking about how much she'd lost was overwhelming. She'd often lie in bed at night consumed with sadness and misery. Brynne had never expected to be alone on a rented bed in a crappy furnished apartment in the prime of her life.

She thought about her conversation with Kenzie in the car outside her mother's home a while ago. She wished she had listened to her then. Kenzie was right that Martin would leave and her life would change. Boy, had she misjudged Kenzie.

While she lay fully clothed, listlessly sinking into her nightly melancholy under the covers, the doorbell rang, but she didn't move. She wasn't expecting anyone. There were plenty of transients in this complex. Some would ring her bell to see if she wanted to get dinner. But Brynne wasn't interested in socializing. She wanted to get the heck out of there. She was focused on a steady income and a permanent home.

The bell rang again.

"How about some dinner?" she heard Jasmine call as she let herself into the studio apartment and set a few bags on the table. "I don't think it's wise to leave your door unlocked. Anyone can just walk in."

"Was it unlocked? Oh no, I meant to lock it," Brynne said from beneath the covers.

"You can't just lie in that bed every single night, Brynne," Jasmine said as she started to unpack the bags. "I stopped at the market and picked up some things for you. You're losing too much weight."

"I'm fine, Ma. But thank you for getting the groceries," Brynne said as she pulled the covers over her head.

"Brynne, you're not taking care of yourself!" Jasmine shouted as she placed items in the cabinets and refrigerator. "You're a shadow of your former self. You're working too hard and not eating."

Brynne got out of bed and walked to the kitchenette. She sat down and watched as her mother continued putting food in the cabinets.

"You know what they say, Ma," Brynne said. "You can't be too rich or too thin. I had rich, now I'm going for thin."

"Why don't you see someone, Brynne?" Jasmine stopped what she was doing and looked directly at her. "This is a terrible loss. I can't imagine you can just get over this that easily. I remember when your father left, I saw a therapist. He helped me get back on my feet. Might do you some good."

Brynne lit a cigarette, which Jasmine hated, and Jasmine fanned the smoke away to show her disdain. Brynne opened the door and stood on the balcony she shared with the other tenants, smoking, while her mother continued unloading the bags.

"I'll be okay," Brynne said as she took a long drag on her cigarette. "I'm doing well at Macy's. I'll get there. You know I'm tough. I'll make it."

Jasmine folded the bags and put them under her arm. "Put that thing out and come sit here."

Brynne crushed out the cigarette and sat next to her mom at the small table. Its legs were unsteady; the table lurched from side to side.

"I want you to have something," Jasmine said as she reached into her purse and pulled out a cashier's check. "It's just a couple thousand dollars."

"Huh?" Brynne's jaw dropped. "What? Where'd you get this? Who's this from?"

"It's from me," Jasmine said as she placed her hand on top of Brynne's. "It's a loan but with no interest due. You can pay me back when you're ready."

"Where'd you get this? I can't take your money. You barely have any, and I—"

"I have plenty." Jasmine laughed. She stopped, then looked at Brynne and smiled. "I worked and saved. Just because I didn't live large doesn't mean I wasn't financially astute. When your father walked out, I was determined to make it on my own. And you may remember I took plenty of classes and worked my way through college. I not only got myself several degrees, I learned how to manage my life. I didn't need the accoutrements to show how well I did. This is just a little something to help you along. But mostly I want you to learn how to manage your money so that you'll be financially independent and never, and I mean never, have to rely on someone else. You hear me?"

Jasmine got up to leave, but Brynne stopped her.

"Ma . . . I . . ." Her throat closed. "Thank you," she said. "I'm just—"

"You're welcome," Jasmine interrupted. "But, Brynne, your happiness won't come from external wealth. I always told you that. It'll come from your intrinsic values, from your personal growth, relationships, and all the good you bring to others. Now get yourself out of that bed, put some meat on those bones, and work hard so you can get out of debt and get on with your life. We are resilient folk." Jasmine kissed Brynne on the cheek and then waltzed out the door.

KENZIE

It was opening day at Grayson Downs.

The place was bustling. The parking lot was full, and crowds swarmed the entrance. Kenzie strolled the plaza just beyond the turnstiles, where she saw women decked out in summer dresses with pretty, wide-brimmed hats checking out the various vendors lined up on both sides of the concourse. Manicurists, hairdressers, jewelry designers, dating advisers, career counselors, horse trainers, breeders, financial consultants, personal shoppers, home improvement pros, safety experts, restaurateurs—and, yes, even a psychic—had set up shop. There were people everywhere. Old and young, veteran racetrackers and new customers. Men and plenty of women. She'd never seen anything like it.

And, of course, the longest line was to meet the "talking horse" from the promotional video. Fans waited for more than an hour to get their photos taken with the legendary horse.

"You did an amazing job." Gemma wrapped her arms around Kenzie. "I'm proud of you. I knew you could do this. You can do anything."

"I'm just thrilled you're here," Kenzie said.

"Hey, I brought my assistant, Adam, and two other execs from the studio with me," Gemma said as she looked around the concourse for them. "Oh, there they are—in line for a selfie with the robotic horse!" Gemma laughed. "Look at this place. You are back, kid. You *are* back."

Gemma gave Kenzie a big hug. "I'd stay longer, but I want to get over to that psychic's booth. I'm sure you're just dying to know what she has to say."

"Fine, but I don't want to meet her. Okay? Ever. Promise?"

"Believe me," Gemma said, "if she's a real psychic, she already knows she doesn't want to meet you and wind up like Annalisa."

"Very funny. Give her my best," Kenzie said as Gemma took off.

Now Matt seemed to appear out of nowhere. Dressed in a pair of black jeans, a white shirt with the sleeves rolled up, cowboy boots, and his trademark Yankees cap, he looked strong and masculine. He approached cautiously and stood a few feet from her. "How you doing?"

"Good . . . I'm doing well." They'd only seen each other briefly, in passing, since he brought her flowers a month ago.

"Leo said this is the largest opening day in Grayson's history." Matt's eyes were focused on hers. "Your marketing expertise really paid off. And look at your women's expo. It's like a singles bar with manicures instead of mojitos."

"Yeah, who would've thought a home improvement booth would attract more women than men? And look who's lined up for the dating service—men." She laughed, trying to ease the tension between them. "Brynne really came through. She recruited a bunch of these vendors. I mean, Saks, Vince, L'Occitane? Out here in the middle of nowhere at Grayson?"

"Don't forget Macy's." Matt's gaze shifted to a booth in the corner. "Brynne's taking care of her business, too."

"Wearing a designer dress, canary hat, matching pumps, handing out business cards attached to washcloths," Kenzie said.

"Hey, how about my pal Craig Susser, free chocolate bread pudding for the masses," Matt said.

"And he's here because of you. Thank you," Kenzie said softly. She took another long look around the concourse. "Look, there's Sarita and Damien," she cried as she pointed to a booth at the far end. "I'm so glad Sarita's here. Her father's funeral was just a few weeks ago. And yet there she is pimping Goth body artists to racing fans. That's amazing."

"The racetrack is a place where everyone's equal." Matt surveyed the premises. "Famous jockeys, hall-of-fame trainers, wealthy owners, and two-dollar bettors, all sharing the same space. Everyone's welcome, and that's what the expo is about. It has something for everyone. Not just women."

Kenzie stared at him. "You get it. You really get it." They shared a long glance.

A flash of red from the corner of her eye distracted her. "Oh, wow, there's the tram taking fans on the backstretch tour," Kenzie said. "Those tours are the most fun. Nothing like getting up close and personal with the talent."

"And look at Leo." Matt grinned while he stuffed his hands in his pockets. "He and Glenn strutting around like they own the place. Like it was all their doing."

"Leo deserves plenty of credit," Kenzie said. "He hired me. He let me do my job. He had amazing faith in me. More than I had in myself."

There was a silence.

"I had faith in you, too." Matt gave her a subtle wink.

Kenzie knew. But she didn't have the courage to say it. She looked off in the distance, counting the house, trying to collect herself.

"Well, I'd better get going." Matt started to amble away. "First post in less than an hour. But congratulations, well done."

"Wait." Kenzie looked up at Matt. "Wait. I have something to tell you." She paused, looked down, then raised her eyes to Matt's. "First, I owe you a belated thank-you for rescuing me when you did onstage. And second, I'm sorry," she whispered. "You were right when you said I'm afraid to really love someone. I just . . . well, I just don't want to suffer more loss. But I learned something from Gemma. Sometimes you have to push past the fear and take the chance. It took me a long time to understand that, but—"

"It's okay." Matt reached for her hand and drew her closer to him. Then he wrapped his arm around her shoulders, and she nestled her head against his chest. It felt so wonderful. So warm. So secure.

"And yes, the business with the ring was eating at me," Kenzie said. "I know you're not the owner. I had to let that go, too. I was obsessing over the fortune-teller's prediction. But I feel happy when I'm with you. And that's what I want in my life. I want to feel happy again. I don't want to lose you, Matt. I'm so sorry for, well . . . everything."

Matt caressed her arm and kissed the top of her head. "I missed you terribly. I never wanted to lose you. Never. And I've never stopped thinking about you. Not once. When I'm with you my world lights up. I've never loved anyone as much as I do you. I'm so happy to have you back in my arms again."

"Let's just call what happened a hiatus," Kenzie said softly as they both instinctively started to move away from the crowds and into a corner under the grandstand so they could be alone. "And pick up where we left off."

"Deal." Matt stood across from her with his hands on her shoulders. He looked into her eyes and then lowered his voice. "Not a day went by that I didn't think about you and miss the good times we shared. I didn't care how much time it took, I was never going to give up on you."

Matt's penetrating gaze never broke from hers. He cupped the back of her neck and pulled her tenderly toward him. He kissed her softly, then long and deep. After a moment Matt gently stepped way. "I want you to enjoy today." He tucked a stray strand of hair behind her ear. "This is a huge accomplishment, Kenzie. It's yours. And nothing's going to take that away."

Kenzie smiled as Matt squeezed her hand, and they moved out from under the grandstand and back onto the concourse, joining the crowd that continued to grow. As they headed for the boxes, Chase Fielding approached. At first Kenzie was taken aback. She didn't expect to see him here on opening day.

"Hey, Kenzie, looks like a great turnout!" Chase said. "What a job you did selling this place. Look at the crowd."

"Thanks, Chase, so glad you could come out. I'd like you to meet Matt Gibson, the best jockeys' agent in California."

As they shook hands, a young woman came over to Chase. He grasped her hand and introduced her to Kenzie.

"And this is my fiancée, Ellen. She was the hospice nurse for my mom," Chase said as he draped his arm around the woman's shoulders and then pointed to the ring on her finger. "My mom's ring. We thought it was lost, but I found it when I went through her things."

"I'm glad," Kenzie said. "Nice to meet you." She was happy to see that Chase had such a sweet-looking girlfriend and relieved to know that he'd found his mother's ring.

It hadn't been *her* ring after all. Of course. "Well, nice seeing you, Chase. Have a good time, and congrats to you both."

"The director, right?" Matt asked as he watched Chase and Ellen walk through the concourse and into the grandstand.

"Yep," Kenzie said.

"Is he the one who got away?" Matt asked.

Kenzie looked up at Matt, reached behind his neck, and brought his face close to hers.

"No, Matt. You were the one who *almost* got away, and I'm glad that didn't happen."

Matt lowered his head and kissed her sweetly.

"So, I just want to be clear. You're done with the ring now? We're going to put that behind us?" he asked when they broke apart.

"Yes. Yes, we are," she said fervently. "I loved it. It was beautiful and had such a wonderful history, but it wasn't mine. Sold it on eBay last week. It's over. I don't want to hear about it anymore," Kenzie said.

"Hope you got some good bucks for it," Matt said as he took her hand.

"Of course I did. Would you expect anything less from the person who got this track back on its feet?" Kenzie cocked her head.

"I would expect nothing less of you, Miss Kenzie Armstrong. Now, shall we go bet some of that money and turn it into something even bigger?"

"Of course!" Kenzie and Matt walked hand in hand toward the betting windows.

GEMMA

"Happy birthday!" Adam said. He greeted Gemma as she entered her office. He was holding a beautiful white cake with pink roses.

"You're the best assistant ever. Thank you. I want a piece right now, I can't wait."

Gemma tossed her bag onto the sofa as Adam placed the cake on her desk, grabbed a knife, and sliced a generous piece onto a plate. He handed it to her.

"The perfect way to start my day," she said, taking a bite. "Although I have to admit I ate too much at opening day yesterday. The aftertaste of the corn dog does linger."

"I want to get out there again soon. Had a great time," Adam said as he walked back to his desk just outside her office.

"Kenzie would be thrilled to hear that. Tell her." Gemma reached for a napkin to pick up the crumbs that had fallen onto her desk.

"I think it will be a light day here," Adam said as he grabbed the call sheet, then returned to her office. "You don't have a heavy schedule."

"Great news. Best present," Gemma muttered with her mouth full. "Anything going on?"

"Not too much, except Stephen had to attend a memorial this afternoon. His office asked if you'd take one meeting for him at three o'clock, so I moved your two conference calls to tomorrow, and then at five o'clock you have drinks with Lizzie Rawson, the ICM agent at the Four Seasons."

Gemma trusted Adam to organize her day. In fact, he was a much better assistant than she ever was. He was thorough and disciplined and made sure every detail was in order. He made Gemma's life easy in every way.

Gemma sat at her desk and pulled up her emails. She was happy to do anything for Stephen. He'd given her a great opportunity and continued to offer generous support and guidance.

"Okay, so what's the three o'clock meeting about? And who's coming?" Gemma asked.

"It's with Clark Lisbett, the screenwriter, and Jake and Kyle Hobson, producing. I think there are some other producers as well. They're pitching a film based on a book. I think one of them is friendly with Stephen, which is why the meeting was set with him," Adam read from his notes.

"Okay, fine." Gemma didn't look up from her computer. She knew Adam had it all under control.

"By the way," Adam said, "you had a zillion calls already, many of which were birthday messages. I emailed them to you."

"Okay, thanks. Now I'm going to give myself a birthday present and relax this morning. Since that rarely happens, I figure that's a pretty good gift, don't you? Please get the usual salad delivered so I can read some scripts through lunch, and then I'll take that meeting. I want to enjoy this light day," Gemma said.

"Great idea," Adam said as he closed Gemma's door so she could be alone.

Gemma was comfortable, in a good place. She already had three films in production. She knew Stephen had great confidence in her abilities.

Now that Jeffrey was out of her life, things were easier. Their meeting at the restaurant last month would be with her forever. And even though she was extremely hurt by what he'd said—and more than once considered sending him a letter telling him what a no-good bastard he was—she'd said what she had to say and could now move on. She'd adhered to his wishes and hadn't contacted Scarlett again. And even when Scarlett texted, she didn't reply.

In the meantime, Gemma and her mom had become much closer. Gemma had begun to really understand how difficult life had been for her mother. And now she appreciated why her mom had gone to such lengths to hide the truth about Jeffrey.

Gemma spent the morning reading scripts and answering emails. There were no fires to put out. No one walked off a set. No one demanded more money. No one complained about their budget. No one begged for a new director. Every day it seemed there was some drama, but today there was just blissful calm.

Which ended at three o'clock when Adam opened the door to Gemma's office, and the guests burst in like a tornado.

Gemma didn't know what hit her. Nine men with big personalities took over the room, all fired up and ready to get their project sold. Adam announced their names in rapid order. Gemma couldn't keep up. She had no idea who was who. She hoped they'd all fit on her couch and chairs. It wasn't unusual to have large meetings, but this was certainly one of the biggest. She did her best to focus on the screenwriter, Clark Lisbett, and the two producers, Kyle and Jake Hobson, whom she knew well and who sat right in front of her on the white sofa.

Adam passed out bottles of water to the guests seated on three sides of the glass coffee table. Gemma sat down on a white upholstered chair, alone on the fourth side, and crossed her legs. It was at that moment the door opened and another person entered.

Jeffrey Kahn.

What the heck was he doing here? Without glancing once at Gemma, he moved quickly, taking the one open seat to her left.

She swallowed hard, determined not to betray emotion. "So, gentlemen, as you know, Stephen had an emergency today. He asked that I meet with you," Gemma said. She had a sudden, terrible twitch in her right eye and had a hard time catching her breath. She repositioned herself, switching one leg over the other, hoping to get more comfortable, and kept her eyes fixed on the others.

"Thank you for taking the meeting, Gemma," Kyle Hobson said. "This came about in a strange way. My attorney, Jared Rogers, pitched our idea to Stephen at lunch, and he thought it might make a good movie. He asked that we come back with a story. So we're here to tell you what it's about." Kyle Hobson was a big, overweight man with a Southern drawl. "Did he mention it to you at all?"

Before Gemma even had a chance to respond, Jeffrey spoke.

"Sorry to interrupt. I'm Jeffrey Kahn. My partner, Jared Rogers, couldn't make it but asked that I cover for him. Just not sure we should take this meeting with . . . uh, with Gemma," Jeffrey said. "Jared wanted Stephen to hear the pitch, but his office just sent me over here. I think we oughta hold off and present it to Stephen when he's available."

"No, I think we're fine. We'll go ahead," Kyle Hobson said. He was annoyed.

Jeffrey held his ground. "I think we ought to do this another time."

"All due respect, sir," Kyle said. "We know Gemma. She's a great executive, and we're going to pitch to her. She has excellent credentials."

Gemma sat quietly. Kyle smiled in her direction, trying to save this awkward meeting. Jeffrey insisted that the men huddle for a moment. Gemma's leg bounced nervously as she waited for them to arrive at a decision.

After a few moments Jeffrey stood up and said the group would return when Stephen was available. It was clear to everyone that Kyle and Jake did not agree. But Gemma knew Jeffrey couldn't bear being in the room one moment longer. She held the cards, and he couldn't stand it. When everyone got up from their seats, Gemma asked them to wait.

"Gentlemen," she said, "please sit down. I'd like to say something before you leave."

She waited as everyone took their seats.

"You're certainly free to reschedule this meeting with Stephen. I'm sure he'd understand and welcome you back. However, I want to mention one thing. I believe I can speak on my boss's behalf when I say that we'd prefer that when you return, it's not with Mr. Jeffrey Kahn. I'm sure none of you are aware that Mr. Kahn is my father."

There were audible gasps as they all stared at Jeffrey, who was seated on the sofa. He closed his eyes and looked down at the mention of his name.

"Yes, he is. We've been estranged since my birth. You see, he got my mother pregnant at his best friend's bachelor party, and though he owned up to it financially, he refused to acknowledge that I was his daughter. I sought him out recently, but he wanted no part of me. In fact, he was downright mean. So I don't ever want to see this man again. I'm sorry you weren't able to pitch your project to us. My assistant, Adam, will provide parking validations. Thank you so much for coming in today."

The men hadn't moved. They were flabbergasted and speechless. As Gemma gathered her paperwork and purse, she saw Kyle

Hobson's face turn beet red. He glared at Jeffrey, who sat on the couch with his head in his hands.

"Oh, and one last thing," Gemma said as she moved toward the door. "It's my birthday. Thank you for making it so special. It's certainly one I won't forget."

Gemma smiled sweetly, held her head high, marched out of her office, and never looked back.

SARITA

Sarita was having a hard time regaining her focus. She'd start to run an errand, then forget where she was going. At home she'd sit on her bed and stare into space, fully expecting to hear her father knocking on the door.

The funeral, food, flowers, notes, hugs, and the warmth of her community had happened all at once. Now she was alone with her thoughts, and she continued to feel her father's absence. Somehow she'd managed to get through opening day earlier that week, even though it had only been three weeks since her father passed.

She'd read Papa's note so many times that it was already worn and stained, but it would be the last note she'd ever receive from him. She had to keep it forever. Despite their tumultuous relationship, Sarita believed that when he'd squeezed her hand, it symbolized a rapprochement. Reconciliation. Her mother said it was his blessing. He had given her what she always wanted: acceptance.

Even so, grief took its toll on Sarita. She felt guilty about not living up to her father's expectations and yet was relieved that she could live the life she wanted. There was no rebellion anymore, no anxiety about being the daughter her father wanted. She was free from Thursday-night suitors. She didn't have to sneak around and hide her identity anymore.

"Sarita!" Mama was calling from downstairs. "Your boss, Kenzie, is here. She wants to see you. Can you come down?"

Sarita jumped off her bed, opened the door, and ran down the stairs. Kenzie had never been to her home. She wondered why she was there. Kenzie stood in the doorway holding Sarita's backpack high in the air.

"Forget something?" she asked with a sympathetic smile.

"Oh, gosh, I didn't even know I lost it. That's so nice of you," Sarita said as she met Kenzie in the living room and invited her to sit down on the couch next to her.

Mama had left quickly to continue a card game under way in the dining room.

"I'm glad you were able to come to opening day this week, and it was good to see you back at work the last few days," Kenzie said gently when they were settled. "It means a lot that you're so devoted to your job. But, Sarita, you need to take some time. To grieve. To feel the sadness."

"Yeah, I know." Sarita lowered her eyes.

"Don't pretend it's not there. 'Cause it'll catch up with you, like it did with me. I don't want that to happen to you."

"I can't believe he's gone," said Sarita after a pause. "I miss him."

"I know." Kenzie took her hand. "It's hard losing a parent, especially when you're so young. I'm not surprised you left your backpack at work. Grief does that to you. It makes you kinda feel like you're in a daze sometimes."

"Yup, I'm easily distracted," Sarita said.

"You will be for a while. But I understand." She smiled and then stood. "I have to get going. Just wanted to drop this off."

Sarita walked her to the door. "Thanks for bringing it over. And thanks for being there for me." Sarita hugged Kenzie, then watched as she walked down the sidewalk and got into her car.

She thought about what Kenzie had said. She wished she could get out of this fuzzy reality and back to herself. But she felt an overwhelming sense of sadness. How could anything good come from her father's death? How could she ever feel anything but pain over the loss of her papa?

She was reluctant to leave her mother. She wanted to stay in her home, on her bed, looking at photographs, reading poems, and writing songs. She felt the need to be around her father, around his things. For a time she couldn't wait to get out of there, but her feelings were far different now. She wanted to do all the things her father had wanted when he was alive. She felt tremendous guilt that she hadn't allowed herself to be more open to his ideas.

With so little energy, she couldn't imagine participating in the singing contest in a few days. Weeks had passed since the last time she'd performed at Deathrock Bar. But Moody Gray, the lead guitarist in Witches of Skeletal Symphony, had been on tour. Now he was back, and he wanted to be the one to crown the winner. With a break in his schedule, the final competition was imminent.

And yet Sarita was mired in grief. She lay on the living room couch and thought about how her father's death created so much conflict about the choices she'd made. Were they real choices or just childish rebellion? She thought about Damien, who was the polar opposite of her father. Damien didn't follow a script. He lived in the present, enjoyed his life, and encouraged Sarita to do the same.

Damien checked on Sarita constantly. Mama was impressed with his affection for her daughter. Both he and her mother encouraged her to get out of the house and go to the club. They thought she spent too much time in her room, brooding. Enough time had passed—it was time for her to resume life.

But that was the problem. Sarita wasn't sure what life it was.

"Everyone misses you," Damien said as he plopped down beside Sarita on the chair in her bedroom. "Your mom said Kenzie stopped by earlier today." Sarita nodded. "So . . . do you feel like going to the club tonight?"

"I don't know," she said, staring at the floor. "Not sure I'm ready to go out. I feel like I should stick around here."

Damien sat quietly. They'd had so many of these conversations lately. He'd ask her to come to the club, and she'd offer the same answer. No matter what he said, she'd never go.

"I might make plans to go to India, like my father wanted," she said. "Maybe I should go sooner rather than later." Damien put his arm around her and pulled her close. "I'm questioning so much about my life and the choices I've made."

"Take the time you need," he said. "I'll be here no matter what you decide."

Sarita placed her hand in his and took comfort in his words.

"I wish I could move beyond this, but I can't," she said. "I just wasn't prepared for him to be gone this fast. I feel lost. I didn't realize how much influence he had."

Damien rocked her in his arms and kissed the top of her head. She turned and gazed into his brown eyes. His emerald-green Mohawk, deep-black bushy eyebrows, silver nose ring, and giant ear piercings were beautiful to her. Her father must've been terrified of Damien, but he never knew what a kind and sensitive man he was. She wondered what he would've thought had they gotten to know each other. He'd probably be shocked to learn that Damien was more like him than he could ever imagine. Damien was well read, full of ambition, and close to his own family. If only her father had been more open. If only he had appreciated the impact Damien had on his daughter. If only he had understood how respectful Damien was and that, like him, he wanted only the best for Sarita.

But even if Sarita had agreed to an arranged marriage, would she and her father have agreed on a suitor? Never. It never would've happened. They locked horns on almost everything. So why was she pretending her father was some saint when he wasn't? Why in death did he appear to be someone other than who he was in life?

"Text me if you change your mind," Damien said as he got up to leave. "I'm gonna hang out with the guys for a while and then catch a set or two at the club."

Sarita smiled as he leaned down to kiss her. When he opened the door, Mama was on the other side, waiting to enter. She embraced Damien and offered him some food to take.

How odd that her mother, who had been horrified by Damien's presence in their home several weeks ago, was so accepting of him today. Sarita watched as her mom placed her hand on Damien's shoulder and kissed his cheek. She couldn't help but wonder what her father would've thought. She believed he would've been furious.

"You don't want to go out tonight?" Mama asked.

"Mama, what has happened? Weeks ago you would never have approved of my relationship with Damien. And now, now that Papa is gone, it's suddenly okay?"

Mama sat down beside her on the bed and wrapped her arm around Sarita's shoulders.

"Parents have a choice in life," Mama said. "They can accept their children, work hard to change them, or reject them. Despite what you might think, Papa and I had our disagreements, too. Perhaps not in front of you but certainly behind closed doors. He wasn't always right, my dear."

Mama smiled as she smoothed Sarita's hair.

"Do you think Papa would've accepted Damien?"

"Eventually," Mama said. "We were certainly surprised to learn about your lifestyle. But you are still our daughter. Our precious Sarita. Papa was set in his ways. But in the end I'm not sure he'd really abandon his youngest daughter. And, of course, I would never have let that happen."

Both of them sat still as Sarita thought about her mother's words.

"I'm trying to figure out who I am now," Sarita said. "For some reason I'm more confused than ever. I don't want to disappoint Papa. I've been thinking about giving up singing. It's really a frivolous endeavor. Maybe I should take over Papa's business, as he wanted, find a suitable husband, and settle down. It was something I never in my wildest dreams wanted, and yet now that he's gone, I feel confused, like nothing really matters anymore."

"What was that song you sang to Papa?" Mama asked. "Wasn't it the one about following your dreams? Wasn't it what Papa sang to you all those years? Did you forget about that song already? Did you forget that Papa squeezed your hand? Did you not know what he was saying?" Tears welled from Mama's eyes as Sarita started to hum the tune.

Of course she remembered. That memory would be with her forever.

"Papa is still with you, my love. His life is over, but yours is just beginning. He would want you to live your life. Not his."

As Sarita snuggled in her mother's arms, she sang the song again. Mama closed her eyes. The powerful sound of Sarita's voice filled the air.

She was sure Papa was listening.

BRYNNE

"Sam liked the sheets," Patty said as she passed by the stockroom. She placed the new bedding she intended to purchase next to the register and then returned to the door of the stockroom. "You were right. I've come back for more."

"Glad they worked out." Brynne was busy restocking the shelves. Patty walked back to the register and waited for Brynne to finish what she was doing.

"How is everything? Are you doing okay?" Patty asked as Brynne stood up, straightened her suit jacket, then walked over to the register. She began plucking through the items and scanning the codes into the computer.

"Doing well, and you?" Brynne asked politely. She'd moved up to assistant manager of the department in just a few weeks and had become adept at dealing with all kinds of personalities. Her goal was to be a bright and shining star to all her customers, because the more they talked about how great she was, the more promotions she'd receive and the more money she'd earn. She'd figured it out quickly. But then, Brynne was a quick study. She'd also learned that salespeople were the scapegoats for customers' bad behavior. She couldn't believe the rude attitudes, the grand sense of entitlement, and the demeaning comments. But of course, she had once been that way, too.

"I'm doing well," Patty said as she watched Brynne expertly scan the merchandise into the machine. "I've not told anyone you're here. I wouldn't do that to you. I didn't want to make you feel ashamed. Instead, I thought I'd help by buying some more linens from you."

"That's so kind." Brynne grabbed a few bags from under the counter. "But it's okay to tell others. I'm not embarrassed at all."

"Really?" Patty asked. "I mean of course, you're right, what was I thinking. No, nothing to be ashamed of. I just thought, well, I guess none of us ever expected that you, Brynne, that you of all people would be a *salesgirl*."

Brynne stuffed the sheets into the bags and handed them to Patty.

"I'm assistant manager of this department now," Brynne said. "I've had what the HR person describes as a meteoric rise. I'm quite pleased. It's definitely been challenging. But I'm doing well."

"Well, great," Patty said as she grabbed her bags. "Much good luck to you, Brynne."

"And to you and Fred," Brynne said as Patty moved away from the counter. Brynne bit her lip through the entire conversation. She knew Patty didn't even realize that her tone was condescending, offensive, and hurtful. But Brynne wasn't about to point it out. Instead, she thought about mentioning what she read in the *New York Post* last week. That Fred only had to serve two years instead of four for embezzling company funds. It had been a well-kept secret, until now. Fred would be going to prison once his appeals were exhausted. Now *that* was something to be ashamed of.

The old Brynne would have blurted that out the second Patty arrived. But not now. She enjoyed her job and didn't want to jeopardize anything. She loved the paycheck. That was the most fun. More important, she was less judgmental and felt good about herself. Patty couldn't define her.

Brynne's fancy suits were perfect for her new role as assistant manager. Granted, she looked far better than the other employees in her expensive duds and was often mistaken for a customer. She was learning how to capitalize on what she had to continue moving up the ladder.

Her mother's check certainly helped, but drawing a paycheck and building a career was far more exciting. She hoped to pay her mother back soon. It had been a good lesson for her. If her mother managed to succeed above her dire circumstances, then so could she.

Brynne was no hypocrite. She would be the first to say she missed a lot about the life she once had. She particularly missed Grayson and her horses. She laughed, thinking about her days as the grande dame of Grayson Downs. But being back there for opening day earlier this week had been bittersweet. She'd felt a pang of sadness when she drove home that evening.

At night she was glued to her computer, learning about women who had exited careers to have children and returned to the working world later in life. She read about starting new careers. She spent the rest of her time learning about finances. She took seminars on the weekends and webinars at night. Her mother gave her excellent advice. Investing was something Brynne had never considered while married to Martin, because he'd taken care of everything. She'd never realized how important it was to be an independent person in a marriage, and not just someone's appendage. She had lost herself in Martin. His identity was hers, but not the other way around.

While she was studying the materials for her "Fundamentals of Investing" seminar the next weekend, her mind wandered to her girls. She longed to hear more from them. Marianne had told her about a cooking class she was taking at school, while Brianne was into gymnastics.

The twins were growing up fast, and Brynne was no longer privy to the details of their lives. When they Skyped, Brynne tried to get them to open up, but they shut down. They were focused on the good things. Brynne remembered that mode well. Only the Positive, Not the Negative. It was her motto. However, seeing it in her daughters made her sad. They wanted to put on a good front even though their lives had fallen apart.

Brynne and Martin would share temporary joint custody, but it would be awkward. The girls would have difficulty returning home this summer. The home they'd left would already be sold and inhabited by another family. And now Brynne worked and wouldn't be available to them all the time. That, too, would take some getting used to.

Brynne thought more and more about her mother and what a wonderful role model she could be for her daughters. She decided right then and there that Brianne and Marianne would spend more time with Jasmine. The woman was a scholar, for heaven's sake. She had a wealth of information to pass on.

Though the girls wouldn't return to Los Angeles for two more months, Brynne hoped to have saved enough money by then to rent a nice house, or maybe even put a down payment on a condo.

She was exhausted. Working extra shifts and rushing home to study every night after work was taking its toll. She tried to stay focused on her computer screen, but her eyelids were heavy and her eyesight began to blur. She barely heard the text tone on her cell phone. But when she did, she grabbed the phone, hoping it was a text from one of her daughters.

Gemma and I are having dinner nearby. Wanna join us? Kenzie texted.

Can't tonight. Gotta study, but I'd like to another time, Brynne wrote back.

Okay, want to thank you for all you did to make opening day such a success.

My pleasure. See you another time?

Kenzie sent her a smiling emoji. Thanks to Sarita, Brynne had learned how to do that as well, and she sent her one back.

Brynne sat back in her chair and smiled. Who would have imagined that she would have girlfriends she could share her troubles with, as well as her triumphs? She took another sip of wine and continued working at her computer until the phone rang.

Carla Ringwald, the head of human resources at Macy's, was on the line. "Brynne," she said, "sorry to call you at home, but I have something I wanted to run by you."

Brynne held the phone close to her ear. "Sure, Carla, happy to talk to you. Is anything wrong?"

"As a matter of fact, no," she said. "You're doing an outstanding job in the linen department. But perhaps we ought to discuss your becoming a buyer. You seem to have a good eye, and we could use a woman with your expertise on our management team. But we'd need to train you in various departments to see where you'd be best suited. Oh, and of course there'd be a substantial increase in pay."

Brynne smiled broadly. She felt her muscles relax. She took a deep breath and closed her eyes.

"Yes. Yes, of course." She sighed. "Thank you."

"Great. Stop by my office in the morning, and we'll get you started," Carla said.

Brynne tore off her cardigan sweater and flip-flops and walked to the kitchen. She drank the last drops of her glass of red wine, then collapsed onto a chair. She put her feet up on the table, leaned back, and smiled. What a relief.

The hard work was paying off.

KENZIE

"Well, you did a hell of a job, kid." Leo was waving a piece of paper as he crossed into Kenzie's office, which was still full of half-empty gift baskets, wilting flowers, and other leftover congratulatory gifts. "I knew you could do it, and you pulled off a winner. A real winner."

"Thanks, Leo, I'm glad you're happy," Kenzie said as she leaned back in her chair.

"So, tootsie, listen to this." Leo put on his glasses and read the information from the paper. "We got attendance up to an average of 5,378 per day, for a three-week total of 64,536. That's almost 11,000 more in one meet than the 53,820 we totaled the last five years." Leo removed his glasses and looked at Kenzie. "Outstanding. Ole Grayson will be back to see another year. We can relax a bit, and then, well, you're gonna have to do it again."

"So Grayson's not going to become condos?" Kenzie asked.

"Not yet. We're getting more trainers, filling up the stalls. I think we can ride it out another year."

"Great." She smiled, a weight lifting from her chest. "Then I need a little break. Can I take a few days off this month?"

"Yeah, yeah, take as much time as you want, but after New York," Leo said as he dropped into the chair across from Kenzie.

"New York?" Kenzie asked, leaning forward.

"You're gonna be speaking to the Ad Council at their annual conference. In two weeks. They want you, tootsie."

"What do you mean? Speaking about what?"

"They wanna know how you did it. How you turned this little itty-bitty ugly track into an event for three weeks and quintupled the attendance. It's great. You're a star, baby."

Kenzie stared. "No. No, I'm not a star. Okay? No," she said. She got up from her seat, folded her arms in front of her, and walked over to the sliding door, agitated. "I'm not going to New York. And I'm not speaking at their event."

"Okay, look, I had a feeling you were going to say that. But listen, I got in touch with your previous boss who told me to contact your old limo driver—Fernando something—so I got him for you. And I got Grayson to put you up at the Regency Hotel. You're going to be treated like royalty. And you get to talk all about the track and get us even more publicity, and maybe we can get the California Horse Racing Board to extend our meet from three weeks to five. So this is really important, tootsie. Really. For the track. You gotta do it. You're gonna be fine."

Kenzie looked at Leo, who was pleading with her. She could see it in his eyes: he was determined to get a yes. But she wasn't budging. This was not happening. She was not going back to New York. Not speaking to virtually the same advertising sales group she spoke to almost five years ago.

"Leo, I'm sorry," she said. She returned to her desk and sat across from him. "I just can't. I have a terrible phobia about speaking, especially doing it there—the scene of the crime. I can't. I'm sorry. You heard what happened. Brynne filled you in on the details, remember?"

Leo leaned across her desk and took her hand. He'd never done anything like that before. Kenzie knew he was going in for the kill.

"Kenzie . . . there's no better way to conquer a phobia than to deal with it head-on. Guess what? I was afraid of heights. Yeah, me. Afraid to go to a high floor. In fact, I just would never go to one. I'm not kidding. It was so bad, I couldn't tell anyone. If I ever had a meeting and had to travel beyond the fifth floor, I'd take a pill. And then I was absolutely worthless 'cause I was a zombie."

"Well, I can't be on drugs when giving a spee—" Kenzie said.

"I got over it," Leo interrupted. He sat back in his chair and changed his demeanor. He was suddenly far more serious. "I had a girl once. A girl I was really into. I was going to marry that girl. But she got hit by a car and was in a hospital room on the sixteenth floor of NewYork-Presbyterian. She was dying. And I had to see her. I walked onto that floor and avoided all the windows. I knew her room had a beautiful view of the city, but I didn't want to see it. I'd close the shades and sit by her bed the entire day. I'd glance at the window but would never go near it. Then one day I went over and looked down. I felt sick and dizzy. But I made myself do it again. And again. Every couple minutes till the nausea stopped."

Leo paused and looked away. Kenzie was sure he had tears in his eyes. She couldn't believe it.

"I never left her side," he said softly. "Slept right next to her on a cot and held her hand when she passed. It was a weird thing. I lost the love of my life, and yet I managed to conquer my phobia."

Kenzie stared at Leo. She'd never heard him tell a heartfelt story. Ever. That he had done so told her how important this speech was to Grayson. She'd come to love this place. And Leo had given her the chance to come back from the brink.

Kenzie sighed. She got up and walked over to the sliding door again. She glanced at the walking ring, which was being replanted for the meet next year.

"I understand why you want me to do this," Kenzie said, staring at the paddock, her back to him. "Give me some time to think about it."

"Okay, tootsie," Leo said as he walked toward the door. "In the meantime, Richard Grayson gave us a new budget for next year. I'm going to give you a raise and a staff so we can start building this sucker into something big."

Kenzie waited till he left her office, then crashed onto her chair. She understood the importance, the visibility this appearance would give the track. She pictured herself standing onstage again. At the same podium. In virtually the same place, speaking about much the same thing. She reached for a Hershey's Kiss, which had come in one of the congratulatory baskets she'd received after opening day. She unwrapped one, then two, three, four, and more and more. Soon she was throwing handfuls into her mouth. When she couldn't look at another, she decided to call Matt.

"I heard," Matt said when he answered his phone. "Leo wants me to work on you. As if you'd listen to anything I had to say on the subject. I already told him forget it, you'll never do it."

"Why am I not surprised he told you before he asked me? Of course he'd want you to change my mind. But you know I can't go back there. I don't want to ever do that again. Why would I?"

"I don't know, why would you?" Matt asked.

"I wouldn't."

"Why not? How about showing them how far you've come? That you weren't destroyed. That you got back on the horse, no pun intended. That you are successful yet again. That you have nothing to be ashamed of. How about sticking it to them? How about that?"

Kenzie didn't respond. Instead, she tossed a few more Kisses into her mouth.

"Hello? Are you still there?" Matt asked. "What're you eating? It smells good."

And then the door opened, and Matt walked in with his cell phone attached to his ear. He put the phone in his pocket as he leaned against the door.

Kenzie quickly swept all the silver wrappers into her wastebasket and swallowed the last of her Kisses. She put the phone down. Matt was looking as good as ever—tan Justin cowboy boots, stonewashed denims, crisp white shirt, blue windbreaker, and New York Giants cap. His clear blue eyes lit up the room.

All she wanted to do was rush into his arms and have him hold her like he'd done so many times, but she wasn't going to this time. She knew he loved her. Their relationship had matured. She'd even begun to trust him, something she hadn't been sure she could ever do with anyone. She walked to the window and stood with her back to the paddock, facing Matt.

"I'm afraid. Afraid of what might happen again," she said.

"Nothing's gonna happen," he said. "You had a panic attack because you had just lost your mom. You hadn't even dealt with that. It wasn't about the so-called shame and humiliation of exposing your butt to the audience. You were dealing with grief at that time, but things are different now. You're a different person, and you're dealing with issues head-on, not running away like you've done in the past. Grayson helped you. It healed you. I know you can do it. And I think you know it, too."

"How do you know?"

"Because I'll be there. And you know who else is going to be there?" he asked.

She shook her head.

"She's gonna be there. Your mom," Matt said as he thumped his chest with his right hand. "She's going to be right inside you, in your heart. You are going to carry her up onstage with you this time. And she's going to be there, rooting you on, just like me. You know she'd want you to do this. You know that."

Kenzie heard Matt's voice echoing the same thoughts she'd had about her mother so many times, and she had to blink away sudden tears.

"Okay," she said after a long pause.

"Okay what? I want to hear you say it," he laughed.

"Okay . . . I'll go."

GEMMA

"I'm sorry," Adam said. "I came downstairs to get you, 'cause this girl, well, she just walked in, sat down on your sofa, and wouldn't move. She had a security pass, but I didn't call one in for her. She says you know her well. Her name is Scarlett."

Gemma exited the elevator with Adam in tow. They walked down the hall toward her office. She peeked through the door and saw Scarlett seated sullenly on the couch.

Gemma was having a rough day. Another studio had outbid her on a project; an actor had fallen out of a current deal; the first set of dailies on her big-budget film were disappointing; and she'd discovered her favorite lipstick had been discontinued. When she entered her office, she told Adam to hold her calls.

"I'm surprised to see you here," Gemma said. She put the salad she'd just purchased on her desk and sat down.

Scarlett kicked off her Uggs and folded her legs under her skirt. She stared at the green rubber bracelet she was playing with on her wrist. Her long dark hair had been trimmed to her shoulders. Gemma noticed that Scarlett had the same curvature in her nose as Jeffrey's. There was a time when she might've been envious of that, but not now. Not anymore. Jeffrey Kahn was out of her life. Sealed in the past. She wanted no part of him ever again.

The thought of Jeffrey and his family made her feel embarrassed. She regretted her behavior during that time. The sneaking around, pretending to be someone who worked at the homeless shelter. Befriending Scarlett, a fifteen-year-old. What had seemed so normal then seemed absolutely insane now. Gemma didn't want to think about it.

"How'd you manage to get a security pass? It's not that easy to get in here," Gemma said.

"My girlfriend's dad works in postproduction. His assistant got me the pass," she said without looking up.

Gemma was impressed. She knew Scarlett was smart and kind of liked that she'd beat the system. She moved away from her desk, closed the door, and walked over to the same white chair she'd sat in a few weeks ago when Jeffrey was there.

"So how've you been? Everything okay?" Gemma asked. She tried to sound upbeat and bright.

"My dad told me you're my half sister."

Gemma's eyes widened. She sure wasn't expecting to hear that. "At first I didn't want to believe it because, well, it didn't make sense. I mean, he never said anything about you or that he had another daughter. And you never said anything, either. And then the other night . . . Well, things have been crazy lately. I'm not sure he even wanted to tell us . . . but he did . . . he told us about you."

"Well, I'm sorry. I really am. I didn't handle it all that well." Gemma's jaw clenched as she shifted uncomfortably from one side to the other. "And your dad, well, he . . . he wasn't real thrilled."

"He's your dad, too," Scarlett said.

"Yes. Yes, he is."

"I Googled you," she said. "I should've done that earlier, but I didn't have any suspicions about you. I took you at your word. I thought you really were a volunteer."

"Scarlett, I'm sorry," Gemma said as she sat up straight in her chair. "I made a mistake. I should've come clean with all of you. Sooner. I just wanted to meet my . . . well, Jeffrey."

"It's okay, you can say it—he's your father, too. He's *our* father," Scarlett said as she leaned forward, plucking at the rubber bracelet on her wrist.

Gemma didn't know what else to say.

"Dad left Mom the other night," Scarlett said. "My mom found out that he'd been having an affair with Lauren, his assistant." Gemma took a breath. Scarlett got up from the sofa and moved over to the wall to look at Gemma's photographs. They were personal ones of Gemma's family and friends. Scarlett examined each one closely. "She doesn't like to be called his secretary, which is what mom calls her. She'd always correct her and say, 'No, Mrs. Kahn, I'm his assistant.'"

"I'm sorry to hear that, Scarlett," Gemma said quietly.

"Who is this photo of?" Scarlett pointed to a framed photograph on the wall. "Is it your mom?" Gemma nodded. "She looks nice."

"She's a good mom," Gemma said as Scarlett took her own personal tour of the office, focusing sharply on every detail. "Your mom is nice, too. But I'm sorry to hear your dad—"

"He's your dad, too," Scarlett interrupted.

"Yes. Anyway, I'm sorry he left."

"He screwed up our family," Scarlett said as she crashed onto the couch and spread out in a prone position. "Before he left that night he told us that he got your mom pregnant, never saw you, never knew who you were, and then I guess you guys had lunch or something and you told him."

Gemma didn't want to rehash the meeting with her father. She certainly didn't want to share the details with Scarlett. But she was surprised he'd told his family. Maybe he'd felt the need to come clean. But she still wasn't sure why Scarlett was there.

"I'm so sorry to hear all this. You've really been through a tough time. What can I do?" Gemma asked sympathetically, leaning forward in her chair.

Scarlett removed her green rubber bracelet from her wrist and started stretching it. She wrapped it around her other wrist, then flicked it back and forth between her fingers. She seemed completely engaged and uninterested in answering Gemma's question.

"I'd really like to help you," Gemma said softly.

"What's it like being raised by just your mom?" Scarlett asked. She didn't take her eyes off the rubber bracelet, and her inflection didn't change. "What was it like not having a dad? 'Cause I'm sad that he moved out, but I think it's probably best. Mom hates him. After he told us about you and she busted him about Lauren, well, they had a big blowup. It was ugly. I was kind of scared. I took off and ran to my friend Isabella's. Then my parents were mad at me 'cause they had to tell Isabella's mom what happened. And my mom was crying. It was pretty gross."

Scarlett took off the rubber bracelet and flung it across the room like it was a slingshot, then smirked when it hit the wall behind Gemma.

"I see why you're upset. You have every right to be and—"

"We're sisters," Scarlett interrupted.

"Yes. We are," Gemma said, "but that doesn't always mean—"

"Why is it okay for you to hang around me when you want something, yet when I come to you, it's like, well, like you don't want to know me anymore? I'm not my dad, you know. I'm different. I thought we were friends. I helped you when you wanted something. And now, well, I need you."

Gemma lowered her eyes and then took a beat before she said anything. "You do need me. You're right. And I will be there for you." Gemma looked up. "We're sisters. And sisters look out for each other. We need to do that."

Scarlett's eyes were glassy and the corners of her mouth drooped. She started to say something but couldn't get the words out. Gemma thought she was fighting back tears. "Hey," she said, offering a smile, "how about we do something fun? Like go Rollerblading or something sometime?"

Scarlett looked up at her hesitantly. "You'd do that? Aren't you kind of old for that?"

"Well, that's not a great thing to say. I've done my share of Rollerblading on Venice Beach. I bet I could beat you."

"Okay." Scarlett gave a tentative smile. She sat up on the couch and slipped her feet back into her boots. "I'm sorry to mess up your day. I know you're a busy person, but I wanted to see you."

When Scarlett stood, Gemma walked over and embraced her, and as soon as she did, Scarlett started to cry. Gemma comforted her and smoothed her hair.

"I hope I can be like you someday," Scarlett said. Gemma consoled her, saying that eventually things would be all right again. Just a different kind of all right.

"Dad said I should try and be like you," Scarlett went on. "He said you would be a good role model."

Gemma froze. "Really? He said that? When? Frankly, I'm surprised to hear that."

"When he left he was crying. So was I. And when he hugged me and said he'd see me soon, he told me that it's a good thing he didn't raise you, 'cause you turned out all right. And that maybe I should try and be like you. He told me you had a big job and where you worked." She stepped back to the couch to grab her backpack and then wiped her hand across her nose and sniffed loudly. "Anyway, I have to get back to school. I ditched fourth period to come here."

"You're welcome to come over anytime," Gemma said as she draped her arm around the girl's shoulders and walked her out. "Give me a little notice, though, next time."

Scarlett laughed as she and Gemma embraced again. Gemma opened the door and asked Adam to escort Scarlett to the elevator.

"Take care!" Gemma shouted. "Text me when you can go Rollerblading."

Adam turned around and eyed Gemma with a puzzled expression, which made her laugh.

Gemma closed the door and walked over to the wall of photographs that Scarlett had studied. She looked at the photo of her mom. The real hero. Her mom chose to keep her when she could've easily given her up.

She had given her the gift of life.

And, though she'd learned her father wasn't so wonderful, Gemma had discovered that his daughter, Scarlett, was an exceptional young woman.

So maybe she lost the same father twice. But she certainly did gain a sister.

She scooted to her desk, kicked off her shoes, pushed back in her chair, and punched in a phone number.

"Hi, Mom. I wish you were there and that I didn't have to leave this message on your machine. But it's really important. I want to tell you . . ." Gemma began to choke up. "How much . . . How much I really love you. I'm not sure I've done that lately, or frankly enough . . . Before they were just words. But now they have much more meaning. I'm so grateful that you're my mom. That you made the decision to keep me and then sacrificed so much to raise me on your own . . ." Gemma looked over at the photo of her mom on the wall. Her eyes welled up with tears. "I love you, Mom."

SARITA

Sarita wished she were more confident. She hadn't been to the club in a long time. She hadn't sung before an audience in months. She wasn't feeling excited and energized, the way she had in the past. Grief had overwhelmed her. But tonight was the final performance. Moody Gray would decide who would be the lead singer in the Witches of Skeletal Symphony, who were preparing to go on tour. Sarita wanted the gig. She had to finish what she started. That was what her mother told her.

Damien met her at the Deathrock Bar. He looked stunned to see her clad in traditional Indian garb. She wore a blue-and-green silk sari over a matching petticoat and short-sleeved, midriff-baring blouse. The major portion of the sari, the *pallu*, hung over her left shoulder and was heavily embellished with fine embroidery. There was no red wig. There was no white powder on her face. There were no visible piercings. Her dark hair was parted in the middle and hung straight. Damien was the only one who knew who she was. He took her hand and brought her inside the club.

"You look beautiful," he said as they sat at the front table. "But I sure wasn't expecting to see you dressed like this."

"I know," Sarita said, reaching across the table and pouring herself a beer from the full pitcher. "I just wanted to express a different side of me tonight."

She'd be taking a risk. It was the final competition between her and just one other singer. No one at the club recognized her. The Sarita they knew was a hot Goth chick. She looked around at the folks she knew, but to them this Indian chick with Damien was a stranger.

"I'm a little nervous. I hope they'll accept me . . . you know, looking like this. Are you okay with it?"

"I'm okay with anything you do, and frankly, I can't stop looking at you. You look pretty and sexy in a way I've not seen before."

"I'm more than just the Goth girl, and I wanted to show that today . . . a different side . . . My ancestral side . . . I'm proud and don't want to hide it."

"I love you no matter who you are, Sarita." He leaned in and talked to her softly. "No matter what you wear or what you look like. Honestly. It's great you've embraced your ancestry. You've worked hard for tonight. This is all you've ever wanted—to sing in a band. You need to feel it from within. It's not about what you look like. It's about who you are inside. You have to sing from your heart."

Sarita brought her hand under his chin and felt the rough stubble of his beard, then kissed him softly on the lips.

The other contestant was introduced and began singing with the band. She was energetic and agile. She danced fluidly across the stage while singing, and never once did her Katy Perry–like voice waiver despite all the gyrating. Sarita wasn't a dancer—her voice was everything. She could reach the highest notes with ease. But this girl was a performer. She was killing it. And the audience loved her.

Now it was Sarita's turn. She stood and approached the stage cautiously, tentatively. Before she got there she turned to Damien one more time and saw Mama sit down with him.

"Mama!" Sarita ran to the table and greeted her mother with kisses on both cheeks. "What're you doing here?"

"Damien invited me. I wouldn't miss it for the world," she said. "You look lovely. But it's not exactly what I expected."

"It's exactly who I am, Mama. Who you raised me to be," Sarita said, and then looked at Damien, who watched her proudly. "I just think . . . Well, I thought tonight I'd be who I really am."

"But, Sarita, you know who you are," Mama said. "What you wear is just a way to understand who you are at that moment. But we are made up of a lot of personalities. Is this the one you want to project tonight? Is this the appropriate dress for the song you'll be singing? Is this what a lead singer in this band would wear? Or is this something to wear at another time?"

Then her mother handed her a plastic bag.

"You forgot these." Mama smiled.

Sarita looked in the bag, but then her name was called. She walked to the stage, holding on to the plastic bag. She reached for the microphone and waited for the audience to quiet down.

"As some of you may know, I lost my papa last month," she said. "And I'm still . . . Well, I'm still mourning his death. I've learned that this kind of loss doesn't exactly disappear that quickly, that you find yourself doing and saying all sorts of things you wouldn't ordinarily do." She looked at the crowd, which had grown quiet and still. "I know you've never seen me dressed like this. Well, I rarely, if ever, am. But tonight I wanted to honor my father and sing this song in his memory. And I thought it would be nice to dress the way he'd like to see me. But then I realized despite our conflicts in the past, and we had plenty, that he really just wanted me to be happy. And I'm most happy when I'm free to be me. And as you know, *me* is much different from this." The audience laughed, and she laughed along with them.

Sarita started unraveling her sari. "It's amazing what one can wear underneath this thing." The audience watched with rapt attention. As each layer was removed, the garments underneath became more visible. "My dad's death made me question who I am. It got pretty confusing, because I wanted to be me, and yet I didn't want to disappoint him. But I learned that like everyone else, I'm a lot of personalities. In some ways these two outfits are a metaphor for what I've been struggling with for so long. These were the two personalities constantly at odds with each other. But tonight"—she let the sari fall to the ground—"this one won. It just happens to be the one you're most familiar with." She was left standing in her blue midriff top, black short skirt, red-and-black striped hose, and army boots. "I put this on just in case I changed my mind." Then she reached into the plastic bag. She placed her hair under the red wig, put a ring through her nose, and slid bracelets on her wrists. Within a few seconds Sarita had transformed into the person they knew so well. Once the change was complete, there was loud applause. She smiled as the band started playing and then she began singing.

Sarita's voice produced beautiful sounds as it searched up one and down another octave. One minute it was raspy and deep; the next, full and rich like that of an opera soprano. It conveyed a sense of desire and passion and had its own distinct style. By comparison, her competitor's voice was wispy and delicate. She couldn't come close to Sarita's vocal talent.

At the end Sarita was spent. She had given it her all. She took a deep bow and began gathering her sari. The audience was cheering and whistling. Damien was on his feet applauding wildly. Amidst all the praise and demands for an encore, she pointed to her mother and asked her to stand up.

"My mama is here tonight. Everyone please welcome her."

Mama stood up and smiled broadly.

Sarita watched as the crowd applauded more. She was so proud to have her mama there. She clapped along with them. She didn't even care if she won. She had already won. She had a wonderful boyfriend and a mother who had not only embraced her but had also encouraged her to pursue her interests and restore her identity. She realized that she was still the dutiful daughter, proud of her Indian heritage, and the hard worker at Grayson. But this was where she felt the most comfortable. Right here. Onstage. She'd wanted to be a singer for as long as she could remember. Her night was almost complete.

Almost.

And then it happened.

Sarita was declared the winner. The place erupted. Damien leaped onto the stage, took her in his arms, kissed her repeatedly, and then spun her around.

Sarita stopped for a moment, looked up toward the sky, closed her eyes, and whispered, "I did it Papa. I did it."

BRYNNE

"Brynne," Martin said. "Can I come in?"

Brynne was reluctant to open the door. But Martin kept knocking and she didn't want to create a scene or wake the neighbors, so she unlocked the door and let him in.

She hadn't seen Martin in months. The dapper and handsome man she'd once been so in love with looked like he had just come from the Salvation Army, wearing whatever they had available. It was a shock. She'd never seen Martin like this. Didn't his girlfriend take care of him?

His dark-blue jeans hung loosely from his frame, his denim long-sleeved shirt improperly buttoned and two sizes too large. His loafers were scuffed, something Martin would never have allowed to happen before. His eyes were puffy and his face looked as if he hadn't shaved for three days. Brynne was surprised.

Martin looked around briefly, then sat at the kitchen table. Brynne handed him a bottle of water and watched as he emptied it in one long gulp.

"You look terrible," Brynne said after several moments of uncomfortable silence.

"I don't expect any sympathy," Martin said as he stared into space, unable to look at Brynne. "To say I fell on hard times . . . Well, let's just say things aren't working out. I made a terrible decision when I left. And things have continued to go downhill."

Once Brynne would have given anything to hear these words, but now they left her cold. "Aren't you living with . . . with . . . her, your *career* woman, anymore?"

"For now. But it's been over for a while," Martin said.

"No sex? Sleeping in separate bedrooms already?" Brynne couldn't help but get a dig in. "I hope you're still paying for the girls' boarding school."

"My parents are footing the bill," Martin said. "But they've cut me off."

Brynne was surprised to know Martin's parents felt that strongly about keeping them at boarding school. But she didn't like that no one had consulted her about whether they should stay there. She made the decisions regarding her children. Martin always left that up to her. Her in-laws were never involved. Just because they were the ones with money didn't mean Brynne was going to let them call the shots. Particularly when it came to her daughters. She was furious. This would never happen again. And money wouldn't dictate their lives the way it had before. Not anymore. The girls could stay at boarding school till the end of the term. But then, in the summer, she'd discuss the future with them. They were going to live within their means.

"Things are very bad." Martin looked directly at Brynne. "I moved in with Marcella, but all my belongings couldn't fit in her home, so we put them in storage. The unit caught fire and everything is gone. The insurance didn't cover one-tenth of the value."

Brynne took a sip of her wine and moved about the room. She didn't feel comfortable sitting next to Martin. She stared out the window and looked toward the mountains, which were snowcapped and beautiful. She remembered driving through the hills toward Grayson, the place where she'd once spent so much time but now rarely visited. She sighed, recalling the life she'd once had, the one that had been given to her and taken from her by the man sitting at her kitchen table.

She poured herself some more wine and offered Martin another bottle of water, and then she returned to the table and sat across from him.

"It's a good story," she said. "But I don't believe you."

Brynne got up and walked over to the kitchen counter. She picked up a manila folder. She opened it up and showed Martin several photos of him and Marcella, dressed to the nines, leaving a party in San Clemente, where he'd bought a new home. She showed him photos of the house.

"Good show, Martin." Brynne looked at his shirt. "But when you wear a denim shirt like this, you want to make sure the Hermès label stays tucked inside. I know all about the foreign bank accounts. Not to mention your parents' fortune. I've got a good job, Martin, and even better lawyers who hire great private investigators. We're going to nail you, baby. And your prenup? I'm challenging that. And pretty much everything else. So cut out the act. You're not on the verge of homelessness . . . yet."

Brynne took a sip of wine and leaned against the counter. "Martin, this has been a really good thing for me," she went on calmly. "Because I discovered me."

Brynne tossed the folder back onto the counter and then continued. "I manage a department at Macy's now. And I'm in their buyer program. I guess you could say *I'm* a career woman." Brynne stared at Martin as she let those words sink in. "I'm earning my own money, and I'm going to make even more. The good news is that once we settle the divorce, I won't have to rely on you for a penny.

I'm making it on my own. You played with me for a long time, Martin, but I'm not your toy anymore."

Brynne stopped. She gritted her teeth and clenched her jaw.

"I trusted you. I never dreamed you would hide our money and create this wild story about how you lost it. Or that you'd hold me to an abusive prenup signed almost twenty years ago. I thought I knew you well, but I didn't. You duped me. But I know a lot more now."

Martin raked his hands through his hair and started to get up. But Brynne came over, put her hand firmly on his shoulder, and pushed him back into his seat.

"It's not time to leave yet," Brynne said. "The cheating, the stealing, that was nothing. The biggest mistake you made, Martin Tomlinson, was making me your enemy."

Brynne raised her glass and threw the rest of her wine in Martin's face.

He flinched but said nothing. He used his shirtsleeves to dry off. He lowered his eyes and didn't move. She placed the glass on the counter. Brynne was surprised at his passivity, but then, she had caught him off guard. He clearly wasn't prepared for what she had to say.

Brynne had become another person. An independent woman.

"I want my daughters," Brynne said, breaking the silence. "And don't even think of challenging me on this. When they come home this summer, they'll be with me until we work out permanent joint custody in court."

There was a long pause.

"They're here." Martin said it so softly she almost didn't hear. "In the car."

"What?"

Martin nodded toward the door. "They asked to come in this weekend. I thought they wanted to see me. But they didn't. They wanted to surprise you. I just picked them up from the airport."

Brynne opened the door and looked at the parking lot. The sun had set and the lot wasn't well lit. Her eyes searched for Martin's car. She didn't know what kind of car he had now. She scanned the area and then there they were. The girls came running toward Brynne.

"Mom!" they screamed.

Brynne watched as they approached. Even though they appeared older and more mature, and were wearing clothes that Brynne hadn't picked out and would never approve of, they were still her babies. She was overwhelmed. Tears streamed down her face. She took both girls by the hand and led them into her home.

When she turned to close the door, she saw Martin get in his car and drive off.

KENZIE

She was in Fernando's limo again. Everything was exactly as it had been five years ago. As if no time had passed. As if nothing had changed. As if this had always been her life.

But like Gemma, Sarita, and Brynne, Kenzie was now a different person.

"We certainly missed you out here, Miss Armstrong. Been a long time since I've seen you," Fernando said.

"It has, Fernando. And I missed you, too," Kenzie said.

Fernando winked in his rearview mirror and she smiled back. Just like all the other times.

They pulled up to the back entrance of Avery Fisher Hall at Lincoln Center. Kenzie cringed when she saw the door, the same door she had entered with great expectations, and the same one she'd exited shamed and humiliated. The thought made her queasy. When Fernando came to a stop, Kenzie let herself out and was greeted by Jennie, who would assist her backstage. Jennie grabbed the garment bag from Fernando and handed Kenzie a bottle of water as they entered the building.

As they approached the dressing rooms, Kenzie began to feel jittery. Her stomach turned and her palms were sweaty. She took a long breath to calm herself.

She stopped when she saw her name on the black nameplate next to the archway, engraved in white lettering just like before. There it was: *Kenzie Armstrong*. She traced the letters with her finger.

When Jennie opened the door to her dressing room, Kenzie saw Brynne, Gemma, and Sarita, all with raised glasses. She stood speechless in the doorway.

"You're not going it alone this time," Gemma said. "There's no way anything is going to be stuck in . . . well, anything, while we're here. We've got your back!"

"Oh my God!" Kenzie cried. "What're you all doing here?"

"Well, let's just say you've certainly been there for all of us," Gemma said. She hugged her best friend and escorted her into the room.

"Thank you." Kenzie felt as if her heart would burst. "Wow, thank you. You're all here. For me? Really?"

Brynne offered Kenzie a glass of champagne. "Yes, we're here for you. Because—as I learned the hard way—that's what women do. They support each other." Brynne smiled and then hugged Kenzie. "Good luck, hon."

Kenzie blinked away the moisture in her eyes. "Thank you."

"And, when we're back in LA," Sarita said, "we're all going to celebrate again. In my new apartment."

"You moved out?" Kenzie asked, clinking her glass with Sarita's. "So proud of you."

"Furnished by Macy's," Sarita said.

"With my discount, I might add," said Brynne proudly.

"But for tomorrow night," Sarita said, "I want you to put on your nose rings and best wig and come to the Black Hole. It's a new club right here in Greenwich Village. My first gig with the Witches of Skeletal Symphony. It's just your style, Brynne."

"Hardly, but I'll try it." Brynne clinked her glass with Sarita's.

"But you will happily tag along, right?" Matt said. He had been sitting in the corner the whole time, but Kenzie hadn't seen him. The second she heard his voice, she set down her glass and ran over to him.

"I'm so glad you're here," she whispered in his ear.

"Me too," he said. "Seeing Brynne all warm and cuddly was well worth the trip."

"I heard that, Matt." Brynne marched over to Kenzie and Matt. "Don't get too carried away. This trip happened to coincide with a management seminar at Macy's, which I could not miss. You know I'm in their buyer program."

"Yes, we definitely know that, Brynne." Matt smirked.

"Can you believe this group?" Kenzie whispered to Matt. "Who would've thought Gemma, Sarita, Brynne, and I would become such good friends?"

"All because of you," Matt said. "You gave them the strength to make their wishes come true . . . Now it's your turn."

Jennie popped her head in the room and told Kenzie she'd better get dressed.

"Okay, we'll leave her in your charge," Gemma said. "But please watch her back before she goes onstage."

"Don't worry," Jennie said. "I have strict orders from the man in the corner over there. I'll make sure."

Gemma, Sarita, and Brynne set down their drinks, grabbed their bags, and hurried out of the room to their seats, lavishing Kenzie with hugs and good wishes as they departed.

Matt brought Kenzie's hand to his lips and kissed it.

"I can't believe this. I'm just in a state of shock," she said. "It's like I'm living the greatest dream in the same place I suffered the biggest nightmare."

"You're back, baby," Matt said. "I'll be in the front row. Right below the podium." He got up to leave.

"No laughing this time. Promise?" She smiled.

"Cross my heart," Matt said. "I love you. Good luck."

Once Matt was outside, Kenzie leaned against the door and closed her eyes. She smiled as she recited her mom's words out loud: "Be strong. Believe in yourself."

Minutes later, Kenzie was dressed and ready to go. Jennie was outside her door. She heard her say, "Two minutes." Kenzie opened the door and followed Jennie down the hall and into the wings alongside the stage. Five years had passed, but it could have been yesterday. *"Be strong. Believe in yourself."* This was the exact route she had taken last time. She peered out from the curtain into the crowd. Her knees weakened. She could hear the rumbling of the audience. And then she heard her name. She asked Jennie to carefully inspect everything on her body. Jennie smiled, winked, and gave her the thumbs-up.

Kenzie stepped onto the stage. Once again she was greeted with a huge round of applause. Again the lights shone brightly on her face, and the room was a sea of black. When she reached the podium at the center of the stage, she had taken a moment to find Matt. He was right where he'd said he'd be, in the front row a few feet away. Dead center. The teleprompter lit up with Kenzie's speech. Her hands were shaking and her mouth was dry.

"Be strong. Believe in yourself."

And this time she did.

She took a deep breath and began her speech. Occasionally she'd reach behind herself to make sure everything was where it should be, but kept on speaking.

And then it was over.

No laughter. No heckling. Just wild applause.

The lights went up, and Kenzie could see the audience, which was even larger than she'd expected. She stepped out from behind the podium and took a bow. More applause.

She made eye contact with Matt, who was on his feet, along with Gemma, who had tears streaming down her face, and Brynne, who was taking photos with her iPhone, and Sarita, who was whistling and fist pumping.

And then Kenzie did what no one was expecting. She reached into her suit pocket, produced a shocking-pink lace thong, and waved it high in the air.

The audience howled.

She did it.

KENZIE

Kenzie's head was resting in Matt's lap while they watched TV in their New York hotel room.

"You did a great job today," Matt said, sweeping a few strands of hair off her face.

Kenzie looked up at Matt as she mulled over her recent past. "Kind of interesting how it all turned out, isn't it?"

"Whaddya mean?" Matt's eyes were focused on the TV.

"How it all started here," she said. "I remember being in Fernando's limo on my way back from Avery Fisher Hall to the hotel. I was numb. I couldn't wait to leave. I never thought I'd be happy again. Ever. My life was a mess . . . And now here I am."

"Here you are." Matt made eye contact with her and smiled.

"But it's all so strange. Had you not been the stage manager then, who knows if anyone would've come to my rescue. If I hadn't broken down onstage, I wouldn't have gone to Grayson. If I hadn't worked at Grayson, I wouldn't have reconnected with you, and I wouldn't have met Brynne and Sarita, who've become good friends. That dreadful day onstage led me to some of the greatest people in my life. You all helped me to grow and embrace life again."

Kenzie sat up and yawned as she gathered her hair in a ponytail. She took a sip of Coke and watched some of the game with Matt.

"I know you're watching the game and not listening to me babble on, but I wonder if fate brought us together. I mean it brought us together twice. Here onstage and then again at Grayson." Matt rubbed his eyes and lay on his side so he could watch the game at a better angle. "Life can be strange that way. And then there's that stupid ring. Annalisa's prediction so overwhelmed me that I almost lost you. That really makes me mad. I never believed in psychics and mediums and all that crazy nonsense. It really makes me angry that people spend money on that crap. Like Gemma, who still believes in that stuff."

"Relax . . ." Matt muttered, his eyes fixed on the game.

Kenzie got up, walked to the other room, put on a sweater, and then returned to the sofa.

"I never told anyone this." Kenzie sat down next to Matt and stared at the TV. "My mom asked a friend who was a healer to come over after she was diagnosed with cancer. The healer clutched the locket on my mom's necklace—the one I'm wearing now—in her hands. She closed her eyes and said mom was going to make it. That she would beat the cancer."

Matt stopped watching TV and looked up at Kenzie. Her lips began to tremble.

"Of course, she didn't make it," Kenzie swallowed hard and then continued. "I hated that so-called healer for making us believe in something that was never going to be. Yet I really wanted to believe her."

Matt sat up and rested his hand on Kenzie's shoulder. She just stared at the TV.

"It's all I thought about when I returned home after the speech in New York. It never left my mind. Why wasn't my mom there that day? Why did that healer want us to believe that everything would be okay when it wouldn't? Why did she give us false hope?"

"Because you can't give up. Ever." Matt draped his arm around her. "You have to believe. Because sometimes miracles do happen." He drew her very close, then rubbed her shoulder and kissed the top of her head.

"It's been almost six months to the day that Annalisa predicted the owner of that ring would enter my life." She looked right into his eyes. "I wanted it to be you. I wanted to believe in the fairy tale that a ring I found on the beach would lead to true love. I wanted to believe magical things could happen. I couldn't get it out of my head. Even though the healer didn't save my mom, I still wanted to believe she could. I held that secret of wishful thinking for the past six months."

Matt lay back down on the couch, and Kenzie leaned against the seat cushion and propped her bare feet on the coffee table.

There was a pause as Matt adjusted his position again for a better look at the TV.

"Sometimes its not just wishful thinking," Matt said.

"Really? How's that?" Kenzie asked.

"Can you hand me the remote?" He sat up again.

Kenzie took the remote off of the coffee table and started to hand it to Matt but noticed something underneath it. She studied it carefully, then picked it up.

"Oh my gosh, there's a ring . . . Wait . . . this is *my* ring." She examined it closely. "The ring I sold on eBay."

"You mean it's *my* ring." Matt wore a mischievous grin. "The one I bought on eBay. The one I own."

Kenzie turned toward Matt. Their eyes met instantly.

"So this ring . . . this ring I found on the beach belongs to you?" she asked.

"Yes. Yes, it does." He nodded.

"You planned this!"

"I planned it." Matt kissed her softly on the lips.

Kenzie's eyes were wide. She was smiling broadly. "Wow. You own the ring? You are the one who owns the ring . . . Oh my God . . . I guess this is how it was supposed to happen."

"I guess so." He smiled. "Are you surprised?"

"Am I surprised? I'm shocked! But how did you know I put it on eBay?"

"Well, let's just say I know someone who sold it *for* you on eBay since you didn't have time."

"Sarita . . . She must've told you that she listed it there." Kenzie flashed a sly smile. "Someone who knows a little bit about matchmaking."

Matt nodded and then placed his hand behind her neck and kissed her longer this time. He brushed his hand against her cheek and gazed into her eyes. "Would you like me to put it on your finger?"

Kenzie beamed as Matt took the ring from her. "This ring belongs to your future husband. But this is not the ring I intend to use to ask you to marry me."

Kenzie's eyes widened. "What do you mean?"

"That's a different ring. One that's being made for you right now. It's an engagement ring. Because you see, I've fallen deeply in love with you, Kenzie. And I can't imagine spending my life with anyone but you. So I'd like to ask you to marry me. Will you?"

"Of course, yes, of course!" Her eyes welled up with tears.

"So for now this ring will have to do." Matt slipped it on her ring finger. "But it was never mine, it was always meant to be yours."

There was a long pause as Kenzie admired the ring on her finger. She walked over to the window and gazed at the semiprecious stones' vibrant colors: white, green, and violet. She'd never really appreciated how beautiful the stones were or grasped their significance till now.

"This ring represents the power of female friendship." Kenzie spoke softly as her eyes stayed focused on the gems. "A suffragette's ring. Women who weren't just political activists but who also formed deep bonds with each other. It was intended to show strength, to unite women, to give them the opportunity to have a voice." Kenzie raised her hand and held it up to the light as she continued to admire the ring.

"It brought a lot of people together. Gemma, Sarita, Brynne—and us," Matt said. "Maybe that was its intention all along. That's why it belongs on your hand."

Kenzie stood at the picture window and gazed down on the magnificent streets of Manhattan. "Ya know, Matt, all I ever wanted after that speech was to be happy again." She turned away and looked at Matt, who was still seated on the sofa. "Losing my mom nearly destroyed me. And yet here I am, five years later, with the man of my dreams, a wonderful new career at Grayson, and good supportive girlfriends who powered me through the difficult times. I'm happier than I ever imagined."

"Occasionally wishes do come true, and sometimes things work out."

Kenzie walked back to the sofa and sat down next to Matt. She cupped his face in her hands. "I couldn't be happier than I am right now with you. I think we'll be together for a long time. And you know what?" She smiled. "I don't think that's just wishful thinking."

ACKNOWLEDGMENTS

"Be strong. Believe in yourself." That wisdom actually came from my own mother. I'd like to thank her for those kind, supportive words that have guided me throughout my life. I wish only that she had lived long enough to hear me express my gratitude.

Thank you to my agent, Jane Gelfman, whom I adore, and to her excellent team at Gelfman Schneider. A special shout-out to her colleagues Victoria Marini and Cathy Gleason, and to Ted Chervin and Hrishi Desai at ICM.

To my fabulous editor, Danielle Marshall, for her passion, guidance, and unyielding support. And to my terrific team at Lake Union Publishing, including Robin Cruise, Dennelle Catlett, and Gabriella Van den Heuvel.

Thank you to Sahiba Sarna Krieger, who patiently answered my questions and helped me understand Hindu customs and traditions.

Thank you to the gang at Santa Anita Park, especially Keith Brackpool, Nate Newby, and Katie Abbott. I'm also deeply grateful to the team at Del Mar Thoroughbred Club: Joe Harper, Josh Rubinstein, Craig Dado, and Nancy Bonforte. And a very special shout-out to Mac McBride, director of media for Del Mar.

And thanks to the wonderful and dedicated people involved in horse racing, all of whom have answered questions, given me tours, and introduced me to a sport I've grown to love. They include Bob Baffert, Jill Baffert, Molly McGill, Kim McCarthy, Dana Barnes, Jimmy Barnes, Jim Pegram, Scott Chaney, Luis Jauregui, Dr. Dana Stead, Harris Auerbach, Madeline Auerbach, Barry Abrams, Bill and Margie Strauss, Scott and Holly Shepherd, and Arnold and Ellen Zetcher. And a very special thanks to Chuck Winner and Bo Derek, members of the California Horse Racing Board.

Thank you to my first readers: Jennie Fields, Megan Crane, Debby Simon, and Deborah Reed. Also to Jared Levine and Alex Kohner for their legal counsel. And to the extraordinary young women in my life and leaders of tomorrow: Sydney Kaltman (Mini-Me), Paige Adams, Elizabeth Higgins Clark, Merisa Lavie, Ali Nuger, Catherine Davis, Jensen Davis, and Alina Kupchak. Another special shout-out to my brother, Professor Rob DeKoven, and to Dr. Jeannette Davis, Marilyn Adams-Gogul, Didi Kaltman, Cindy and Ron Levine, Hy and Edith Israel, and my dad, Sidney DeKoven, who passed on way too early—and whom I continue to miss so very much . . .

Most of all, I want to thank my girlfriends. There are too many to mention, but you know who you are. You're always there for me and I treasure our friendships. You were the inspiration for this novel, and I'm so grateful to have you in my life.

ABOUT THE AUTHOR

Lindy DeKoven is the bestselling author of *Primetime Princess*. Following stints at Walt Disney Television and Warner Bros. Television, she was executive vice president of NBC Entertainment. *The Secret Life of Wishful Thinking* is her second novel. She lives in Los Angeles with her husband, David Israel. Connect with her at lindydekoven.com.